I0651571

Aaron Stevens Hayward

Nature's Laws in Human Life

Aaron Stevens Hayward

Nature's Laws in Human Life

ISBN/EAN: 9783337370435

Printed in Europe, USA, Canada, Australia, Japan

Cover: Foto ©Andreas Hilbeck / pixelio.de

More available books at **www.hansebooks.com**

NATURE'S LAWS

IN

HUMAN LIFE:

AN

EXPOSITION OF SPIRITUALISM;

EMBRACING

THE VARIOUS OPINIONS OF EXTREMISTS, PRO AND CON;

TOGETHER WITH THE AUTHOR'S EXPERIENCE.

BY THE AUTHOR OF "VITAL MAGNETIC CURE."

BOSTON:
WILLIAM WHITE AND COMPANY.
158 WASHINGTON STREET.
NEW YORK AGENTS: THE AMERICAN NEWS COMPANY,
119 NASSAU STREET.
1872.

Entered according to Act of Congress, in the year 1872
BY WILLIAM WHITE & Co.
In the Office of the Librarian of Congress at Washington.

DEDICATED

TO ALL SEEKERS OF TRUTH IN HUMAN LIFE FORCES.

CONTENTS.

PART IV.

NATURE'S LAWS

IN HUMAN LIFE.

INTRODUCTION.

THE literature of Spiritualism, comprising the history of its phenomena, and the enunciation of doctrines which have received either the unqualified and credulous assent of believers, or called forth the criticism of opposers, remonstrant, argumentative, captious or cynical, has already become very voluminous. Lecture after lecture, uttered either in the normal condition, or as claimed by the speaker, delivered through the inspirational influx from a higher source of intelligence, the human organism being employed as the medium of communication with the outer world, has been reported and published. Treatises, from the modest pamphlet to the more pretentious book of large proportions, have so rapidly appeared, that as to quantity the supply has become almost oppressive. Yet no one has thus far been presented to the world, having the precise scope, which it is the purpose of the present undertaking to comprise. Much that has found its way to the

reading public has been highly objectionable to many
minds, upon whose pre-conceived ideas, derived from
educational bias, the subject matter has made revolutionary encroachments; to others it has been curious
and startling; and again by others it has been accepted
as a new revelation, having the weight of undeniable
authority.   In proportion to its real or supposed importance, has it thus met with unlimited praise, indifference,
or violent denunciation.   While we cannot regard
practical issues with indifference, but must, in common
with all observers of passing events, form some sort of
opinion upon topics which, in the march of progress,
agitate the public mind; we do not presume to make
our convictions the test of any one's orthodoxy, but
yield to all full freedom in exercising the right of private judgment.

Unquestionably the truest method of securing a right
appreciation of the merits or demerits of any subject, is
to place it before the investigator, in all its various aspects, rather than to present a partial view drawn from
the prejudiced representations of interested partisans.

To this end we have collated the respective opinions
openly expressed in advocacy or repudiation of the
main tenets, giving the facts alleged to be the basis of
support to these opposite opinions, and the practical
consequences to which, it is claimed, they severally
lead.   This contrast gives ample facility for comparison, and leaves no one who will bestow upon it a
candid investigation, in ignorance of the real bearing
of the whole subject.

Following this order of narrative, we append a

statement of the facts derived from our own observation and experience, with such reflections as seem to form a legitimate deduction. These are sufficient to enable the reader to answer categorically, in his own mind, the question whether there is truth at the foundation of the claims set forth in reference to Spiritualism.

But were we to rest merely with the collation and comparison of the basic facts and inferences, much that is of philosophical interest and of practical value would be left out of consideration. We therefore proceed to the discussion of a variety of topics which necessarily depend upon either the affirmative or negative answer to the main question.

If it is conceded that the phenomena themselves have actually occurred, as represented now by innumerable witnesses, there must be a significance in them. Either the world has been imposed upon by a stupendous fraud, or a wide-spread delusion on the one hand; or involving as it must, if true, the future destiny and welfare of the human family on the other, its importance is unquestionably paramount to that of all other moral forces.

With the diffusion of intelligence, the public mind becomes emancipated from the thraldom of dogmatic authority. But freedom from such restraint must be authorized only by substantial knowledge, patiently acquired, and well grounded. Liberty must not degenerate into license.

In treating the subject adversely, there has been a strong tendency, as will be seen from the passages cited, to depart from the strict controversial line, indulging in sweeping charges against the personal character of its adherents. The morality of mediums and advocates has been impeached, their motives impugned, and the most sordid and charlatanic disposition attributed to them. And occasionally the critic who has assumed an antagonistic attitude, has descended to vituperation and ribaldry.

Not all however, are thus uncourteously inclined. Among disbelievers there are those who see in its progress, as viewed from their stand-point, nothing but destructive radicalism, sapping the foundation of revealed religion. Not imputing to the inquirers into the meaning of the phenomena, intentional sin, they nevertheless conscientiously regard the search as the indulgence of an unholy curiosity. Such a pursuit they consider not merely frivolous and unprofitable, but quote from their sacred records passages which according to the interpretation which they put upon them, expressly forbid it; consequently that their eternal salvation is jeopardized thereby. With such conscientious convictions, as the result of the application of their theological education, it becomes their religious duty to warn their fellow beings against the continuance of unwarrantable investigation into the nature of prohibited phenomena. Not disputing the manifestations, of many of which they have themselves been eye-witnesses, and failing to find a satisfactory solution in any of the numerous explanations heretofore offered by skeptical observers, they attribute them at last to satanic agency, and hence the tocsin of alarm which they have vigorously sounded, warning their people who were attracted to the investigation, to flee from the impending divine wrath. Many religious teachers there are who, notwithstanding the rigidity of the same method of culture through which they have passed, are liberal minded. They do not interdict such a line of investigation, as unwarrantable in persons religiously disposed, but are willing to acknowledge with the poet that truth should be accepted wherever found, "on Christian or on heathen ground." Recognizing certain facts, established by unimpeachable testimony, they endeavor manfully to dispose of them by referring them to the operation of some previously known law, but which is now expending its force in a new direction. It has been customary to refer every thing which was not understood, to electricity, which evades responsibility, and gets rid of the trouble of seeking for a cause of new phenomena. This still continues to be accepted by many as a sufficient explanation, yet the most delicate electrometer has failed to detect any variation in the electrical conditions of the surrounding atmosphere.

It will at this day scarcely be credited that certain physicians in Buffalo, N. Y., at an early period in the history of the modern manifestations, gravely asserted that the sounds known as raps, heard to be made on tables or other articles of furniture, or solid substances of various kinds were caused by the snapping of the medium's toe-joints. So far as that wild explanation was concerned, it was easily to be tested by any one of common sense. But little progress had then been made in the curious facts developed. If up to that time, there had been nothing seen or heard beyond mere physical phenomena, apparently destitute of meaning, any person of ordinary acuteness was capable of ascertaining whether the sounds were or could be produced by throwing the toes out of joint, and in again, a circumstance familiar to every one. There was however, no resemblance between the sounds which can be thus produced, and those which were heard during the sittings of mediums. The latter sounds will be readily recognized by the thousands who have heard them, if we decribe one of them of a medium degree of power, to be midway between the sharp concussion heard on the emission of a spark from an ordinary magneto-electrical machine, of moderate intensity, and that caused by striking the knuckles upon the table. It conveys an impression, as if proceeding from the interior of the wood. Toe-snapping causes no such sound. As regards the fact, it was soon settled beyond controversy, and surely those who had ventured upon such a ridiculous hypothesis, must now be heartily ashamed of their hasty wisdom. But we will not anticipate.

Mental phenomena following immediately upon the physical, the explanation began to tax the ingenuity of philosophers and scientists. Facts known to the investigator exclusively, were given in response to specific inquiries, and then spontaneously without the putting of leading questions. But the facts belonging to this particular class being already known to him, the suggestion was at once made, and in all fairness, that they were educed by the reflection of one mind upon another. Science would have accepted this as a final explanation had the limit of development been reached. But how would it apply to the elimination of new facts, not previously known to either the medium or the inquirer? A source of intelligence must exist somewhere in such cases, and it puzzled the brain of the philosopher to find it in any field of inquiry which he had hitherto explored. We trust sufficient light will be thrown upon it in the following pages, to relieve any new inquirer, who has not had opportunity, or inclination to agitate the subject in his own mind, from the embarrassment which beset the earlier seekers.

Going a step still farther, what shall be said of prophetic communications? We have supposed in reference to the class of facts last named, that they, or some of them were known to some one, although not to either of the parties immediately concerned in the inquiry, nor within the possibility of verification at the time, but which were subsequently ascertained to be true by indisputable evidence. If reflex cerebral action failed to account for these, how much more difficult is it to explain a forthcoming fact, still unknown in our mundane sphere? But again, we must not anticipate.

Besides those occupying the middle ground of comparative indifference—friendly neutrality or who exercise a spirit of toleration in reference to all that may have grown out of the development of the phenomena, there are the unwise extremists among believers, who not only surrender their own reason in the extravagance of unquestioning faith, but propagate dogmas which are fanatical in theory, and carry out in daily practice, the premature conclusions of an unbridled fancy. Repudiating the authority of what they term old theology, they submit to the new and unknown authority received through their medium, setting aside the injunction of John in the Christian scriptures, and endorsed by the best reasoners to "believe not every spirit, but try the spirits." They repose unlimited confidence in the validity of the statements given to them in that way. In some instances, they have by their practices, shocked the moral sense of the community in which they live, or have temporarily sojourned, so as to bring disrepute upon the cause they were professing to advocate ; thus putting themselves on a level with the degenerate portion of their opponents in and out of churches, who have strayed from the path of rectitude ; instead of showing to the world a purer practice resulting from a more elevated philosophy, and revelation of truth.

A further class to be included in the public exponents, are the imposters, who pretend to believe whether they do or not, in the facts of Spiritualism. The reader is supposed to be sufficiently intelligent to supercede the necessity of any exposition on our part, of the character, and lack of moral worth of such people. So numerous are the adventurers in this world, in the present state of society, that there has never yet appeared a genuine production without its counterfeiters, more or less numerous. The best organizations—societies both secular and religious, of the highest pretentions, furnish sufficient examples of this, to make the honest man blush for the human race.

Such are time-servers, who always espouse the popular side. Their vacillating opinions and varying conduct destroy the value of their testimony on either side of any cause. If an umpire should put them in the scale in weighing the testimony for and against, they should be classed with the opponents of the cause they profess to advocate, (for it is with them that they really fraternize) or they should be thrown out of the estimate altogether. Every good cause suffers by wolves in sheep's clothing. In his false dress, the wolf is much more dangerous to the flock than the open raider, whose ferocity is undisguised.

Among the evidence in favor of Spiritualism, we have selected passages from the published discourses of Normal, Trance, and Inspirational Speakers, which of course, are expected to embody the best representative opinions on the affirmative side.

Although the spread of Spiritualism has been very rapid, and large accessions are constantly being made to the ranks of its adherents, it is still on trial in the minds of vast numbers of earnest seekers after truth, and it behooves each one to bring to its study a determination to conduct the research in an unprejudiced manner, so as to ascertain the exact truth. It is contrary to the spirit of the age to ignore facts, lest they should be found to interfere with previous misconceptions; or to refuse to institute a candid, honest inquiry into the existence and meaning of phenomena alleged to be new, because they are irreconcilable with a favorite theory. The manly course to pursue is to use the God-like reason with which we are endowed, and which is given us that we may be enabled to search after truth successfully, and ascertain for our-

selves the laws of Universal Nature, wherever that
search may lead us and whatever may be the result.
There are not wanting instances of men in high social, political and professional positions who began
such an investigation into the alleged facts and philosophy of Spiritualism, with the expectation of being
able to expose its groundlessness ; but who were imbued
with a spirit of candor, who had before them a scientific and a moral purpose, and considered the public just
as much entitled to the results of their investigation in
case of failure, as in the successful realization of their
expectations.

The fact of immortality is admitted to be of the highest importance, and if there is a future life, we must learn
about it sooner or later ; and there must be a decided
advantage on the part of those who place themselves in
a condition of receptivity, so as to learn as much of the
revelations concerning it, while passing through the ordinary earth experience as possible. He who neglects
his opportunities in this respect, sustains the greater
loss. Our earthly life at the longest is but short, and
a continued existence in a future state of being, must
necessarily be designed for higher development, giving
opportunity for increased happiness. To attain this our
life here must be regulated in accordance with moral
and spiritual laws ; discharging its duties with fidelity,
assuming its responsibilities with cheerful patience, and
endeavoring by all appropriate means to place ourselves
in a condition of due preparation for the enjoyment of
the privileges of the higher life. This is a practical
consideration in which all are equally interested, and

is obviously of sufficient moment to justify us in inviting the reader to an earnest examination of its claims upon his attention. A subject which so profoundly concerns human destiny cannot be passed by with indifference. As means to an end, there are also in this life numerous practical questions of a moral and social nature, which should enter into the consideration of all systems of moral philosophy and of religion, whose teachings, carried out in daily life, stamp an indelible impress on character and conduct. Spiritualism professes to comprise within its work whatever has to do with the welfare of the human family. The measures thus comprehended will be discussed in their proper order.

PART I.

———

TESTIMONY AGAINST SPIRITUALISM.

"The dead know not any thing." Eccl. ix, 5.
"If a man die, shall he live again?" Job xiv. 14.
"What positive proof have we of immortality?"

Before quoting the statements of fact, and the adverse opinions which have been deduced from them on the one side, and gone forth as the well pronounced judgment of responsible critics, whose names are appended to their animadversions, we shall enumerate a list of assertions which have passed from one to another, without the responsibility of authorship, until they have become common property. The less thoughtful, and the least reasoning portion of a community acquire their opinions by appropriating common gossip, and perverted statements as the basis, avoiding the trouble of experiment, reading, inquiry or reason. They reach conclusions by a short cut; and though their process of reasoning is superficial, they become enthusiastic and zealous partisans, the side which they espouse depending altogether upon accidental surrounding circumstances. How far the assertions enumerated are amenable to the foregoing criticism, can only be judged of by the reader, after he shall have weighed the evidence on both sides. We desire only that pre-conceived opinions, and the prejudices resulting from mis-statements, after hearing one side of the question brought up for consideration be laid aside, and that the same candor be exercised in forming the judgement, which would be brought to the discussion of any other question.

GENERAL ASSERTIONS.

Spiritualists are a low set of people.

They are immoral.

They have no respect for the sabbath.

They are licentious.

They drink intoxicating drinks ; chew and smoke tobacco.

The female mediums are no better than prostitutes.

Speaking mediums often after giving a lecture, go off and get drunk.

Mediums and the believers in Spiritualism delight in making inharmony in the marriage relation, and try to break up families.

They have no respect for good society, and are unfit associates for decent people.

Those embracing the doctrines soon become demoralized, inattentive to business, losing their property, and finally bring up in the Insane Asylum.

We thought well of such and such persons, until they became Spiritualists.

We can trust them upon all subjects but one, and that is Spiritualism.

He is going crazy since he has become a Spiritualist.

No sensible, thinking person believes in the doctrines. Those who do are in their second childhood.

Spiritualism has never taken any but persons of weak brains.

They ignore the Bible as authority, and Jesus as God.

They have no respect for our minister, or the laws of the country.

They should not be allowed to utter their sacriligeous doctrines before the public ; the authorities should arrest them ; there should be a law to stop their proceedings.

Spiritualism is nothing but electricity and magnetism.

Spiritualism is all of the devil.

It is frequently asked "What good has Spiritualism done?"

If true, we are safe, but if not where are you?

If it is true, what of it?

PASSAGES FROM A TRACT ON SPIRITUALISM,

BY PROFESSOR AUSTIN PHELPS D. D., OF ANDOVER.

Spiritualism is not science. It has never yet assumed the order, the self-consistency, or the dignity of a science. Open its authorities, and what do you find which has built up astronomy, chemistry, geology, or even the more mobile science of political economy? In comparison with these, Spiritualism plunges us headlong into "chaos and old night." Specially, its laws of evidence are not those which science is wont to honor in other things.

Take the question of the personal identity of "spirits," for example. How can you answer it? Who is wise enough in the laws of spiritual being to tell us what is logical evidence of spiritual identity? How do I know the resources of chicanery in other spheres of existence? I have tolerable means of protection against the trickery of this world; but, when it comes to the possible trickery of the "seven spheres," woe is me! Nothing but downright miracle can settle this elementary question of identity.

Yet it is amazing that multitudes of inquirers, quick-witted in other things, ignore this whole question of spiritual identity, in testing the Revelation of the Seance. Men not used to the melting mood break down in tears at the assurance that a departed mother, wife, child, is addressing them in the harangue of a medium; but, when pressed for the proof of identity, they point to things which they would laugh at if used as evidence of fact in the sale of a horse. They would not buy so much as a jack-knife on such evidence.

So we say to the Spiritualists, "With all due respect to your intuitions, we would like to have Lord Bacon and the rest subpoenaed, and put into the witness-box. Your craft is not a science till it can stand a trial by jury." The most scholarly of American defenders of Spiritualism is evidently staggered by this questioning of identity.

Is it like God to set going the machinery of the supernatural world, for the sake of recovering a lost earring? Is it like God to send " spirits from the vasty deep," as in the case of one of the afflicted, to discourse upon pumpkin-pies?

Excuse us, gentlemen. Whatever else this may be, it is not religion. It hoots at our grand Biblical theology. It degrades our beautiful Christian ideal of heaven. It bedraggles our most sacred hopes of immortality.

Spiritualism is not good morals. Good men and women are among its believers, no doubt. Afflicted ones seek in it communion with their sainted dead, with no thought of wrong. Restless inquirers search it for some wiser adjustment of nature to the supernatural than they have found elsewhere, with no profane curiosity. Christian believers, of pure lives and Biblical faith, think they can accept a fragment of it here and there, in an electic fashion, without damage to their holier experience.

But after all, and to these exceptional believers it should be said in sad faithfulness, the drifting of this modern theurgy is to loose morals.

More than all else, they breathe a deadly antipathy to the Christian theory of the relations of the sexes. Where else do denunciations of the servitude of marriage find so congenial a home as in a spiritualistic library? Where else such loose theories of divorce?

Where else so much nonsense about "affinities," "spiritual unions," " twin-spirits," and the like?

Spiritualism, taken as a whole, is not good sense. Not that the admission of a certain modicum of fact in its alleged phenomona is unreasonable.

It is not good sense to receive the rhapsodies and incoherences of clairvoyants as a substitute or a supplement of the Christian Scriptures. It is not good sense to interrogate a modern witch of Endor, to get something better than Paul's testimony to the immortality of the soul. It is not good sense to ask or answer the irreverent question whether Jesus Christ was anything more than a spiritualistic medium, and whether his miracles were like the table-tippings.

Ignorant men may believe it till they know better. Silly women may be led captive by it till they are wiser. Sick nerves may dance to such music till their possessors get more protoxide of iron into their blood.

But solid, sober, sensible men and women, whose fathers and mothers were of healthy stock, and who have inherited a right to large, well-balanced brains, " looking before and after," have no proper place in that assemblage.

At this point, candor requires some concessions to Spiritualists on the part of their opponents.

We must concede to them a certain basis of phenomomenal facts. Precisely how much must be yielded may not yet be certain; but fair criticism will grant something. Bad and foolish as the modern necromancy is, it is not an unmitigated humbug. Bees do not swarm upon nothing. Neither do believers plunge in crowds into an absolute vacuum.

As little reason have we to cavil at the character of a certain portion of the testimony by which the toughest facts of Spiritualism are supported. Some of that testimony, so far as it respects the sanity, the culture, the integrity, and the opportunities of the witnesses, would convict a murderer in any court in Christendom, outside of New-York City.

It is too late also to set down the spiritualistic phenomena as only a re-vamping of old, or an invention of new, feats of jugglery. Their advocates are not to be censured, if they decline to argue with a man who comes to them, as from the detective police, with the logic of invisible wires, and of sleight-of-hand, and of leaden plummets concealed under crinolines. We might have been excusable for such innocence twenty five years ago ; but it will not do now. Signor Blitz, who probably knows as much as most men of the capacities of jugglery, has been heard to say, that nothing on record in the history of his professsion could account for that class of facts on which Spiritualism chiefly builds. Robert Houdin also, who claims to be the inventor of most of the tricks performed by the fraternity of modern jugglers, has declared his inability to equal or to account for the so-called spiritual occurences which he has witnessed. Similar testimony is borne by M. Hamilton, a Parisian expert in legerdemain, and by M. Rhys, a maker of the conjuring implements used by Houdin.

Moreover, the theories of scientists thus far announced cannot fairly be held to cover all the facts of the case. Electricity, magnetism, odic force, nervous disease, unconscious cerebration—do not any or all of them exhaust the demands of candid science in explanation of the phenomena?

After all these deductions, Spiritualism is apparently right in claiming that a residuum of fact remains, which goes straight to the point of proving the presence and activity of extra human intelligence. For one, I must concede this, at least, as a plausible hypothesis.

What are the facts of our faith on this doctrine? On the same testimony on which we hold other Scriptural facts, we hold these : that a malign being exists in the universe, who is distinct in his personality ; that he is at the head of a vast organization of subordinate kindred spirits ; that they have a limited, yet immense, spiritual power ; that they are especially malignant towards the person and doctrine of Jesus Christ ; that they have peculiar affinities with the most grovelling of human vices ; that to a certain extent the elements and laws of nature are subject to their use ; that they have access to the abodes and hearts of men.

Have we not, then, in the " devil and his angels," of whom the Scriptures forewarn us, the " sufficient cause" which philosophy requires for all that there is in Spiritualism which science cannot otherwise explain? Are we, on the one hand, asked to imagine unknown and unknowable laws of mind and of matter? What for? Are we on the other hand, required to muddle ourselves with extra-biblical conjectures of the organization of Hades?

But it is claimed that Spiritualism is not devilish in its moral spirit. Not only do some good men and women believe it, which is nothing to the purpose, but some inspiring truths, it is said are affirmed by it.

"If evil angels come, why not good angels?" We answer they do. "Are they not all ministering spirits?" But not after this table-tipping, lying, swearing fashion. The evidence of the evil in the phenomena is superabundant : the evidence of good is no more than a device of temptation must have. Do you suppose that Satan would aim at anything less than this, if he should set about creating a wide-spread delusion for the capture of souls?

The devil and his subordinates may do a great many silly things, but they are not fools. He will never concoct, nor they execute, a system of temptation which is all falsehood or all vice or all nonsense. He will never organize a set of agencies which shall show themselves up at the outset as pure malignants. That would tempt nobody, and would make him the laughing-stock of the universe. He knows better than to paint himself with horns and hoofs.

Spiritualism, then we claim, on the hypothesis, that, so far as it claims religious authority, it is of Satanic origin, is cunningly adapted to its end. Senseless as it seems to sedate and Christian logic, it is very crafty as a compound of temptations.

When the late President Day, of Yale College, first

had his attention called to Spiritualism, a quarter of a century ago, said he, "Either nothing is in it, or the devil is in it." No candid man, who knows its history during these twenty five years, will now affirm the first wing of the president's alternative. The second is as philosophical as it is Scriptural.

Dr. Gulick, late of the Hawaiian Islands, says that American Spiritualism has no marvels which equal those of the Hawaiian Paganism, testified to by eye-witnesses of them not long ago living, and used by the Pagan priesthood as miracles in support of the national religion.

OPINIONS OF REV. W. T. DWIGHT D. D.

The following paragraphs are extracted from a sermon preached against Spiritualism by W. T. Dwight D. D. of Portland, Me. The distinguished position of this divine, as an expounder of Orthodoxy, enables him to wield a powerful influence, not only over the minds of his own parishioners and among the people of his own denomination, but among many others whose religious predilections accord with orthodox views, for it is said that he stands as the representative of three quarters of all the Congregationalists, Baptists, Methodists and Episcopalians in the State.

For convenience, several sentences not in immediate succession, but having a kindred sentiment are included in one of the paragraphs. They set forth in strong terms the belief that any leaning towards Spiritualism

is condemned in the Bible, from which necessarily follows its condemnation by the church.

"God has purposely confined the knowledge of these
things to Himself.   This is the reason why they are secret, or why they have not been revealed : 'they belong
to Him,' and not to men, not to creatures.   * * * It
is alike irreligious and fruitless on our part to seek to
know them ;"   "He keeps us in ignorance : He keeps
absolutely secret with Himself what He intends to do,
and most of what He is constantly doing."

"It is not only the prerogative, but the choice of God,
to hide Himself, or to withhold from His creatures,
in many respects, the knowledge of His nature and His
operations."

"We are also in utter ignorance of futurity, and of
what is now taking place in any other quarter of the
universe, or in any other world.   It has been also, as
we see, with perfect certainty, God's intention to keep
ourselves and our whole race [including, of course, Swe-
edenborg] in this very state of ignorance—an ignorance
inevitable and absolute, so long as we live on the earth.

"God's spiritual essence, His self-existence, His eternity, His omnipotence and ominscience, and His infinite
moral perfections ;—these are not only subjects, but
they involve facts and realities, directly concerning Himself, which we are as incapable of knowing as is the in-
sect ; the archangel can as little comprehend them.
They are all secrets of God."

"Among these secret things are to be included the
purposes of God."

"Aside from the word of God, he knows not that the

internal fires, which have been ever raging within the earth, may not burst forth ere to-morrow's sun, and consume our race and all the vestiges of humanity."

"The future, and by this term is included the persons and the events belonging to all coming time, is also secret with God."

"The state of the Invisible World is absolutely secret with God."—"The World of Spirits, and I include here Heaven and Hell, their respective localities—so far as they have locality, the actual condition of departed persons individually, and all intercommunication with such persons and with the dead universally;—all this, excepting the few and general revelations which are contained in the Scriptures, is entirely hidden from men."—"God has determined that we should possess just so much knowledge of the World of Spirits as can be acquired from His own announcements by inspired prophets and apostles and the saviour; and He has also determined that we should possess no other knowledge. The fact that He has revealed to us, in the Bible, what we thus actually know respecting the invisible world and its inhabitants, is in itself decisive evidence that He has purposed we should know nothing additional. What we have there revealed to us, He has disclosed to us for our profit: what He has not there revealed, He has withheld for the same reason."—"We know that God, as the Infinite Ruler who has given the Bible to men, and Christ, as the crowned Mediator who now rules directly in the World of Spirits, will permit no such knowledge to be communicated from any other source."

"The light of the Gospel was introduced into Iberia, a province of Asia (now called Georgia), in the following manner : a certain woman was carried into that country as a captive, during the reign of Constantine ; and by the grandeur of her miracles, and the remarkable sanctity of her life and manners, she made such an impression upon the king and queen, that they abandoned their false gods, embraced the faith of the Gospel, and sent to Constantinople for proper persons to give them and their people a more satisfactory and complete knowledge of the Christian religion."

" I am willing to grant, that many events have been rashly deemed miraculous which were the result of the ordinary laws of nature ; and also, that pious frauds were sometimes used for the purpose of giving new degrees of weight and dignity to the Christian cause. But I cannot, on the other hand, assent to the opinions of those who maintain that in this century, miracles had entirely ceased ; and that at this period, the Christian Church was not favored with any extraordinary or supernatural mark of a Divine power engaged in its cause."

- "Descriptions of the unseen world and of the state of the departed [by spiritual mediums], have been stolen * * * from Emanuel Swedenborg, when describing his seven spheres or heavens, or from others ; or if original are just fit to fill the pages of a fourth-rate novel."

"They [the secret things of God] are secret, because He [God] has not revealed them to men ; and because it is His purpose not to reveal them while the Christian dispensation is continued."

"Literal verity when affirming, that in all the published volumes of these pretended revelations, there is not one original and valuable thought."

"If the Bible and the God of the Bible are not both a lie, Spiritualism, in all its claims to supernatural communications, is the most contemptible, the most mischievous, and one of the most wicked, among existing delusions."

"Neither good angels, for they would utterly loathe the whole matter; nor bad angels, for God will not permit them thus directly to act in the affairs of men; nor departed saints, for they are at rest and in transport with their Savior; nor lost spirits, for they are in prison; are active here."

"It professes to hold direct and constant intercourse with the invisible world, or with the region of departed spirits. Christians who have died in the Lord, and reputable men of the world—together with murderers, drunkards, and harlots, who have not died in the Lord, can at almost any time be brought into immediate communication with any persons who desire it. Primitive martyrs and Christ's apostles may be thus summoned. Ancient prophets and patriarchs may be thus summoned, etc. We are assured that at spiritual meetings, which are now held in certain regions in Europe,—whether such blasphemies are yet practised in our own country, we know not,—the Lord Jesus Christ is thus summoned and catechised; and he communicates the desired information."

Animal magnetism is described by Dr. D. as follows:

"An influence or element in some respects resembling electricity and natural magnetism, and in others

independent of both : an influence or element partly
physical, and partly pertaining to the human body, in
which in different persons it exists in very unequal degrees."

"There shall not be found among you any one that
maketh his son or his daughter to pass through the fire,
or that useth divination, or an observer of times, or an
enchanter, or a witch, or a charmer or a consultor with
familiar spirits, or a wizard, or a necromancer. For all
that do these things are an abomination to the Lord."

"They who did this [sought unto the spirits of the
dead] were, by God's own appointment, as the Penta-
teuch informs us, to be capitally punished as traitors to
God, the theocratic sovereign of the nation. That punishment indeed ceased, and properly, with the final
overthrow of idolatry among the Jewish people."

"It is not hyperbole, but literal verity, when he affirms that its spirit [the spirit of Spiritualism] is anti-
Christian and heathenish."

OPINIONS OF ELDER JACOB KNAPP THE BAPTIST REVI-
VALIST.

On Friday evening, March 10th, Jacob Knapp, from
Illinois—the celebrated Baptist revivalist, whose language is so potent to stir up the emotions of fear in the
breasts of women and children, and whose ideas on all
things seemed warped by his doctrine—held forth on
the above subject in Tremont Temple, Boston, to a
large audience, composed of many of the "faithful," and
a considerable sprinkling of free-thinkers and Spiritual-

ists, who were attracted to see what kind of treatment
their belief was to receive at the hands of this wielder
of the "Jerusalum blade," as the printed sheets of songs
distributed among the audience denominated him.

Elder Knapp was then introduced. He showed that
the hand of time had dealt kindly with him. He appeared, a thick set, strongly knitted frame, a firm-
drawn face, crowned and edged with silvery gray hair
and beard, and a very magnetic power seemed to gleam
in his eye as he walked the platform and gazed abroad
over the congregation.

The Elder assured his hearers that "Our Jesus" was
not represented by that infidel ideal which was so generally held up by the free-thinkers. The devil could
not walk off with Jesus under his arm ; but as for the
Unitarian Jesus, the devil could take him off his feet
pretty quick. The speaker instanced, among other
passages in the Bible, to prove the presence of the devil in heaven—that is, that he was not yet excluded—
those referring to the false prophets—or the lying spirit in the mouth of Ahab's prophets, which led that king
to his destruction—and declared that the spirit who then
offered his services to God to go down to earth and be
that lying spirit, was the devil. The case was also
mentioned occurring in the Book of Job, where it was
recorded that "there was a day when the sons of God
came to present themselves before the Lord, and Satan
came also among them to present himself before the
Lord."

The lecturer therefore declared that though the residence of the devil is on our earth, yet he has some ac-

cess to heaven and the presence of the angels of God. To trace the conflict between the seed of the flesh and the spirit in the history of the race was very easy.

And so they went up and up in their labors to raise a pathway to the skies, till God came down in wrath and confused their language so that they could no longer build, and they were scattered over the globe. Just so the Elder said the Unitarians want to get up to heaven without Jesus Christ, but they will meet with a similar fate.

The same conflict was to be seen in the family of Abraham, wherein one child Ishmael, was born after the flesh, and was the servant of the devil, and the other, Isaac, was born of the spirit, and God recognized him as the seed of the woman. When they were but mere lads, the child of the flesh persecuted the child of the spirit.

But why, asked the Elder, should the whole world rise against all the high priests of the living God? Because they belong to the devil, and by his command they seek to slay the prophets. Why should John the Baptist be cut off from the world as he was, and only be allowed to preach for a brief time? He bore malice toward no one—he was working that men should prepare a way for the coming Lord of Life; but the seed of the serpent had a deadly enmity against the seed of the woman, and the followers of evil determined to put him out of the world. And when Jesus himself appeared, they hated him and hastened to nail him on the cross— to their minds it was not good to have such a fellow on the earth. And who, at the present day, was so much hated by the servant of the devil as Jesus Christ?

Here was a case in point, to the mind of the Elder; the true prophet foretold the destruction of the king, while the false prophets—inspired by the devil of course —sought to lure the man on, and therefore gave pleasant words to his ear. The Elder declared that God never asks us to believe without evidence, and referred to the signs of supernatural power given by Moses before Pharaoh. Here the magicians and diviners of Egypt —the Spiritualists of those days—were able with their "enchantments" to imitate the miracles of Moses, till they reached the changing of the dust to insects. This they were unable to do, and they said unto Pharaoh, "This is the finger of God." In all their previous efforts, filled with the evil spirit, they had endeavored to destroy the faith of the people in Moses, who was the servant of God, and the seed of the woman.

We are told by Jesus, said the Elder, that in the last days " there shall arise false Christs and false prophets, and shall shew great signs and wonders, in so much that, if it were possible, they shall deceive the very elect;" that is, men who were calculated to deceive— and many women also—should come filled with false teachings, being the instruments of the devil in his efforts to overturn the truth of God; and many souls should by them be led blind captives to his will, till he plunges them into the bottomless pit, there to howl and agonize for an eternity of woe. The Elder said that as, in our rebellion, the rebels tried to get all the States and all the men they could to join their ranks, so the devil is constantly looking up recruits for his

great rebellious army, that is marshalled against the
Lord God under the black banner of hell !

This devil, according to the Elder, has many ways of
working out his pleasure among the people.   No one
scheme will answer for a long time.   Bald Atheism had
had its day, and was powerless for harm ; and Deism,
Parkerism, Unitarianism, Universalism, and, worst of
all Spiritualism—a universal conglomeration of all the
others—have been instituted to do the devil's work in
turning souls from the Lord Jesus.   They say that there
are four millions of Spiritualists in the United States
this very day, and many of the Universalists and Unitarians, and all the rest of God's enemies, who are fight-
ing against the heavenly watchward of "Union," and
under the ensign of the devil, are drifting towards Spiritualism.

The Elder desired it understood, however, that, while
he acknowledged that there is a great deal of jugglery,
mesmerism, deception and perfect fraud in the manifestations of the spirit mediums, there are yet those things
existing among Spiritualists that cannot be accounted
for except by the exertion of a superhuman diabolical
power.   No mesmerism can make a table rise up
without hands; there is some power there.   It is the
power of the devil.   I want you to see the devil's object.   He knows that there is a strong desire on the part
of humanity to know something more about that future
that God does not reveal.   We all know that we are
very anxious to learn what they are doing who have
passed beyond our sight.   Oh, how I felt about my
son who fell on the field of battle !   All I have in this

world—I thought—I would give if I could see him and have five minutes conversation with him. So I felt till I hushed myself, and went back to the Word of God, and thought that there he had given us all we ought to know. And there are many men who are trying to get a knowledge of the future. The speaker referred to many men who were "thinking men but not Christians," who wanted to know about the future, and instanced the case of Dr. Greely and a friend, who once entered into an agreement that they would hang each other—the subject to be suspended as long as possible ere death should supervene, and then to be cut down and restored. Dr. Greely was hanged first, and almost died; but when he was brought to consciousness he had nothing to tell—he had not been able to penetrate the mysteries of God. The Elder recited the case of the [to him] dead Lazarus, who, after lying four days in the tomb, did not bring anything back with him when Christ, by a miracle, restored him to his sisters and friends.

When God completed his revelation, he said, "It is finished; the world has all the light it will ever have; no new revelation will ever be given to the human family." This revelation was sufficient. Man didn't understand a millionth part of it; and yet some dissatisfied ones were seeking to know more, and were for that purpose calling in the aid of the devil, in direct contempt to the revealed will of God. The devil knows just what men want when they seek to penetrate God's mysteries. If he wants to lead a man to hell he tells him what he desires, the man believes, and goes his

way to the eternal fire.   The Elder said the Spiritualists point triumphantly to the intelligence manifested
and the information given at their circles—but where
did it come from?   The devil, of course.   Depend upon it, it is he that brings you the intelligence.   You go
into a room where all who are assembled are perfect strangers to you, and you ask the medium whether
you have children—if any are dead—how many years
ago they died, and where, perhaps desire their names
—and you are answered correctly in every particular.
Now, where does this knowledge of your family affairs
come from? Why, the devil knows where and when and
how they died ; he keeps a record, and sometimes, when
you ask a question and he is n't ready to answer, he asks
for time—he has got to go and bring an answer from
some other devil.   I have had to wait for hours sometimes for a reply.

You will remark that the devil denies occasionally
the inspiration of certain portions of the Bible ; he
won't deny it all at once, and again he tries to sweep it
away, and will say "It is out of date ; it is designed for
a darker age ; but you are to expect many revelations
from truthful sources to supply its place."   If the person to be approached is Orthodox, he will tell him that
it is n't an eternal hell into which the wicked are plunged,
but that by-and-by they come out of it ; and the next
thing—when he thinks the man will bear it—he tells
him there is n't any hell at all !   Then he will destroy
his belief in the Bible, and leave him, without compass
or chart, beating about upon the waves of a shoreless
sea, till he dashes upon the rocks and goes down into

the deeps of everlasting misery ! So you see, [said the speaker,] that the devil is all the time deceiving men and women, and making them believe they are communicating with their friends whom they have lost, or with the spirits of persons who on earth bore good reputations for knowledge or morality. Again he arrests their attention by performing many remarkable things, many of which I have witnessed—far more than I ever saw in print. If you don't believe my statements you can write to Mr. Hook, of Stockton, Cal., or to Dr. Grattan ; they will tell the same story, and endorse cheerfully all I say : Some three years ago I started for California, but before I had arrived, or before it was known that I was coming there, in the family of Mr. Hook occurred many strange things. His wife was a Baptist ; Hook was an unbelieving man, though well known in the community, being a member of the City Council ; and Yates, his neighbor, was the clerk of the Court ; but still both were irreligious men. And while I was on my way to California, there appeared a strange being in Mr. Hook's house. The Elder said they had no family but by adoption, and one of the children, a little girl, used to complain of a hideous figure she saw, who threw water on her and her companion when they retired to bed. The bed being moved did not mend the matter. The chamber being searched revealed no possible chance for the ingress or egress of a human being undiscovered, yet the individual still appeared, throwing water—and dirty water at that. Sometimes the slats were removed from their trundle-bed during the night, and they would be let down upon the floor. By-and-by the apparition began to talk to them. The girl was the medium; she could see him; she was an honest girl—didn't know anything about Spiritualism, or about the Elders coming. She would describe correctly the spirits, or beings, she saw around people in the house, so that they would be recognized as representatives of those who had been known on earth by the parties. To the question of why the rest could not see these things as well as the girl, the speaker replied that all persons were not alike. Balaam could not see the angel in his path, but the unthinking ass perceived him; so the devil may be seen by one person and not by another. Following the appearance of the speaking phase came a curiosity on the part of Messrs. Hook and Yates, with their families to know something regarding its powers of conversation, so they met and questioned of the presence—whom the Elder considered to be the devil—whether Elder Knapp was coming, and the answer was, "Yes he has sailed, and is now on his way." They asked if there would be a revival of religion in the neighborhood on his arrival, and were told there would be, and that Mr. Hook and Mr. Yates would be converted.

The Elder thought it did not require any great amount of prescience to perceive the source of the replies. "Of course the devil keeps his eye on me; and he knew when I left New York, and he also knew that there would be a revival on my arrival in California, and that these two women—who were praying women—would plead strongly for the conversion of their ungodly husbands; he could make such assertions without the least risk." Mr. Hook asked him if there was a hell, and was affirmatively answered. The questioner, who did not believe in hell, was quite "taken aback." These conversations and singular manifestations occurred for some three weeks previous to the Elder's coming to the house, and the families witnessing did not mention anything of the matter among the people outside. They were perfectly at a loss to know what to make of the sights and sounds, as they did not believe in Spiritualism.

The Elder arriving, questioned the parties, and was shown the discoloration made by the water that had dripped from where it had been thrown by the mysterious agent, and also some still remaining upon the window-glass of the room where the child medium had lately slept. They asked the apparition his name, and he answered, "Elijah Greenfield." That was the name of Mrs. Hook's first husband, and he pretended to be the same, but contradicted himself in several of his statements; and when reminded of it, he replied by asking them, with a laugh, if they supposed he was bound always to speak the truth? The Elder was of opinion that the people in question ought to have known enough about the devil to know that he is the father of lies.

Then "Elijah" began to throw things about; then "he" took the girl's pillow and threw it into another room, dashed the spittoons about so rapidly that the family could not stop them; and they did not know whence the power proceeded which hurled them around the room : "he" took two China vases and broke them,

and two statuettes that cost Mr. Hook twenty five dollars, shared the same fate, being dashed to pieces in a
corner of the room.   As fast as these things were broken up, the family would take the pieces and put them
out of the house, keeping the matter a secret for the three
weeks above stated.   Finally, one day, a young man—
afterwards a minister preaching in California—was sitting at the table, who knew nothing of the matter in the
house, when his coffee-cup was taken up and thrown
over his head without any visible agency : after which,
the tureen dishes—one with meat, and the other with
potatoes—were thrown after it.   The startled family
explained the matter as best they could.

But by-and-by the mysterious being begun to get
tired of throwing water, and threw fire !   This did not
burn, according to the Elder's description, but only
sparkled and produced a redness on the medium's arms
and hands ; so he thought it might have been phospho-
rus, or something of a kindred nature.   [Laughter.]
"You need not laugh over that," said the Elder ; "it is
a solemn fact—one to be prayed over—when you re-
flect what a masterful power of evil is at large in your
midst."   If the devil could slay the servants and cattle
of Job, and afflict him with such sufferings could he not
break a few dishes or destroy a little furniture ? asked
the speaker.   "If God lets out his chain he can do
more."   The Elder said at present the power of the
devil was stayed, for beyond the breaking of the furniture the demon had no power—at least according to his
experience.   The demon, however, tried to accomplish
evil for the little girl by advising her to leave her kind

friends and go to another place which he recommended, and failing, tried to frighten her by telling her he would kill her. He said to her, "If I can throw water and fire, can I not take your life?" Her mother, in this emergency, told her to call on Jesus, and the devil immediately retreated. "The devil can't stand Jesus," said the Elder, triumphantly; "I can go and pray the devil out of any medium, or out of any circle. He will fly; but Christ is stronger than the strong man armed. Christ has the power to take away the capability of the devil to do these things."

One of the most powerful revivals of religion occurring in modern times, we are assured by the Elder, followed his preaching in that vicinity, and the singular manifestations appeared to be all over—indeed, all parties concerned were congratulating themselves to that effect, when the devil again appeared; notwithstanding nightly prayer meetings were held in the house, and other holy disinfectants were put in use, the devil showed his presence unto the praying band by hurling a big book that was on the table across the room. The devil taking—as is mentioned above—the cognomen of her first husband—according to the Elder —told Mrs. Hook he would drive her out of the house —which was quite consistent with his character on earth, he having tried to kill her just before his own death, also having threatened to haunt her as long as she lived. The Elder said he supposed Greenfield had got the devil to go back to trouble his wife, and the task must have been eminently pleasant to him, especially to persecute a wife who had done so much for a brutal husband.

The Elder said he always knew Spiritualism was of the devil, because he saw Universalists, Unitarians and Atheists, and all bad men flocking to its standard. During the last of his experiences in California, while sitting in a room with Mrs. Hook and the young girl above referred to, a spittoon was thrown at him from the next room through the open door, striking near him and breaking into many pieces. No one was in that room, nor could there possibly have been any one without his being able to discover him. It certainly was the devil himself, invisible to his sight. Similar occurrences of remarkable things had taken place at least once in about every hundred years of the world's history, from the days of the apostles till now ; and these last exhibitions of demoniacal power in our day were only a proof of the devil's determination to take advantage of the universally rebellious spirit of the age against God.

The speaker lamented the sad decay into which the Unitarian sect had fallen, as to their manners, at least. Why, thirty years ago they were quite respectable. They would never have descended to hire a miserable stool-pigeon like Hatch to stand at the doors of a church and peddle infidel tracts to deceive the people going in, who would take them, supposing them to be evangelical. "Hatch is a child of hell, and he knows it." In the old days they were very honorable to him, and never accused him of using bad English. They then said that Knapp believed just as all the Orthodox ministers did, and that they had just as soon be sent to hell in plain language, as to be "bowed and scraped" into it by softer speech and more graceful gestures. But now Unitarians were going out among the infidels and denying the Lord that bought them, and striving to undermine the whole Christian scheme of salvation, being among the chief apostles of his Satanic Majesty.

Now just look, said the Elder, at the Spiritualists, and the tendency of their system. The Bible says: "By their fruits ye shall know them." We know that Wesley was knowing to these things, and could not account for them, except they were done by the devil. The Elder declared that there were just as many devils in the world to-day as there ever were. He said that the Spiritualists never had done a good thing. The Wesley girls, who nicknamed him, could never get the devil to do anything in the house that was useful, even to brushing a room out, although he played numerous antics there. Now mark, said Knapp, how many there are who have been driven absolutely mad—have become inmates of a lunatic asylum, under the influence of Spiritualism. Hundreds and thousands, from the shores of the Atlantic to the shores of the Oregon. See how they look, exclaimed the Elder, who have given their time and thought to these things—lank, long-haired, wild-looking, careless and slovenly in their appearance, for the devil is uncleanly in his habits, and when he threw water at Hook's house it was dirty water. You will see them going on from worse to worse, the dupes of Satan. You can see by their very looks that they are but mere walking temples for devils. The Elder said all the old witches in the days of Saul were but emissaries of the devil, and were doing his

work. He called attention to the many families which
he asserted had been broken up by Spiritualism, which
never failed to introduce "Free-Loveism" wherever it
went. Those who had paid more attention to the subject than he had, had informed him that ninety-nine
one-hundredths of all the women believing in Spiritualism were common strumpets. "I wouldn't have one
of them in my house any sooner than I would have the
Old Fellow himself!"

He then proceeded to retail the following pathetic
story, saying that in Battle Creek, Michigan, some
years since, a lecturer on Spiritualism came along, and
he became acquainted with a widow lady, and he wanted
to make her a medium, pretending she would be a good
one; so they concluded to go around the country to
give lectures and hold their meetings with Satan; and
he expected to make it a good speculation, because
people are such miserable goslings that they will pay
out their one, five, or ten dollars, for the service of the
devil without a word of complaint. She had three
children, and since they had decided to travel, these
were in the way—they must be got rid of. So they
poisoned them, and they died. And thus these three
children were cut down in their young days, and died
under the influence of Spiritualism. These persons
were lying in prison when I went to California, because
the State of Michigan don't make use of the gallows.

The Elder said the drift of the Spiritualist lecturers
was to deride and ridicule or defy the Bible and its
teachings. He had heard one of these speakers in California say that if a man did not deny Jesus Christ, he

had no true fellowship with Spiritualists. Their speeches about Jesus were enough to make a Christian's blood run cold, and it was awful to think of their unrestrained blasphemy, and of what was to come in consequence.

Again, Elder Knapp in his discourse in Tremont Temple complained bitterly of the opposition which his revival movement was receiving from what he terms " the uncircumcised and ungodly infidels," Unitarians and Spiritualists in Boston. They were possessed, he said, by a legion of devils, 40,000 strong, and were led on by the infamous tract distributor to do battle against " the Lord's anointed." They found all manner of fault with him for his plainness of speech and fidelity to the truth ; but he had no doubt that if the Lord Jesus Christ was to come to Boston and preach three weeks, they would think and say that he (Knapp) was "quite a decent man compared with him." They had not even that outward respect for an ambassador of Jesus which many unconverted persons had. He remembered well that before he was converted he had a great reverence for a minister of the gospel as such ; remembered sleeping with one once, when a young man, and he had such a feeling of awe and reverence for the holy man that " it seemed as if God was there in bed with him." But these men were so depraved as to have not only no such feeling, but the opposite one, of bitter hatred and supreme contempt for those who preached the gospel with fidelity. The Elder was particularly severe upon the Spiritualists. Possessed with licentious devils, the Spiritualist women, he said, were leaving their families to shift for themselves and getting up houses of ill-fame all round the city. He had said the other day that 99 per cent. of the women Spiritualists were no better than strumpets. He now said that they were, without exception "old, rotten, dirty, stinking hags," and were running after Hatch and every other vile and unprincipled fellow who would consort with them.

The Traveller says "The National Convention of Spiritualists, at its session in Troy last week, besides choosing the Woodhull woman president, afflicted the world with some of the most absurd and wicked trash ever vented. One man defended profanity, boasting of his ability to swear in twenty languages, and claiming a "God-given-right to damn anything and everybody" he pleased. Another declared it was as natural for him to swear as for some people to pray, and it did just as much good. But even this was not the worst. Others indulged in declarations which would shame Atheists, and one woman declared unblushingly in favor of abolishing the institution of marriage and substituting therefor that of "natural affinities." A suggestion that the association should appoint regular officers whose duty it should be to solemnize spiritual unions between "affinities" in this world was received with general favor. No wonder the Woodhull found fit companions and satellites here.

FROM THE BOSTON HERALD.

A writer in the Boston Herald says "And I was once as blind as Denton and his comrades, but the loving Jesus had compassion on me, and called me to Himself by a direct revelation on the Christmas eve, 1835. Since that memorable night I have known and understood that Jesus is the Lord and Savior. I dare to declare that I am his eye-witness, for I have both seen His lovely face and form and heard His sweet voice, and further that the generally prevailing and promulgated doctrine that there can be no revelations, inspirations and other spiritual manifestations now-a-days is entirely false; that whatever was in old times can be also to-day, but under the same conditions and by the same laws; that the modern Spiritualism which claims, and also has indeed the above mentioned spiritual manifestations is of entirely different kind from the divine spirituality of the ancient saints, and of Jesus the King of the saints, as much as mud is different from clear water, it being condemned by the divine law and by the holy Scriptures as idolatry and rebellion, as a satanic system.

William Denton, in concert with all Spiritualists, asserts that Jesus was a clairvoyant and healing medium, and there are now as many good and righteous mediums "as Jesus ever dared to be." This is all false. These mediums are not worthy to wear the shoes of

Jesus, for they are of Satanic order, consulters with familiar spirits and idolaters, whereas Jesus was and is divine, filled and influenced by the Holy Spirit. These mediums find their equals in the woman called the Witch of Endor, in Simon Magus, called the sorcerer, and in the magicians, necromancers, enchanters, diviners and soothsayers, but not in the prophets, and Jesus whom they revile wickedly.

STATEMENTS OF DR. W. A. HAMMOND.

The real and fraudulent phenomena of what is called spiritualism are of such a character as to make a profound impression upon the credulous and the ignorant. * * * Such persons have probably from a very early age believed in the materiality of spirits, and having very little knowledge of the forces inherent in their own bodies, have no difficulty in ascribing occurrences, which do not accord with their experience, to the agency of disembodied individuals whom they imagine to be circulating through the world. In this respect they resemble those savages who regard the burning-lens, the mirror and other things which produce unfamiliar effects, as being animated by deities. Their minds are decidedly fetish-worshipping in character, and are scarcely, in this respect, of a more elevated type than that of the Congo negro who endows the rocks and trees with higher mental attributes than he claims for himself!

He has "witnessed many spiritualistic performances, and has never seen a single one which could not be accounted for by the operation of some one or more of the causes specified. No medium has ever yet been lifted into the air by spirits, no one has ever read unknown writing through a closed envelope, no one has ever lifted tables or chairs but by material agencies, no one has ever been tied or untied by spirits, no one has ever heard the knocks of a spirit, and no one has ever spoken through the power of a spirit other than his own."

The "causes specified" in the above remarks are diseased nerves, indigestion, hysteria, etc., and the writer, in his book against Spiritualism, advises the use of protoxide of iron, and other medicinal preparations, to dispel the delusion.

CHURCH OPPOSITION.

The progress of Spiritualism has taken such a wide range, and numbered among its adherents so many recruits from the various religious organizations, that the official authorities of a number of sects, either on their own account, or by instigation of zealous members among the laity, have felt conscientiously bound to take cognizance of what they considered a dangerous encroachment of heresy. Within a very few years such a case occurred in Laconia, N. H. Two ladies of the Congregational Church, yielding to what they declared to be the evidence of their senses, and a mental conviction arising from what they considered an irrepressible power acting upon their minds, came in conflict with the authoritative opinions of their rulers. The minister and certain of their fellow-members visited them, and informed them that their supposed evidence of spiritualism was a delusion, at the same time threatening them with expulsion from the church, if they continued to advocate the new doctrine, or to entertain the belief in the truth of the phenomena. Their crime consisted in the fact that music was heard in their presence, as if produced by instruments, while no such instruments were visible. The ladies having, as they aver, had no agency in evoking the harmonious sounds, and therefore being unwilling so summarily to yield their conscientious convictions, were accordingly expelled.

Other denominations have taken similar action in relation to members who felt themselves irresistibly attracted to the subject.

FATHER HECKER'S CAUTION.

Some years ago Father Hecker, editor of the *Catholic World*, and one of the distinguished divines of the Roman Catholic Church in America, lectured against Spiritualism, which he termed a delusion. In one of his lectures, delivered in Chicago, he said that the path Spiritualists were treading, was a dangerous one, and that his audience should avoid it as they would a snake in the grass.

The Roman Church claims to have spiritual communications in isolated instances, as a gift to the favored, but she interdicts the practice of mediumship.

This large division of the Chrstian Church is not alone in her opposition.

The Protestant Church as we have already shown, by reference to the remarkable bitterness of spirit indulged by prominent representatives of several sects, when speaking of the subject, exceeds the opposition of the Romish priests.

The Swedenborgians with few exceptions, condemn it, assuming that the founder of their sect is the only medium of special inspiration in modern times.

In what is called the liberal portion of the Protestant Church in America, the discussion of the subject is treated with gentlemanly courtesy, yet several instances have occurred in which not only doubt has been expressed, but its pretensions have been treated with sarcasm.

Besides these, the expounders of Hebrew Theology, and the Liberalists, called by their enemies, by way of opprobium, Infidel have been to a great extent, arrayed against it.

The positions of these several controversialists will be further considered in subsequent pages.

The Rev. Justin D. Fulton D.D., the Rev. Mr. Morgan, and the celebrated showman, P. T. Barnum may all be placed in the category of out-spoken opponents, not only of Spiritualism, but of spiritualists.

The Baptist divine is scarcely less censorious than his confrere, Elder Knapp; and has spoken of believers in the strange phenomena in terms of malediction, even more severe if possible than his celebrated denunciation of the character and life-work of the late Charles Dickens, which so sorely afflicted the vast multitudes of admirers of the latter's genius and of the humane tendency of his writings. He quotes passages from the Bible, the interpretation of which, he claims, proves that the spiritual phenomena are the works of the devil; and asserts that there is no good thing in it.

The spiritualists complain that Mr. Barnum spares no occasion to traduce them and their cause.

Mr. Morgan, in a discourse delivered in the Music Hall, Boston, made grave charges of fraudulent practises, against certain travelling healers, which however, have been as stoutly denied.

These persons have denounced the practice of seeking spiritual knowledge in the way pursued by spiritualists, as dangerous, and a curse to society, which should be arrested.

Scientific men have generally ignored the claims of Spiritualism. This has been a source of complaint among its defenders. It has been attacked and denounced both by certain scientists individually, and by some in their collective, organized capacity. The action of the authorities of Harvard College, for example, in expelling a student of the Divinity School for exhibiting mediumistic powers, is not forgotten.

Recent events furnish examples of a decided tendency in the other direction, as will be seen in the sequel.

PART II.

CONSERVATISM.

THERE is a class of public speakers and writers who have not expressed themselves with boldness upon either side of the main question discussed in these pages. Unwilling to array themselves with some, at least of the opponents who have acquired prominence by their undisguised expressions of opposition nor to commit themselves against it, in the language of Mr. Knapp and persons of similar character; yet having a disposition to inquire into the significance of the phenomena, they have spoken and written as nearly definite as the signs of the times seemed, according to their own conscientious scruples, to require of them. They occupy an intermediate position, owing allegiance to neither.

They admit the occurrence of spiritual phenomena, but apparently have not attached much importance to them. They cannot consider the manifestations diabolical in character, at least they have refrained from expressing themselves to that effect. What they intend precisely to be understood to mean, it is not proper here in a simple marshalling of the expressed opinions of the opposing parties, to state. The reader must draw the inference. The definite yea or nay wanting, we class them as conservatives, desirous of leaving the existing condition of things undisturbed. Among such we include the following. Some such persons, desiring at all times to subserve the interests of truth, according to the inpetus given by new occurrences express themselves in a more outspoken manner at one time than another; but do not seem to be fully convinced in their own minds so as to take a definite position on either side.

REV. H. W. BEECHER.

The following abstract of a discourse by Mr. Beecher embraces the proper method of reasoning to arrive at or depart from Spiritualism. If his hearers pursue an independent course of inquiry, it leaves the teacher irresponsible for their conclusions.

Sunday, Nov. 26th, Mr. Beecher's morning discourse was on "Science and Theology." His text, was taken from Tim. iii : 13-17. The end, he said, is more valuable than the means; the house is more valuable than are the tools by which the house is built. The Bible itself is valueless; but so far as it accomplishes good, it is of transcendent value. The adoration of the church and of the Bible are both idolatrous; but if I am obliged to choose between a book—a record—and a living church made up of living men interpreting God's providence, I should say, Give me the church by all means. In the past, the Bible has not been free from controversy and assault; but the actual experience of the hearts of men has overthrown skeptics in our day. The assaults are stronger, better aimed, more vital, and more in alliance with scientific inquiry, armed with an acuteness never brought to bear before; but the preponderance of evidence still remains with the Bible. Nevertheless, the campaign is going to another Waterloo. The ground, to some, seems to be falling away from the word of God. The undermining of science seems to them likely to destroy its foundation. But the all important instrument for this destruction is lacking. Within the sphere of science comes the origin of man, the facts of mental and of moral philosophy, the mysteries of moral and spiritual intuition: but it does not hold within its arms the one great element of moral conscientiousness. The atmosphere of doubt acts in many ways; but that it is acting powerfully and precipitously, few can doubt. Be as little conversant with the terms, the world or humanity, who does not know that over religion there hangs to-day an amount of doubt and uneasiness which may not be computed? While the question, "Is there a God?"—the question which has been the great controversy of ages—is thundering round about us, they that believe in it, instead of fortifying themselves against a common enemy, are virtually knocking down their own bulwarks by disputes about the meanest elements of theological geometry.

A state of doubt is as fatal in its practical consequence as a state of unbelief. Both paralyze. If you attempt by the Bible to establish a perfect scheme of moral philosophy out of intellectual reason you will fail. It is not sufficient for that. The word of God draws the line between duty on the one side and wrong on the other—between lust and virtue, ambition and right. A man might as well go to Webster's Dictionary to find out how Mozart's Requiem sounds, as to endeavor to find advice as to the petty governments of a church in the elucidation of abounding mystery in the Bible. Although my whole life has been spent in the study of the Scriptures, I am not competent to investigate them ; but I am able to know what is best for the true manhood, to know that love everywhere is better than hatred—and so are you. The Bible fashions character. The devotees who seeing the mischief of doubt, refuse to doubt anything, and, not content with denying themselves, though they deny to everybody else, they say : " You have got to take the Bible literally ; you must read it just as it is." What nonsense ! Such a proceeding may be safe to men who were not in danger any way, but for those who don't want to be led by the nose, it is dangerous. You make skeptics of such men—set their pride against belief. The Bible is full of facts, and they must give way. It is said, " In six days God created the earth." The rocks told a different story ; they say it took thousands of years. Theologians grew wrathy and gave the lie to Nature. But to-day the rocks have proved their story, and we know that a day is a season. We take these days for gigantic periods, and geology and theology agree. The rocks have not changed, but the interpretation of Genesis has. I don't say to young men, "leave science alone;" but I say "Don't hurry." I say, "Don't read, but study." The spiritual force of the Bible gains in every generation. So I say to scientists, "Study up the knowledge of man, his adaptability to social life. Join hands with the Philosopher, the Mesmerist,, the Spiritualist and License Demonstration Herself to every Nation." No one knows anything about the Bible until it is to him the same as is a medicine book in actual sickness. The medicating power of the Bible is therefore its life.

A statement having obtained some degree of publicity to the effect that Mr. B. had expressed his belief in Spiritualism in one of his discourses, he took occasion to deny it in the following card :

"In my discourse of Sunday night I did not discuss 'Spiritualism' as that term is now understood, but Scriptural teaching respecting the Divine spirit. Modern 'Spiritualism' was barely alluded to, but without affirmation or denial. If the report shall be interpreted as an expression of my views on the modern doctrine of Spiritualism, I am unwilling to be responsible for its statements. I look with profound interest upon all wise efforts to educe scientific truth from that extraordinary class of phenomena which has become so common in our day, and to which at length, in England at least, the attention of men of the highest scientific attainments has been seriously turned. But I have never yet been convinced that these remarkable modern phenomena originated from the interposition of spirits outside of the human body."

OPINION OF MR. THEODORE TILTON.

The following letter from the above named gentleman indicates his opinion at the time of its publication. The well known liberality of his course, entitles him to the credit of sincerity and earnestness of purpose, upon whichever side of a controversy circumstances influenced his mind to range itself.

"My Friend—I thank you for asking me to attend your convention. Many labors keep me at my office-desk. The phenomena of Spiritualism have interested me greatly. But I have had bad luck with mediums. Sooner or later, nearly all of them (in sitting with me,) have exhibited traces of imposters and cheats. Thus I have known a medium who, after the manifestation of genuine marvels such as would impress and satisfy the most skeptical inquirer, has condescended to the petty trickery of producing raps with his hand, and of moving a table with his foot. There is so much that is genuine, cheering and magnificent in the better and higher phenomena of Spiritualism, that my blood grows hot with indignation at the insincerity of mediums who will use the most sacred of facts as the warp and woof of the meanest of deceits. You ask me to send a sentiment. I would like to send it in the form of a scourge to drive out the profaners of the temple. I hope you will pass a resolution whipping the rogues who steal the livery of Spiritualism to serve their devilish selves therewith. By as much as I love truth, by so much do I hate fraud. My experience with Spiritualism teaches me that, as it is ordinarily seen in the performance of mediums, it is about one-half truth and the other half humbug. I am yours frankly,—"

It is said that his views have become more favorable since the publication of the above letter, but no public announcement of the fact has yet come before us. The candor and out-spoken sincerity of Mr. T's criticism is highly commendable.

REV. W. H. H. MURRAY.

The Rev. Mr. Murray, pastor of the Park-street Church, Boston, Mass., said in a sermon from which the following is an extract:

"To me the spirit-world is tangible. It is not peopled with ghosts and spectres, shadows and outlines of being, but with persons and forms palpable to the apprehension. Its multitudes are veritable, its society natural, its language audible, its companionships real, its loves distinct, its activities energetic, its life intelligent, its glory discernible; its union is not that of sameness, but of variety brought into moral harmony by the great law of love, like notes, which, in themselves distinct

and different, make, when combined, sweet music.
Death will not level and annul those countless differences of mind and heart which make us individual here.
Heaven, in all the mode and manner of expression, will
abound with personality. There will be choice and
preference and degrees of affinity there. Each intellect
will keep its natural bliss, each heart its elections.
Groups there will be, and circles : faces known and unknown will pass us ; acquaintances will thrive on intercourse, and love deepen with knowledge ; and the great,
underlying laws of mind and heart prevail and dominate
as they do here, save in this—that in sin, and all the
repellence and antagonism that it breeds, will be unknown, and holiness supply in perfect measure the opportunity and bond of brotherhood."

PART III.

TESTIMONY IN FAVOR OF SPIRITUALISM.

In the Christian Scriptures, John enjoins his brethren against blind credulity in language that has been often quoted, though it is questionable whether the advice has been heeded, even by those who refer to it as authoritive teaching. He says "Believe not every spirit, but try the spirits, whether they be of God; because many false prophets are gone out into the world." And in like manner, Paul in his letter to the Thessalonians advises them to "Prove all things; hold fast that which is good."

If this advice were followed, the investigator bringing to the task the exercise of the great boon which has been vouchsafed to mankind, the blessed power of reason, there would be little of delusion or crime in the world.

Paul was a hero among the Christians, and his words are treasured up by the followers of the Nazarene in implicit faith, and his teachings obeyed as of undeniable authority.   Entitled to the same weight comes the following language in his first letter to the Corinthians, in which he enumerates a variety of spiritual gifts.

"The manifestation of the spirit is given to every man to profit withal.   For to one is given by the spirit the word of wisdom ; to another, the word of knowledge by the same spirit ; to another faith by the same spirit ; to another, the gifts of healing by the same spirit ; to another, the working of miracles ; to another, prophecy ; to another, discerning of spirits ; to another, divers kinds of tongues ; to another, the interpretation of tongues ;" and then at the close of the chapter he calls upon all Christians to "covet earnestly the best gifts."

In the Hebrew Scriptures we find allusion to some of these things in the language of prophecy uttered by Joel.

"And it shall come to pass afterwards that I will pour out my spirit upon all flesh ; and your sons and your daughters shall prophesy ; your old men shall dream dreams ; your young men shall see visions ; and also upon the servants and upon the handmaids in those days will I pour out my spirit."

Having collated examples of opinions publicly expressed in opposition to Spiritualism, embracing all grades of intensity from the severest down to comparative or absolute indifference, it is now proper to present the testimony on the favorable side.   By pursuing this course impartially, the reader will be enabled to com-

pare the weight of fact and argument as they are presented with greater or less force to his mental compre-
hension, and reach independent conclusions. The sum
of testimony in either case, it is of course impossible to
embrace within the limits of any book of reasonable
magnitude. Enough of the unfriendly quality has been
quoted to illustrate the animus of the various writers
and speakers. But if it has been difficult to compress
within a moderate compass what has been said in the
way of animadversion, sarcastic criticism, stolid incredulity, condemnation, vilification, and priestly anathema,
it is still less practicable to present at one view even an
epitome of what has been given to the world in the
way of simple narration, supported by calm reasoning,
in a truly religious frame of mind on the other side,
much less what has been written and spoken in terms
of extravagant laudation. It is sufficient for our present purpose to give a modicum of each.

The number of Spiritualists in the United States
alone has increased during a period of but little over
twenty-two years from a mere handful of startled
and curious investigators, to a number variously estimated from six hundred and sixty thousand, to eleven
millions. The lesser estimate, it is stated, is for want
of the necessary data much below the reality, while the
larger possibly exceeds it. It is however, unquestionably very large; running into the millions. Among
such a vast number, embracing men and women of culture and scientific attainments, many of them of thoughtful minds having, to say the least, an average degree of
mental strength, it is to be expected that the testimony

now to be offered in behalf of the truth of spiritual phenomena, selected from a voluminous quantity, should
be definite and positive in character.

In the earlier period of its progress in this country,
several periodicals conducted by writers of ability appeared, and entered earnestly upon its advocacy, shar-
ing the fate of most pioneers in almost all fields of
adventure and active enterprise.   After a time they
were suspended, but to be immediately succeeded by
others which nurtured the seed thus sown by brave
hands, and brought it onward to fructification.

The permanent literature, from small beginnings comprehended in a transient newspaper account of singular
physical phenomena, extending to the graver pamphlet,
and thence to the more permanent book devoted to what
are known as the higher manifestations, and the discussion of the philosophy of the subject, has been alluded to
in our Introduction.

A portion of the testimony in this division of our
plan of arrangement will consist of that which relates to
physical phenomena; but what is of more importance
is involved in the question of the reliability of Communications claiming to be received from persons inhabit-
ing the spirit-world.   This was for a long time a delicate
and embarrassing one.   In the family and neighborly
meeting of groups of private friends, the character of
the communications received, after being tested by appropriate means were alleged to be truthful, and highly
satisfactory to the parties immediately concerned.   But
in these the public generally had no part.   All were
learners, and no one at first could take the responsibili-

ty of deciding upon rules which would bring out the best method of conducting meetings for the desired purpose. Individual mediums had their capacities gradually developed, until they were recognized by believers to be reliable, and thus the meaning of the phenomena, the communication of specific facts, and the philosophy of the subject came to be more extensively known.

THE MEDIUMSHIP OF MRS. J. H. CONANT.

At length the proprietors of the *Banner of Light*, the oldest of the periodical publications, devoted to the facts and philosophy of Spiritualism, established on a permanent basis, inaugurated an exceedingly liberal plan for the benefit of the public generally, namely, the opening of an elegant room conveniently furnished, for holding Free Public Circles ; employing a lady of refinement, and of remarkable mediumistic powers, as their medium of communication between the spirit-world and such of the inhabitants of our world as chose to avail themselves of the opportunity of attending the tri-weekly sessions ; the only conditions required, being the preservation of quiet, order and neatness.

The following standing announcement is placed at the head of the Message Department, in their regular issue.

" Each Message in this Department of the Banner of Light we claim was spoken by the Spirit whose name it bears through the instrumentality of Mrs. J. H. Conant, while in an abnormal condition called the trance. These Messages indicate that spirits carry with them the characteristics of their earth-life to that beyond—whether for good or evil. But those who leave the earth-sphere in an undeveloped state, eventually progress into a higher condition.

We ask the reader to receive no doctrine put forth by spirits in these columns that does not comport with his or her reason. All express as much truth as they perceive—no more."

Each meeting is opened by an invocation, of which the following is an example, indicating the temper of mind which governs the conductors.

INVOCATION.

Holy, holy art thou, oh Great Spirit, whether thou art Brahma or Jehovah ; whether thou dost reveal thyself to us through children, or through the more splendid intellect of maturer age ; whether we behold thy footprints upon the mountains, or read thy record in the flowers, in the fruits, in the grains and precious stones ; forever thou art holy, holy, holy. And we, thy children, the living and the dead, do this hour join hands and worship thee, bringing thee the fruits of our experience, reverently laying them upon the altar of time, asking thy blessing to fall upon them. Give us, oh Great Spirit, the power to understand ourselves, the wisdom to read thy mighty, thy precious volume of Nature aright ; and when the hour of our triumph shall come, and we are upon the mountain-top of wisdom, of experience, and shall look down smiling upon all below, then cast thou thy mantle of love, perfect love upon us, and let it be decorated with humility, giving unto it a double lustre in the spiritual kingdom.

THE SEANCE.

Visitors are deeply impressed with the evident sincerity which pervades all parties concerned in the transmission of the messages, the intrinsic character and quality of which differ from each other in the widest degree; presenting in their individual features almost as many characteristic phases as there are disembodied minds communicating. Many contain nothing of immediate importance to the listeners, but are of a personal nature, giving the best possible opportunity, however, of testing their truthfulness to any one who will take the trouble to trace the correspondence between the statements given, and the knowledge of facts in the possession of persons to whom they are addressed. They are simple and familiar in style or profoundly scientific, reflecting positive or negative character, and sometimes imparting new knowledge both present and prophetic. Their versatility excludes the presumption that they are the spontaneous utterances of the lady who is the channel of communication; for this would require an extent of education, and a degree of training in personation that no mortal in human history has ever yet attained. In proof of this, we quote the following remarks of a Chicago gentleman, which corroborate the uniform impression made upon the minds of all observers. Describing spiritual matters in Boston, he writes:

"I was much interested in attending the Banner of Light Free Circle. If Mrs. Conant is not under the influence of spirits, then she must be the most remarkable woman that ever lived. For a pale, feeble woman to answer so many profound and intricate questions and personate so many characters all of her own personal skill, must at once stamp her as the greatest actor and most versatile thinker of the age."

We select two of the communications for the purpose of illustration; the first is from the Rev. Dr. Gannett, a well known Unitarian Minister, whose earthly life was suddenly terminated by the terrible Railroad disaster which occurred at Revere, near Boston in the autumn of 1871, while on his way to fill a ministerial engagement, the time appointed being the following sunday.

COMMUNICATION FROM REV. EZRA GANNETT D. D.

By the kindness of your President, I have been invited to take part in your services this afternoon; but I do so with the full consciousness that I am unworthy, because when in the body, living as I did under the blazing sunlight of modern Spiritualism, I rejected it, and crucified this Savior of modern times again and again. Therefore, I am unworthy to become a recipient of this great blessing; but I believe I am here by the will of

God, by the grace of that Infinite Presence that cares
for us all—that notes the falling sparrow, and numbers
all the years of our existence. I was once told by one
of my parishioners, who was a believer in modern Spiritualism, that he should yet live to see the day when I
would acknowledge myself in the wrong. He is on
earth. I do acknowledge I was wrong, and, like a little child, I am willing to be led in the right way ; for
now I fully understand that, except I become as a little
child, I cannot enter the kingdom of heaven.

My friends are mourning over my sudden departure ;
but I have to say to them that my death was a merciful
one. I suffered nothing ; I took my exit from the body
of flesh probably instantaneouslv ; at least, I have no
recollection of anything but a sudden blow here, [on the
forehead,] and then I found myself viewing the wreck
of matter, and wondering into what state I had been
ushered.

I believe now, more than ever, in the goodness of an
all-wise God—a Supreme Power that guides us through
all the ways of life, and finally saves us, and admits us
into that heaven of perfect happiness which every soul
seeks to obtain. I feel, since entering upon this new
life, deeply impressed with the necessity for great re-
forms upon the earth. I feel that the earth is ripe for
change, and that the angels are ready to record great
events which are to transpire : and one of these great
events is the passing away of mythical religions, and
the establishment of the glorious spiritual religion over
all the earth. Did not Jesus, or the Spirit of Truth
through him, declare that such a time as that should

come, in the history of the earth? I so interpret the words, but when here I did not so understand them. I believed that he referred to the millennium—to the time when the soul should be redeemed from error, and should live in a perfectly happy state upon earth.

My friends say I have been removed from the sphere of my labors. It is not so. I have only been translated higher, that I may do better—that I may be a more faithful laborer in the vineyard of my Father. I have seen, hitherto, as through a glass, darkly. Now, standing as I do in the world of causes, and communicating with the world of matter, I can look forward hopefully—I can work with a will; and I praise my God that he has dealt so mercifully with me. Rev. Ezra S. Gannett.　　　　　　　Sept. 7.

The second communication is from Dr. Wesselhoeft, a physician formerly engaged in extensive practice in Boston, and is said by those who knew him intimately, to be characteristic of him during his earth-life.

COMMUNICATION FROM DR. WM. WESSELHŒFT.

I had ample evidence, before making the change of worlds, that a great many of these people who believe in modern Spiritualism were disposed to make this modern Spiritualism a very ridiculous thing; and I have had greater evidence, since death, that this is a fact— that the majority of those who believe in modern Spiritualism do it more harm than good, for they call upon the inhabitants of the other world to come back and answer the most nonsensical questions that could possibly be propounded; and I am here to answer one, to-day, which is to me a very foolish one. A lady who claims to have been a patient of mine, and who claims. that her daughter, now in the spirit-world, was also one of my patients some seventeen years ago, wishes me to come back, and, for her satisfaction and the satisfaction of her friends, to make a statement concerning the disease with which her daughter died, diagnosing every particular point, so that there may be no mistake, so that she may know, herself, that I am speaking—that her old physician gives the message to which his name is attached, or expected to be. Now, to begin with, I don't know the lady, and never did. My memory is good—just as good in this life as it was in the earth-life; and if such a lady was ever a patient of mine, it was under a different name. I don't know her by that name and never did. Probably she expects I shall be attracted to her because she has called me, and I shall know what her name was, and shall give it to her, thereby doubling the test. I have something better to do now. Although her request may be a very laudable one to her, to me it is a very foolish one. I would recommend to her that she should employ some good wise spirit to give her a few lessons as to what her duty is to the spirit-world as well as to herself. I was a plain-spoken man in the earthly life; I am just the same now. If she don't like it, I've no apology to make. She ought to make one to me. The name the lady gives me is Mrs. Agnes Chesterfield. I don't know her; and if I did, I would probably refuse to

give her what she asks, for the reason that I would not
be very likely to remember all the points of the case she
demands me to work up, for I had more than one patient at the time. I could hardly be expected to write
out a critical case from my memory ; and the lady, if I
understand her, demands something very clear and accurate, or nothing at all. Now then, my lady, go to
school ; go to some good spirits, to teach you. No
matter if they are as cross as I am ; they'll do you good.
Dr. William Wesselhoeft.   Oct. 23.

It will be observed that the name of the communicator
is placed at the end of each message, notwithstanding its having been already prefixed as the usual head-
ing ; a seemingly unnecessary repetition. Our purpose,
however, has been to quote the message verbatim, and
in the precise order in which it was spoken through the
medium. The date is also appended for convenient
reference, in the case of new inquirers.

From two to six of the messages, as the case may be,
are delivered at each sitting. In addition to this, and
immediately after the invocation, questions which have
been propounded by persons at a distance are read by
the Chairman, and immediately answered by the pre-
siding spirit. An opportunity is then given to the audience to ask such questions as they desire, which are
also answered instanter. This privilege all persons
are earnestly invited to avail themselves of, without
hesitation.

RELIABILITY OF SPIRIT COMMUNICATIONS.

In reference to this question which is mooted by all novices, it is only necessary to remark, that it simply requires the application of common sense, and the ordinary rules of evidence.

Communications are made either orally or in writing. When by the former method, the tone and manner of the medium affords an indication of its genuineness.

The faculty of imitation is in many cases a natural endowment; to acquire it artistically necessitates great application and perseverance. Even then, there must be an original from which to copy, in order to meet with success, in an attempt to counterfeit.

Trance mediums are either conscious or unconscious, while in that condition—in the beginning of the manifestations it appeared to be generally the latter; and they are thrown into it with very varying degrees of facility. The displacement of the person's individuality for the time being, is attended with some degree of spasmodic muscular action, occasionally violent, with a sigh or an ejaculation. In the incipient stage of development, there is much more of this than subsequently, and more or less retention of consciousness. Indeed in proportion to the difficulty of suspending that consciousness, will be the incompleteness of the trance condition. If it be retained in the earlier experience of the medium, the thoughts of the communicating spirit can not be trans-

mitted with distinctness. Such is the testimony of mediums, as regards the sensations which they experience;
and the result is a matter of observation, coming within
the cognizance of all intelligent investigators.

The mixed character of mediumship, in certain cases
owing to incomplete development, accounts for the unsatisfactory and sometimes contradictory nature of communications received. The individuality of the medium
is mingled with the communication. If therefore, there
is any want of veracity on his or her part, the matter of
the communication will be to some extent supplement-
ed, or interpolated by something foreign to its purpose.
This is liable to occur in written as well as in spoken
messages.

Complete control having been established, the succeeding entrancement is effected without disturbance of
muscular action, and moreover without suspension of
consciousness. Indeed it is believed that the greater
portion of the best mediums now remain conscious.

These remarks are made on the supposition that the
investigator and the person through whom information
is sought, are entire strangers to each other, neither
knowing any thing of the other's honesty of purpose.
Hence the same rules of evidence are to be adopted
which govern an examination into the truthfulness of
testimony on any other subject.

Fitness for mediumship, or adaptability is a peculiar
organic condition involving qualities which are yet to us
occult; at least the peculiarities of temperament which
were supposed to constitute susceptibility based upon
what was known of mesmerism, do not apply.

In respect to veracity, there are pure and noble souls whose testimony would at all times be regarded unimpeachable. There are others less scrupulous. Herein mediums do not differ from other persons. In the true value of moral traits of character, they are neither better nor worse than the Christians of our day. So far as the benignant influence of the teachings of the doctrines concerning a future life are concerned we should expect them to show better fruit, but this affects them as individuals and not as mediums. In ordinary matters of business this does not concern the inquirer. If he finds it necessary to transmit a message by telegraph to a distant point, he does not stop to inquire what the social position of the operator is, to what church he belongs, or with what political party he affiliates. It is enough for him to know that the person intrusted with that duty is capable, prompt and efficient, that the line of communication is perfect and the apparatus in working order. The question of fidelity comes in, and that is inferentially settled by the interested parties employing his services.

The intrinsic character of the message or communication must therefore speak for itself. If it contains a specific fact which is known only to the person addressed, it relieves the medium from suspicion of fraud. Yet to a third party it is still liable to the objection that it is only a reflection of the mind of the seeker, who in this case is supposed to be present. But if the thought was not present in his mind at the time, and the statement comes to him as a startling reminder, it cannot be explained in that way. And again if he is hundreds or

thousands of miles away, what shall be said of the reflex theory? It has happened again and again, that the
recipient of the verbal communication has solemnly
averred that the circumstances related to him were not
occupying his mind at the time, nor had they been
thought of, for perhaps a long time previous. If a space
of miles in extent separates the parties in the body, that
is the medium and the person at a distant point, who
knows the fact stated, the knowledge must be imparted
to those persons present in the body with the medium,
by means inexplicable by the electrical, the reflex or
any other theory suggested by the objector.

These ingenious though often far-fetched explanations,
if they could satisfy the demands of a reasoning mind,
in reference to the classes of cases just mentioned, are
still at fault in another. We refer to cases where the
statements made embrace facts entirely new and previously unknown to any one in the body, present or absent.

The objection, or explanation which presumes that
the medium is necessarily a pretender, is not only un-
generous, but unjust. True ladies and true gentlemen
who accept this calling in good faith, often against their
will and in spite of their personal opposition to it, are not
chargeable with the false pretensions of counterfeitors,
nor the uncertain character of mixed communications
coming through partially developed mediums who resort to the use of their imperfect gift as a trade for
mercenary ends. They have patiently borne the doubts
and sneers of the ignorant and presumptuous for the
purpose of affording the fullest opportunity to inquiring

minds to test for themselves the truthfulness of their messages.

When a dear departed friend, or a near relative makes an effort to be identified, and to give a friendly or affectionate greeting, it is not complimentary nor is it kind, without an attempt to ascertain its genuineness by reasonable tests, to charge the medium with imposition, and a false persônation. But when after its truthfulness is acknowledged, because it is no longer possible to ignore it, and the communication purports to come from a loving mother, what word shall be employed to characterize the assertion that it is the work of the devil? How must that mother feel to be called a devil? How would she in earth-life feel, if after sending an affectionate letter by the mail, or a message of kind greeting, by telegraph, with precious pearls of advice, the recipient should say it came from the devil?

When information is sent by letter from one person to another, there are means of identification as to its authorship, which are fully satisfactory to the person addressed. Modes of expression arc characteristic as well as the chirography. It has often occurred, when messages have been received from the spirit-world, the person addressed has at once exclaimed "That's just like him." When a circumstance has been related to another who was not present when the message was received, on hearing the phrases repeated, even before the name was announced, the exclamation came spontaneously, "Why, that's from so-and-so, its exactly his manner and language."

A verbal message from one to another in our mundane sphere, may be accurately conveyed, but this depends upon the accuracy of the messenger. We know that scarcely any two persons narrate the same event alike. The difference in memory and the relative facility in the use of language will modify the statement. Its spirit will be occasionally communicated without abatement of intensity, or variation in accuracy of detail. But this is seldom the case. Hence a communication from a human being disembodied to one still in the form must necessarily, except when given through one of the best mediums, lose something of its intensity at least. The reliability must then be determined by the employment of ordinary rules of evidence, and submitted to common sense and reason.

PSYCHIC FORCE.

The array of testimony against Spiritualism in Part I. from prominent divines, aided by an occasional opponent who has attacked it from what he considered a scientific stand point, and scattering newspaper comments, has consisted mainly of negation ; such and such things did not occur as represented by persons witnessing them. What could not be denied, others have attempted to explain. It was still negation, as far as it related to any definite source from which the alleged phenomena originated, excepting the devil recognized by Mr. Knapp and others of like belief.

We do not propose to enumerate the prominent believers as is sometimes done with reference to those who deny, as it is not a mere array of names on the two sides respectively, that would settle the question. Otherwise we might classify a list of Scientists, Professors in Colleges, Judges of Courts, Members of Congress, distinguished Literateurs, Philanthropists, Ministers, officers at the head of the nation, and men in high position in Councils of State, as believers. But no truth can be disposed of by vote.

We prefer to present the statements of facts which have occurred; and to mention the parties who witnessed them, and are personally responsible for the statements. Truth or falsehood in such cases is easily ascertained.

The arrangement of this kind of evidence will include the development of mediumship in its various phases, such as the more elementary or simple manifestations, better known as physical phenomena, and also the higher phases, exhibiting mental and moral characteristics. As the former give proof of physical power beyond that which has been taught us under the laws of mechanics, the latter announce facts which have been proved true, of a character which could originate only in a mental force, by whatever name it may be called.

The nearest approach to fairness in investigation is the course of experiment and inquiry which has been instituted by Professor Crookes and others in England. They are not, like their predecessors, so stubborn as to deny flatly that what are called spiritual manifestations ever occurred, until stupid denial would render them ridiculous; nor continually to evade by suggesting that they proceed from something else than their real cause.

We need not fear the result when men of mind are
disposed to acknowledge a fact, and honestly to ascertain if they can, its relation to any branch of science.
These gentlemen have proposed for the new agency, the
name of Psychic Force. The following remarks quoted, scarcely gives them the credit they deserve, in setting out upon an independent investigation.

"The attempt of a few distinguished scientists to drive
a stake in the realms of soul-life, for experimenters to
tie to when called upon to explain mysterious phenomena,
seems to be stoutly resisted by the old fogy conservatives; while the untenable ground on which they attempt to stand while they drive the stake, makes it
probable that they will have to give it up. It is not
probable that Prof. Crookes and his compeers will be
able to gain admission into the list of forces for their
new article of soul-force while they attempt to explain
the laws by which it is controlled as wholly mundane.
They can quite easily prove the existence of some subtile
force if the phenomena are admitted, but they cannot
prove that it is controlled by any earthly human will;
and hence the ridicule attached to those who attempt to
prove its existence by laws that do not control it. It is
not now probable that the point will be gained in science of establishing even the existence of a psychic force,
because the advocates do not go far enough, and plant
themselves on spiritual life as the power that controls it
and the source from which it emanates. It is a shame-
ful attempt to bring the spiritual forces into subjection
to the human will, and bind them by mundane agencies,
to the old wheel-ruts of physical science. The simple

truth is, spirits are among us, doing many things as they will, and not as we will them, and a large part of the phenomena are utterly ignored by both church and science ; but a few have been witnessed, and cannot be explained by the church without attributing them to a devil, nor by scientists by earthly agencies ; and hence an attempt to bring in a new force, and, to avoid a conflict with the church, to report it subject to only earthly control, and to disconnect it with anything of a spiritual origin. But the church is evidently alarmed by even the name, which trenches on forbidden ground, where science has not yet been allowed to set her unholy foot.

"The position at first assumed by the investigators—and that which the great world of skeptics so greedily seized upon—is capitally sketched by a correspondent, Carl Harter. Wouter Van Twiller—surnamed "the doubter"—he says, gained a great reputation for knowledge and incapability of being imposed upon, by a solemn, mysterious shake of the head and a muttered 'I have my doubts about the matter,' whenever a new question was propounded. So with scientists, who have smoked and doubted for all these years, and have gained a great repute among men by their reticence. He says the various hypotheses of 'sleight-of-hand,' 'humbug,' 'psychology'—self or otherwise—have vanished before the tests of truth ; now the spirit-phenomena are declared to be the result of soul power or mind power : 'but whether that soul or mind is in a mortal body or not will perhaps be determined within the present century.'

"Wonderful psychic power! a table is suspended in mid-air; an accordion is played; a pencil writes intelligent sentences; and all without contact with mortal hands, and under circumstances which make machinery impossible; and the question arises, What is the cause? 'Why,' says the common mind, 'the making of music, the writing of an intelligent sentence, are things that can only be done by a human being; there is no other power that can do these things, and, since the hand of flesh did not prevail in this case, it must have been done by a human being without a hand of flesh—a spirit.' 'Not so,' says science; 'be silent when wisdom speaks; this medium thought write, and the pencil wrote.'"

OUR EXPERIENCE.

It is not uncommon now to see articles and extended narratives entitled "How I became a Spiritualist." The Catholic, the Methodist, the Presbyterian, he whom his christian neighbors reproachfully stigmatizes as Infidel, and persons of other shades of sectarian bias have all answered it. The title page will perhaps have excited curiosity to know what particular event or argument it was which shaped our opinion.

We never had any particular belief in regard to a future life until the facts of spiritualism gave us an insight into its philosophy.

Our earliest evangelical religious instruction was received from the pulpit of the Congregational Church.

Yet we could not feel that interest in the teachings nor perceive the truth in them which others expressed. We then attended the ministration of the Universalist church. In that denomination we saw much that we liked, but no proof of immortality, nor anything that made the subject clear to our mind. After this we listened to the preaching and read the writings of Theodore Parker. What we then learned seemed to be a step in advance. While listening to these discourses, the remarkable occurrences at Rochester took place, and soon after similar events in Boston. At first we were strongly opposed to acknowledge them as true, believing, after having attended several seances, that the whole subject was a disgrace, and that its pretensions would soon explode. Indeed our opposition was so intense that no manifestations would take place in our presence, and we have been requested to leave the room occupied by the mediums for the purpose. Still we could not remain away. We attended a lecture on the subject, but could not understand what the speaker was trying to prove. After stopping a few minutes, away we went. We still felt a desire to attend subsequent meetings, and so followed up the investigation for some time, yet feeling ashamed to be seen in the room or going there. It seemed below the dignity of man. At length our spirit mother, who when in earth-life was a member of the Congregational Church, came with an unmistakable test of her identity. Her first words were "My son, God moves in a mysterious way his works to perform." She gave her religious views, the manner of her death, and many particulars calculated to con-

vince one that spiritualism had in it much more than
we had been inclined to believe, and that it was worthy
of further investigation.   Then the thought was suggested that it was simply mind reading, but soon something beyond that was given—statements of the truth of
which we were not then informed, and were compelled
to inquire into.   One circumstance settled the question
in our mind forever, and satisfied us that the invisibles
can and do tell us that which we have never previously
known.   It was a personal test.

After being thus convinced, we related our experience thus far to our friends, who almost without exception, were incredulous, and rejected the claims of the
revelations to credence.   They thought we were getting
fanatical, perhaps a little insane, on that subject.   An
acquaintance was solicited to converse with us about it,
and persuade us to drop it, for the reason that it would
be injurious or perhaps ruinous to our mind ; and if not
that, our business would suffer from being known as a
believer.   He was not acquainted with its facts, and
asked but a few questions in relation to it, soon realizing that he was not competent to reason upon it, and
must first inform himself before he could point out faults
in others.

The business we had engaged in was not in harmony
with the views of usefulness which we adopted on becoming a believer in Spiritualism, and our interest in
it having increased, we zealously pursued our inquiries,
travelling extensively in order to visit mediums in various sections of the country, spending time and money
in order to ascertain the truth concerning the alleged

manifestations. During our journeyings we heard most of the public speakers, and had sittings with most of the noted mediums, and have learned from reliable sources the character of the manifestations witnessed in the presence of others. For ten years we resisted the influence at work on our mind, feeling unwilling to work in harmony with the authors of the scenes transpiring around us. At length it proved irresistible; a gradual development had been going on, until it seemed beyond doubt that a new calling had been opened for us. We yielded to the impulse, and for several years past, have exercised the gift of healing. Our case in some respects was similar to that of Paul, particularly in regard to the strenousness of our opposition and determination to resist the power which was evidently put in operation to subdue our will by the force of truth.

Since we became convinced of that truth, many of our relatives and acquaintances including some of those who were so solicitous for our welfare, have themselves given in their adhesion to the same cause, from the evidence presented to their minds, and are enjoying the benefits derived from a study of its philosophy. So that now we are not looked upon as so much out of the way, in our conversion to it.

When our mother came in spirit, many questions which suggested themselves, were asked, among which was this. "Is it right for me to attend Mr. Parker's meetings?" The answer was "Follow the dictates of your own conscience. It matters not where you attend church, if you but live right." She went on to say that in the land of the immortal spirit there are no forms,

creeds, or religious ceremonies ; but persons are attracted to their own—those of like conditions of development, intellectually, morally and spiritually, on entering
the spirit-world.   It seemed clear to us that the grada-
tion was something like that which is made in school.
The scholar is not asked what he believes when undergoing an examination, but what he knows, and according to his knowledge he is directed to take his position.
When the hindrances of a material body are thrown off,
the disenthralled spiritual being does not enter a sphere
in which he cannot be harmonized.   If attracted higher
he must by progression be fitted to enter the new and
more elevated plane.   It can be compared to our present material life, whenever the question of comparative
merit is considered.   Each will be placed in his own
order.   This seemed to be the view of the spirit, although not expressed exactly in the same words.   Her
views then given have been corroborated by the results
of our subsequent investigation, and experience in spirit
intercourse.

One of the unsatisfactory dogmas in our early religious instruction was that of a great Judgment Day,
after the manner of our Assize proceedings, the difference consisting in the extent of the trial, the one being
universal, the vast majority of the multitudes assembled
being culprits, while the other is small, puny, and by
comparison, insignificant.   Now the uniform assurance
that there is no such day especially set aside to judge
the spirits, but on the contrary that all days are judgment days, gives us clearer light.   So also of the
doctrine of resurrection of the natural body, and other

peculiar Orthodox teachings included in the same category.

Now it seems reasonable to our mind that when all
spirits who return to us with tidings of their new abode
agree in a statement of fact touching any one point,
upon which they must necessarily have better information than we on the earth plane, and in reference to
which almost as many different opinions have been expressed without knowledge, as there are persons entertaining them, it should be received as conclusive. And
so we are no longer dependent upon the teachings of
Theological Schools established to furnish instruction
in regard to what is true or false in relation to the spiritual world, and what is right or wrong as a matter of
belief. Spiritualism has provided for us a philosophy
which is natural, based upon truth and which affords
satisfaction to the reasoning mind.

We were often annoyed by charges against particular
individuals, who were known as believers, in regard to
their conduct in private life, accompanied with the assertion "we do not want anything to do with it, if the
life of such a person is an example of the fruit of such
a belief." Allusion has already been made to this
point. To such, we have said that they need not wal-
low in the mire because others do. According to the
teachings of the new philosophy each individual is held
responsible for personal conduct. No one's wicked
deeds can be transferred to another, and compensated
for by a vicarious atonement. Every one may go into
as high a sphere as his aspiration leads. He has the
choice of action as a free agent, to the extent that al-

lows him to degrade himself to lower moral and social levels than that which he has attained, if he has no aspiration for the highest good. But there is no escaping the consequence. Infringement of law of whatever kind, is followed by the penalty attached to it. God's moral laws are fixed and invariable as the movements of the planetary bodies.

The benefits to be derived from a study of these laws are open to all mankind, without distinction of race, color, or nationality. No religious sect can alone catch the inspiration and selfishly appropriate it. There is therefore no ground for bigotry or intolerance, neither is there any warrant for the assumption of authority.

As we have said, our experience with mediums has been extensive. There are but few lecturers whom we have not heard, and but few public physical, trance, semi-trance, test, writing, singing, drawing, healing or clairvoyant mediums, in this country, whom we have not either visited, or whose several degrees and varieties of power or gifts we have not seen exercised. Such opportunities, obtained at considerable expense and sometimes inconvenience, have accumulated a large aggregate of results from observation ; which of course if made available, afford reliable data upon which to form correct opinions.

We have observed that there is a greater degree of freedom among spiritualists than among their opponents. Having no fixed creed which all are required to subscribe to, as indisputable authority, they are free to adopt such views as the evidence before them seems to warrant, according to their understanding of its claims. Consequently no two necessarily see alike in all points. Each forms an opinion from his own standpoint. As one ascends the hill of progression with more rapid strides than another and reaches a more elevated point, he has a more comprehensive view, and takes in a wider range of observation. There is as much difference therefore between two persons occupying different positions in the scale of progression or elevation, as there is between high culture and partial knowledge, acquired in ordinary mundane experience in other directions.

There is but one essential point upon which we have found believers in spiritualism to agree, namely, that human beings who once inhabited the earth sphere and have left for the abode of spirits can, when conditions are favorable, return to earth and hold communion with their relatives and friends.

Upon other subjects they differ, and no particular belief is regarded as a test of orthodoxy or heterodoxy, or ground of fellowship.

We have observed among the converts to the spiritualistic faith a strong tendency to credulity. It would appear that one extreme follows another; those who were obstinate in their conservatism, after yielding their assent to the evidence before them becoming enthusiastic, and willing to receive everything that came from spirits. This results in disappointment. It is no doubt to be attributed to the effect of previous religious education. They were taught to believe many things concerning the future life which their recent investigations satisfied them were not founded in truth, and they were compelled to change their opinions. They find that the human spirit after completing its earth-life enters the spirit spheres with the same traits of character that distinguished it before. The change does not produce an instantaneous revolution in character, although there immediately begins a change of opinions, and the correction of errors previously fixed in the mind by false teaching. But their education is gradual and their utterances upon all subjects cannot be accepted as oracular.

They can see better now than before. Secrets are revealed realizing the prophetic declaration "and that which ye have spoken in the ear in closets shall be proclaimed upon the housetops." This is an important practical fact, for who, fully conscious of it would be willing to be discovered in a wrong deed, when a valued friend is an eye-witness of it. It has a restraining effect upon wrong doing. That spirits do thus see passing events here we think will be abundantly proven in these pages.

We consider spiritualism the rejected stone that is to become the head of the corner, and that the Universal Church will be built thereon. It is the broad religion of mankind, which is finally to unite all. It encourages all to perseverance in well-doing. Its philosophy prevents the comparatively unfortunate from giving way to a feeling of disappointment and dissatisfaction with the sphere of life allotted to them, for all have it in their power to improve their spiritual condition.

Notwithstanding our experience has been costly, we have never regretted the time and expense incurred, nor would we part with it. It has been a source of mental satisfaction, settling beyond doubt questions of the most vital importance. By giving it to the world, the course of investigation pursued by others can be greatly facilitated. It is not necessary for all to go through the same experience for themselves in order to satisfy their minds with regard to the same facts. It has too often been insisted on by skeptics that they must see for themselves every thing that has occurred before they will yield an assent to the facts that have transpired. But no one need enter the channels of vice and pursue a vicious career, in order to be satisfied that vice exists. We must accept under proper restrictions, the testimony of others. Otherwise the amount of knowledge in the world would be very limited, the longest life-time affording opportunity to accumulate but a small portion of what is seen, heard and felt in the aggregate. Hence the actual experience of any one individual would furnish but a trifling contribution to the sum of human knowledge. All progress would cease if each was a world in himself, independent of aid from his fellow beings.

In the course of our observation, we have noticed a disposition on the part of some to seek aid from spirits in the prosecution of schemes of pecuniary speculation. Now what would be thought of the sagacity of a person who should stop to inquire of every one, even of his intimate business friends, what he should do in a particular case. Before this can be done with propriety it must first be considered that the person from whom advice is sought, is of superior judgment. Spirits who have passed beyond the veil, are not necessarily more competent to judge of such matters than he who asks the questions. Then there are those on that side, who still have unworthy designs, and the credulous inquirer may be misled, by sacrificing his own individuality, and trusting implicitly to the dictation of another. If a sensitive, excitable person is under their control, he may be led into various excesses, so that they are not always to be trusted, even if they are known at times to influence a good deed.

For the same reason what are called good psychological subjects are not always to be relied on. There are spirits in the form that are able to control mediums far beyond that which is exercised over them by their spirit guides. Caution is therefore as necessary in receiving authoritative instruction from one as from the other.

We do not believe that spirits in the higher life, who have outgrown the material conditions of earth come back to dabble with dollars and cents to any great extent. They often give evidence to the contrary. Their work is to elevate mankind by teaching grand and noble truths, inculcating correct principles, and aiding the recipient of their influence, in the preparation for a higher life, its uses, duties and felicities.

It is not to be inferred that friendly spirits do not sometimes give information and impressions with respect to matters pertaining to temporal welfare. We have known instances where persons had received fine tests from their spirit friends, after which, taking advantage of their opportunity, they questioned those friends upon schemes of money making, and have received answers which wofully deceived them. From what we have seen, we do not doubt that the motive of more than half the seekers of information into spiritual things is to make money out of it, or to ascertain whether they are to bury their partner in married life, having in such cases, an eye on some other person, in case the prophecy is favorable to their desire. Is it a wonder that the life path of such is obstructed?

We have known church members to consult the spirits for the purpose of inquiring where they can find stolen property, where to get a wife or a husband, what prospect there is for them to make money, or to be cured of disease.

But this curiosity, morbid and grovelling as it is, is no worse than that which prevailed in Bible times. The spirit of Samuel was called up to give information concerning the future, and there are other examples of persons seeking familiar spirits for a similar purpose in those days. Jesus told the woman at the well how many husbands she had.

Many have lost property in consequence of resorting to this method with the hope of adding to it. Indeed fortunes have been both made and lost by it, showing that if it is a matter of judgment, there is no advantage gained over the wisdom of this world. Questions asked both in public and private seances, are sometimes refused answers, and the reason very properly assigned is that the information denied would not promote the real welfare of the interrogator, or the cause of justice. When the purpose of the question is good, it is not always that the desired information can be obtained. If

half the interest was taken in ascertaining the true relations of the future life that is manifested in seeking to
promote selfish and unworthy objects, there would be
much more good done. What is life but one continued
existence, giving opportunity for reaching higher and
higher good, inspiration meeting the aspiring soul with
encouragement and reward.

Among what we have seen of this subject are some of
the attempts made to expose it. This has sometimes
been attempted by knaves who have been disappointed
in accomplishing an unworthy purpose by exposing it,
taking first one side and then the other. Occasionally
a good physical medium has added his own feats to the
genuine phenomena in order still more to excite the
marvellousness of his audience. More than one such
might be cited as pursuing this vacillating course re-
gardless of honest principle, for the purpose of making
money. A recent example occurred in New York.
The somewhat notorious B. F. Hatch after losing the
opportunity of longer appropriating the earnings of his
young wife's remarkable mediumistic powers, in consequence of her obtaining a divorce, came out with an exposition first by the publication of a hostile book, then
by lectures and cabinet peformances. The effort made
in Cooper Institute according to the published accounts,
was a ludicrous farce, failing to satisfy even such an
audience as could be induced to listen to it. The pro-
gramme could not be carried out, but the impatient
spectators were dissatisfied, vociferating "Hatch it out."

Not long since we were induced to go to the Boston
Music Hall one sunday evening, to listen to a reverend

Divine, who had announced an exposition of various humbugs, including Spiritualism and Quack Doctors. Some of the Boston merchants had, as we learned, paid for the use of the Hall, in order that their clerks might be taught a lesson of wisdom. We wanted to learn it too, but there was a preliminary fact to be learned, namely, that the gospel was not then and there to be had "without money and without price," a charge of ten cents being made at the door, for the privilege of witnessing the religious gymnastics which followed. We remarked that it was a polite way of making money. It must have turned out well for the exposer, as an audience of three thousand persons had collected. A net worldly profit was doubtless advantageous in enabling the "Minister" to point his moral with additional sharpness. His fantastic gestures made a display equal to that of a puppet show.

His exposition of spiritualism consisted in part of the reading of a communication purporting to have come from the spirit of a little child, who had passed to the fair land too soon to have acquired much of this world's knowledge or wisdom. Hence its language was simple, which the exposer made the butt of ridicule. His ignorance of the law of communication between the world of mortals and that of spirits was apparent to all who had given the subject any degree of attention, in expecting an innocent little child, ignorant in a great measure of this world's lore, to converse in the strains of wisdom and self-importance of a learned divine. Doubtless if it had done so, he would have taken the other tack, perhaps exclaiming with ministerial contempt, "That child needn't put on the airs of a preacher!" He left out of consideration the fact that if a child could communicate its wishes, a strong person of positive power, with well developed intellect, and cultured could also.

In that portion of the moral lesson devoted to quack doctors, he attacked an imaginary healer, stating that one of them took from this city fifty thousand dollars as the fruits of duping the public, and that the "Doctor" had told a friend of his that he had had six magnetic batteries attached to his person; that his patients thought they were receiving his magnetism, when in fact they were receiving it from the batteries. Is this a sample of clerical wisdom and truth? Is it a specimen of the divine exposer's attainments in chemistry, or is it clerical alchemy? Before the pious merchants try to do God service again in this line, they should inquire of some novice whether magnetic batteries can be made, by a special miracle to operate in that way. But what of the truth of the story? We had seen it published three years before in some of the western papers, as having occurred in one of the cities in Ohio. We venture to say that if a reward of a thousand dollars were offered for the discovery of the Doctor, or the friend, they could not be found.

The minister acknowledged that all the personal experience he had had in spiritualism was an attendance at a single seance, for which he paid a dollar. We have seen what a margin he made on his investment. At the seance itself he doubtless got paid in his own coin.

It is a fair question whether the "spoils" of that mor-

al performance had not better have been given to relieve
some of the poor of the city, than to put it into the
preacher's divine pocket for crying "humbug" and the
performance of a series of pseudo-religious gymnastics,
the moral of which consists in teaching young men to
believe a lie.

We have witnessed the exercise of the new faculties
—or apparently new—known as gifts, on many occasions. These have already been enumerated. The gift
of healing is of great importance, and is now very extensively in use. It is undoubtedly the fact that the
possession of this power has in many instances been
greatly exaggerated. There is a strong motive on the
part of selfish deceivers to assume the possession of it
as a means of emolument. It is easier for such by
lofty pretentions to accumulate money in a short time
than by pursuing their legitimate avocations. It is a
fruitful field to operate in. And the more marvellous
the real effect produced by its exercise, the more extensively will imitators push forward their audacious
pretensions. That there is reality in it, however, is a
fact too well established by reliable testimony to be
denied. Cases are related elsewhere in illustration.
We have refrained from giving the names of healers,
lest it may be thought that our purpose is to advertize
the interests of any one or a few to the exclusion of
others, equally useful and meritorious. Instances
might be cited, if necessary, where it had been exercised independently of the will of the medium, and
where the medium was unwilling to accept remunera-
tion for the time employed in dispensing benefits. In

private life also, cases are known where this benefit has been imparted to the sick in a marked degree.

The gift of clairvoyance, or the ability to see spiritual beings is now so common that it is scarcely necessary to cite it as one of the faculties recognized as gifts. It is very questionable whether any one can be found where the subject has been brought to public attention, who has not known of some person in the circle of his acquaintance, who has given evidence of the possession of it. The proof to another's mind is circumstantial; but the circumstances are in themselves convincing to the most incredulously disposed. The sex, the personal appearance, dress, position, manners, voice, modes of expression, peculiarities in detail, not known nor to be anticipated or guessed at by strangers, when given by a medium on meeting a stranger for the first time, together with special means used by the spirits for the very purpose of recognition, to the surprise of the relative or friend who obtains the interview through the medium, are all means more or less positive, of identification. The shrewdest and most skilful, by observing the evidences of nationality may guess at a name, and by the evidences of occupation, by temperament, physiognomy and other physical signs make a case here and there, which is, so to speak, a good counterfeit; but in no case can a specific fact, or a special personal peculiarity be imitated.

Speaking in unknown tongues, by which of course is understood, languages unknown to the medium or to most of the persons listening to the remarks or discourse, is now quite common. Cases have been published several years ago, illustrating this gift in uneducated persons, who could not possibly imitate connected sentences, nor express ideas in a language foreign to them, which they had never studied. An Irish domestic in New York, while in a trance condition was made to converse in modern Greek, with a Greek gentleman present, the only one who could understand and interpret that language.

Drawing, singing, and the performance of instrumental music through spirit power have been of frequent occurrence, the mediums knowing either nothing at all of those accomplishments, or so little as to excite astonishment by the marvellous skill displayed.

Of physical mediumship we have seen much, but as this will be found in other portions of this compilation, we need not consume much time here in the narration. The moving of material objects without contact in the presence of mediums of this class, musical instruments being played upon without the touch of human fingers, the person recognized as the medium merely holding the instrument, as a guitar for example, by its extremity are instances of this kind. The production of likenesses is a remarkable circumstance. We have not personally been present during the evolution of spirit-photographs, but the fact is attested by numerous witnesses.

The impressional and inspirational influence is manifest in so many ways, that it is almost without limitation. Opinion and belief are modified and corrected by it. The inventor, the public speaker, the singer, the physician, the writer, the moralist, are all more or less inspired, and their efforts rendered successful according to the degree of their unfoldment and receptivity.

We have been gratified to know that all doubters are not revilers. Skeptics are generally such, because they are not well informed. The obstinate opposer often makes absurd objections, unworthy of notice. The honest doubter sometimes asks, "If spirit friends come to others why can't my friends come to me?" We reply that it requires not only the desire of the spirit friend, which we may suppose generally to exist, but appropriate conditions. If you wish to send a message by telegraph, you must go to the operator with it. It may be asked why does not the sender deliver his own message? It is simply impossible, unless he goes to the distant city where his friend or correspondent is. While the two remain apart, he must avail himself of the intermediate means of communication. It takes time for the operator to learn how to transmit the message with facility and accuracy. How can we expect our spirit friends to be able to control the subtle forces so as to communicate with us without adequate preparation?

The medium then is employed as an instrument for the conveyance of the message. In many cases a spirit child seems to be chosen as a messenger by the communicating spirit, the child holding possession of the medium. We have thought that the purpose of this was to show the value of artlessness and truthfulness. A greater moral effect is produced thereby, for an adult will bear reproof from a pure child which is the personification of innocence, which they would resent if ad-

ministered in positive terms by an equal. The words
uttered audibly by the medium when thus controlled
are simple, and the manner artless. Familiar names
are given to, and adopted by these children, as "Spark-
ling Water," "Spring Flower," and "Violet." The
influence is persuasive rather than dictatorial. It is
less exhausting than a more positive power to the medium, who is thereby saved from a severe struggle.
Such persons are also revived and soothed after the exhausting effect of a lecture delivered under control.
The same mollifying and recuperative influence continues to be exercised by the spirit child who remains in
these particulars child-like, by a progressive growth in
wisdom. This same blessed influence is employed as a
beneficent power behind that of the spirit who has immediate control.

If spirits can present themselves in a variety of
shapes, and represent different degrees of material
growth to their friends; if they can, as it were, present
themselves for identification in the same dress worn by
them in earth-life, and exhibit well known acts or peculiarities of character, is it not possible that they can
manifest themselves in any other form which they may
desire? Nor it is to be supposed that they really take
on the material form, after having thrown it off by the
change called death.

In relation to the expectation of seekers after spiritual knowledge in visiting mediums we may remark that
it is necessary to submit their request in good faith.
Spirits in celestial life have not lost their acuteness of
perception; rather than that, it has been increased;

hence they know the purpose of the inquirer as well or
better than he does himself, for he may be so foolish as
to deceive himself.   Neither have they sacrificed self-
respect.   If a person, in conscious self-importance, and
with a disposition to raillery, alleges that he wants to
communicate with his grandmother, and wants her to
give her name, he will very likely be rebuked by the
answer that it is "Sam Patch."

They are entitled to as much civility and respectful
treatment as would be required on entering the house
of a person here on a matter of business, and especially
where the party entering is to be the recipient of benefit.   The spirit seeing, and to some extent, anticipating
our needs, whether they pertain to material affairs,
physical health, or spiritual welfare, will meet us with
a cordial, friendly disposition.   They should not be
urgently importuned, nor a desire amounting to a demand indulged.   If the interview reveals the fact that
the spirit is not cognizant of our need, advice would not
be reliable nor valuable, though in such a case it is not
probable that it would be offered.

Many mediums imagine themselves to be controlled
by spirits who in earth-life had acquired high degrees of
distinction ; and who have voluntarily assumed the office
of guides to them.   It is a display of vanity on their
part, although they may have been led to believe that
that relation has been assumed, by a statement of a
spirit at some time previous, getting control.   An eccentric, mischievous, jocular person, of marked humorous talent, may carry with him this peculiar trait, and
play upon the credulity of a medium, without intend-

ing serious or permanent mischief. Another may be less scrupulous.

Sensible persons gain wisdom by experience, and although they may have been led to believe that they were the chosen instruments of great orators and sages, they discover the deception and abandon the claim, preserving their own individuality.

Mediums who are readily susceptible to psychological control, to preserve their usefulness and avoid danger, should refrain from contact with positive persons, whose character is not known. The old adage which affirms that "a person is known by the company he keeps" holds good to this day. Those who can preserve their own independence and do not yield to the power of others, may safely move among a variety of persons promiscuously, and may do good by precept and example. It is the mission of good spirits visiting us from the summer land, to elevate those occupying a lower plane than themselves, and in this they should be emulated by spirits dwelling in the physical form. Sensitives who willingly associate with drunkards, gamblers, or licentious persons, are liable to become contaminated by the evil influence which belongs to such company, which drags them down below their own level of morality. We have seen innocent persons led by the attraction of strong psychological power of spirits both in and out of the form ; and one is as dangerous as the other. The power thus named if employed by a person of good moral principle, will be beneficial, physically and morally, but if put to base uses, much misery will follow.

Mercenary conduct on the part of mediums is stated elsewhere, but a word or two more may not be out of place, as one of the items of personal observation. We have known them, while being paid for their services, to take advantage of the confidence reposed in them, by resorting to tricks of various kinds to compass selfish ends. . Some succeed so thoroughly in ingratiating themselves in the minds of their patrons, as to be regarded in the light of little deities. Their newly made friends could not be persuaded that the medium while under spirit influence was capable of a dishonest act. Their conduct received but little aid, if any, from spirits of any sort. Nervous persons, of great impressibility once yielding their confidence in this way, throwing prudence aside, forget that mediums are human, and subject to human failures.

We know instances where mediums have been guilty of deception, falsifying, and cheating their visitors. Although charity covers a multitude of sins, it is unjust, and a mistaken liberality to cover up a mean act in a way that will encourage its repetition. We should regard it a trifling injury to be robbed of our money in comparison to the pretence of giving us something from the spirit-world, which originated in the machination of the medium, the spirit who is alleged to have given it, not even being present. We have more than one in our mind to whom this criticism is applicable; and if any one feels the application, knowing his own peccadilloes, let him appropriate it, and reform the errors of his ways.

Many mediums claim that they are taken full possession of by the spirit, and are when thus controlled, entirely unconscious. This is true of some, and a portion remain so until the controlling power is withdrawn; but generally they soon become conscious, although still prompted by the spirit, who dictates the utterances.

There are other points in our experience which will be mentioned in their appropriate connection.

MEDIUMSHIP.

Mediumship is one of the most curious and interesting phases of human experience. The subject has recently been so fully treated by Mr. Thomas R. Hazard in a series of articles written for the Banner of Light, and re-published in pamphlet form, that we might omit its consideration, but for the fact that this volume may go into the hands of persons whom the pamphlet might not reach. We desire moreover to present an outline of the main subject, as nearly complete as practicable. We therefore avail ourselves of a few paragraphs, referring the reader to the pamphlet, which will repay a perusal, for a more connected and thorough presentation of Mr. H's views.

The exercise of mediumistic power is not a matter of choice. The peculiar faculty or gift comes unsought. In some of its forms it is very much desired by many who do not possess it, and cannot acquire it by any effort of the will, particularly that of clairvoyance. It is sometimes manifested suddenly, but more generally is a

process of regular, gradual development.   This may be
aided to some extent by observing and complying with
the requisite conditions.   The chief of these is the application of appropriate magnetism adapted to the particular physical constitution of the person seeking to
acquire it.   Such persons sometimes ask if it is best for
them to make use of such means.   We are of opinion
that it is not, a gradual growth being more satisfactory
and practicable than forced development.   The latter
may be compared to the forcing process resorted to for
the purpose of accelerating the growth of plants.   They
reach maturity more rapidly, but do not acquire strength
to resist the power of the wind, as the Oak does, which
grows slowly, but acquires by a sure process, vigor and
sturdiness to resist the violence of the storm.

Injury is done by inharmonious influences brought to
bear by unsuitable combinations of different qualities of
magnetism.   Caution in this respect is therefore to be
observed.   Nor is it wise to indulge an anxious desire for
development.   Time will bring about the requisite conditions, so that it is not necessary to abandon a legitimate business, for the purpose of carrying on the practice of mediumship in any form, as some do, imagining
on receiving the first decided impulse, that they are
called to the work.   Such premature movements only
result in failure, as well as pecuniary loss by the wast-
ing of time.

The impulse, however, may be too strong for resist-
ance, and the subject of it may with propriety yield
obedience to it, if it has been proved, upon being properly tested, to be of a benignant character.

Some go through severe discipline in the process of development. If they are compelled to change their occupation, and devote their time to their new calling, it is of course reasonable that they should be sustained in the work. There is the greatest inequality in this respect. Some of the best are but poorly compensated. Others as soon as they begin to be appreciated take advantage of their opportunity, and charge extravagantly for services rendered. Operating upon a limited scale among neighbors and friends, and particularly the poor among them, their ordinary avocation not being interfered with, they may use their gift gratuitously.

When it is engaged in as a duty, requiring their whole time to be devoted to it, no reasonable person can object to a fair compensation being paid. This can be regulated on an equitable basis, being governed somewhat by circumstances, among which will be the relative pecuniary ability of the party receiving the service, the wealthy not however being compelled to pay extravagantly, and out of proportion to the value of the service merely because of their good fortune. When the latter feel it a duty to pay liberally, and derive pleasure therefrom, it enables the medium to render the same service to the poor who need it, without direct reward. Thus both giver and receiver are alike blessed. Some are so unselfish as to be unjust to themselves in this respect. Excellent healers, although themselves needy, will sometimes unwisely decline compensation altogether.

Spirits from the higher spheres who have outgrown material propensities, have no desire to encourage the accumulation of wealth, and therefore do not influence mediums to that end. Knowing that its use is to clothe and nourish the body, they rather, when that is accomplished, favor the distribution of surplus means where it is needed, and discourage hoarding. This they have been known to do in a marked manner.

The following remarks by Mr. Hazard set forth the trials of mediums.

"How often do superficial or ignorant investigators go to mediums with a lie in their hearts, expecting, at the same time, to get truth in return—a thing as utterly impossible as that the eye of the astronomer should penetrate the heavens on demand of a thick-skulled man, at the very moment that he is pressing his body against the lens of the telescope.

"Contrast the treatment our mediums receive, and the estimation in which they are held, even by many of their friends, with that which is extended to the clergy of all the popular creedal denominations! Wherever these go, they receive greetings in the markets and public places. They enjoy the chief seats at our feasts, and the highest in our synagogues and churches. Every one bows low when they meet them, and calls them rabbis and reverends, doctors and fathers; and when they enter our houses, they become the observed of all observers; and when they go abroad, conductors of railway cars and captains of steamboats hasten to give them the best seats and berths they have at their disposal, free of charge; and wherever they pray, be it in the pulpit of the church, the cabin of the ship, or at the corner of the street, all bow the head and knee in respectful reverence, even though the prayer should be as one of those that Jesus said used to be offered in his day, merely to be heard of men. But how when we meet the poor mediums in the market, whither they may have wended their way to purchase, mayhap, a morsel of cheap food for their day's sustenance? Who of their kid-gloved acquaintance greets them then? Who invite them to their feasts? Who respectfully salutes them as ministers of the angels? Who opens to them the doors of their houses, except on sufferance, or to 'give a seance?' What captain of a steamboat or conductor of a railroad car approaches them, except to demand their ticket, and see that it is paid in full? They partake of none of the courtesies and privileges that are so lavishly bestowed on the clergy of the popular churches, and in fact are, literally speaking, often as poor and as much despised as was that Elder Brother of their order who used to pour out his anguished soul in the lonely garden of Gethsemane, or give it sorrowing utterance in the pathetic lament : 'The foxes have holes, and the birds of the air have nests ; but the Son of Man hath not where to lay his head.' "

The forms of mediumship, as heretofore intimated, are numerous, embracing a great variety of remarkable physical manifestations, as well as astonishing mental phenomena, to each of which we shall allow reasonable space in items to be quoted.

The mediums for physical manifestations have been subjected to great annoyance and suspicion. This is partly chargeable to a most illiberal prejudice in the minds of the ignorant, and partly to the mingling of fraudulent tricks with truthful demonstrations.   Honest mediums, innocent of the slightest attempt at deception have been falsely accused from the time the first raps were heard, to the appearance of hands formed by spirits.   That hands have not only been seen, but have been tangible, we have abundant evidence ; yet the mediums have been charged with using their own hands and feet to produce the effect which witnesses have described, and that by spiritualists themselves, who would have been almost willing to make oath that the hands and feet which touched them were those of human flesh, the latter having shoes upon them, and that they were like the shoes of the medium ; nor could we convince them to the contrary.   This was a painful position for any well-meaning person to be placed in—two friends present, both considered honorable, and both spiritualists, taking opposite grounds, in reference to an alleged fact.   What can be the explanation ?   The conclusion we have reached is that the spirit uses the emanations from the medium for the moment, containing the chemical forces, from the hands and feet, forming temporarily, producing or projecting, as the terms have been used respectively, hands and feet which for the instant were palpable and visible. This is of course, conjectural and may be accepted by the reader, unless he has another hypothesis more satisfactory to his own mind.   Spirit hands thus formed are used for touching, handling, and playing upon instruments. If the medium was not present, the spirits would have none of these subtle, vital elements to operate with.

The force of light, in the case of mediums of ordinary power, disperses those elements, and destroys the manifestations. In one or two of the more recent cases where the mediums have become more highly developed this obstacle has less force. In dark circles, when the instruments were sailing over our heads, sometimes on one side of the moon, and at other times on the opposite side, not admitting of the slightest opportunity for deception, when a light was suddenly created by a friction match, the instrument would as suddenly drop at whatever point it might be arrested. This proves the necessity of conditions being observed, as much so as the use of light for the production of photographic pictures of objects copied. If the law by which these things are done is not understood, the critic should not condemn the conditions which seem to be necessary for carrying on the process.

"If Daniel Webster speaks as tersely and powerfully as he did when he stood in the United States Senate Chamber, he must communicate his ideas to a medium of equal powerful brain structure as he possessed, to have them 'syllabled' with equal force and effect, and perhaps the audience who is listening should be as capable of appreciating the full force of the words as were his fellow senators to give the medium even then full inspiration. As it is, spirits cannot get control of many such brain structures as Webster possessed, and therefore have to impress their ideas on inferior organisms, that are often only able to give them forth indistinctly embodied amidst a mass of their own redundant verbiage and platitudes. In the good time coming when 'Spiritualism' becomes more popular, the defect may possibly be in a degree remedied, unless, as has almost always hitherto been the case, these more talented mediums turn traitors to the higher intelligences, and become of the order of 'rogues (denounced by him of the Golden Age), who steal the livery of Spiritualism to serve their devilish selves therewith,' not only in the pulpit, but on the rostrums or wherever else such daws and popinjays can strut and show themselves decked in their stolen mediumistic plumes.

"As there are exceptions to all general rules in mundane affairs, so there appear to be in spiritual; and I know of many instances wherein persons of certain peculiarities of organization find it very difficult to obtain the necessary conditions for spirit communion, at the same time that they are not at all either personally or spiritually offensive to disembodied spirits.

"The longer I live the more clearly I see that the maxim of Jesus, concerning little children, affords the only safe rule by which investigators of the phenomena that occur through spirit-mediums, can arrive at satisfactory results. Next to pharisaical spiritual pride, the pride of intellect, and that which too often attaches to superficial or mere mechanical learning, offer the most impenetrable barriers to the acquisition of spiritual knowledge, especially if they be coupled with contemptuous feelings toward the medium, and, above all, with spiteful suspicions of their honesty. In the early stages of my investigations, I confess that I was very much addicted to suspicions of this kind, and so long as I indulged in them I obtained but little satisfaction. My constant desire was to obtain tests, which I somehow fancied I had a right to demand, like the Pharisees of old, rather than thankfully receive, in the spirit of the little child, as a free gift. Whilst in this state of mind I seldom received much that was satisfactory.

"There are but few, probably, who have a proper conception of the extreme sensitiveness of a medium's mind, and how easy it is to be psychologized by mundane influences when it is in a condition sufficiently negative to admit of spirit-control. When in that state a medium's mind may be likened to a double-faced looking-glass—the one side reflecting from the spiritual to the mundane, and the other from the mundane to the spiritual sphere; the same psychological laws prevailing in both alike.

"That spirit-manifestations (especially physical) are greatly influenced by the state or quality of the atmosphere, there can be no doubt. I know of excellent mediums in whose presence no phenomena ever occur when the weather indicates rain. And yet, when it was bright and clear, I have known, through some of these, the most powerful manifestations to occur that I ever witnessed."

"It would seem that, in the production of certain kinds of phenomena, the presence of light has a corresponding effect to that of the will, and darkness to that of its absence—the one being positive and the other negative. Thus, at a spirit-seance, in the absence of any exertion of mundane will-power, the medium's mind may be taken full possession of by the 'powers of the air,' and communicate freely of things belonging not to earth; but let a powerful will force be thrown upon the in-

strument's mind, from one or more of the circle, and
the character of the manifestations may instantly change,
or cease altogether, just as they do upon the introduction of light at a dark circle."

The identification of spirits by name is often sought
by investigators with but little satisfaction.   It may be
accounted for in two ways, viz : spirits attach no importance to names as sources of authority, but admon-
ish us that a communication should be estimated
according to its intrinsic merits, rather than because it
was given by a particular person.   Again it seems
probable that when they are born into the spirit-life
they receive a spirit name, as a child does after being
born into this world, and are no longer known by the
latter.   Hence, except for recognition, the name known
in connection with their mundane history is no longer
used.   Spirits recognize other spirits by interior perception, so that in communicating with beings on earth,
they dispense with mere forms.   The probabilities of
deception as to name is considerable, hence personal
identity in respect to form, habits in earth-life, specific
opinions, and in fact all that goes to make up individuality is far better for recognition with them.   The memory of names fades with us here, so that a traveller who
has been absent for some years, on returning readily
recognizes persons with whom they have not been particularly acquainted, and sometimes even others, by physical appearances but fails to remember names.   Is it not
probable that having no longer any use for their earthly name, but laying it aside, when called for at a

circle without any particular need, they may hesitate to give it. Sympathy will keep the memory active as to substantial realities.

The question has often been asked whether the spirit of the medium leaves the body while in a trance state. It is a matter of observation that scarcely any two mediums are affected alike, when under control, in all particulars. Some are psychologically impressed, the medium's spirit being acted upon as a mesmeric subject. In other cases the spirit takes complete control of the body of the medium, his or her spirit being at liberty to roam or to remain quiet by their side. The link binding the two cannot be entirely broken, for that would constitute the change called death.

A few marked cases of certain varieties of mediumship may here be cited to illustrate the intensity of power and skill employed by the invisible intelligences in these particular directions.

Of the writing mediums Mr. J. V. Mansfield has become widely known. Formerly a successful merchant in Boston, he was compelled by those higher powers to adopt the practice of answering sealed letters as a regular business. Retiring from his previous occupation, in obedience to the impulse given him, he has been engaged in his new calling ever since, now a period of fifteen years, and with the most successful and satisfactory results. Thousands of persons have received answers to letters, and had their letters returned therewith, unopened. Mr. M. writes in many languages, although he never acquired the knowledge of any but his vernacular. The letters sent to him to be answered have been doubly enveloped, pasted, tied, sewed, sealed with wax, and their contents concealed in a variety of other ways so that each writer was perfectly satisfied that it was impossible for them to be read unless by destroying the carefully guarded covering.

We once took a sealed letter to Mr. M., containing some fifteen questions, written by an insane person formerly an inmate of the McLean Asylum. As soon as he took hold of the letter, he said he should think the devils had got hold of him. The influence affected him as the lady who wrote it was affected. Every question was answered to the satisfaction of all who knew the circumstances. We have several times tested his powers with great satisfaction.

Mr. R. W. Flint is another writing medium who has a similar gift which we have found to be equally valuable and reliable. He too was compelled to leave his former occupation to engage exclusively in this.

Of spirit artists, Mr. William P. Anderson is a notable example. While entranced, he has executed some of the finest drawings that can be imagined. For some of them which were considered exquisitely finished he received several thousand dollars. Taken from his occupation in a cabinet-makers shop, he was irresistibly led to the adoption of portrait drawing as a business. Mr. Starr, Mr. Milleson, and others were brought out in the same way. Mrs. Blair was controlled in such a manner as to execute the drawing of flowers and wreaths while her eyes were bandaged by several thicknesses of cloth, so effectually excluding the light as to remove doubt from the most skeptical minds on that point.

While thus bandaged she would, in the presence of large audiences in ten minutes time produce a beautiful picture, often emblematical, so that the party for whom it was drawn would recognize its purpose and meaning. Mrs. Hazelton, who was entirely uncultivated in this accomplishment, had the gift bestowed upon her, so that within the last few years she has executed symbolical drawings so skilfully as to astonish the most distinguished artists. No one not witnessing these performances can form any correct idea of the beauty of design and skill in execution displayed in this way.

One of the most remarkable phases of physical mediumship is the elevation and removal of the bodies of mediums from one part of the room to another, or out of one room into another; and even to greater distances. Jennie and Annie Lord at their seances have been taken up in their chairs bodily, and placed upon the table without physical contact. Hundreds in various parts of the country can testify to this statement. Harry Gordon and some others have been taken up in the same way and carried across the room. Truthful citizens of the highest respectability have testified to these facts.

Dr. Willis, N. Frank White, Mrs. Coan, Miss Sugden and Mrs. Hayden are mediums of this class. We have sat in the presence of all of them, both in private circles and public meetings. The spirits would respond to the remarks of speakers on these occasions by raps as loud as if a good sized nail were being driven by sharp blows of a hammer, and heard by all, under circumstances where deception was impossible.

There are thousands of private mediums scattered all over the world, who never make any public exhibition of the wonderful manifestations made through them, but who are constantly giving their friends most convincing evidence of the truth of spiritual phenomena. Many more are influenced in a peculiar manner, who do not know the cause of their peculiar feelings, nor the meaning. Their condition is often mistaken for sickness, and they are plied with drugs with the expectation of affording relief from what is supposed to be physical disease. The physician called to treat the case not understanding the meaning of the singular phenomena that he witnesses resorts to some preparation of Opium or Chloral, which retards the development of the medium, by disturbing the harmony of the forces. Persons undergoing this change are sometimes considered insane and sent to an Asylum, while there is no diseased action to treat.

The necessity of harmonious conditions has been mentioned in connection with manifestations in general. It is particularly to be observed when visiting a medium for the purpose of getting either a written or a verbal communication from personal friends. Harmony must prevail between the seeker and the medium. Mediums are not always successful. One may fail to obtain any thing in a particular case, and another succeed, when both are reliable, the failure in the one case not depending upon any fault in the medium, any more than success in the other is a proof of superior merit.

A good deal of excitement was exhibited for some months in reference to spirit-photographs. Mr. Mum-

ler, the principal artist in this line having been subjected to a prosecution on a charge of fraud, which resulted
however in his acquittal. It is a matter which cannot
as readily be disposed of as those which involve only
the sense of sight, touch or hearing. Professional artists or persons having accurate chemical knowledge are
necessary to aid in the settlement of the question whether the pictures which appear on the plates are genuine,
and not the result of a process within the power of any
photographer to reproduce. Yet if there is an absolute
likeness produced, and no work of art in any style has
been previously executed, from which to copy, the
likeness being readily recognized by any calm observer, not excited by anxious hope, to the verge of imagination, it ought to be considered satisfactory proof.

The weight of evidence is now in favor of the genuineness of these productions. Moses A. Dow Esq.
has given an account of his experience with Mr. Mum-
ler, which afforded him satisfactory proof. Similar testimony has been given by Judge Edmonds and others
of credibility, but not over credulous.

On the doubtful side artists say there is great opportunity for deception. After all it is a question of
recognition, and every person of common sense ought
to know the likeness of a familiar face.

Various questions have been discussed through speakers and writers in reference to the character and the
subject matter of communications, which we quote in a
somewhat desultory manner.

Concerning the phenomena of Spiritualism detailed
in the Christian Scriptures it has been remarked :

"The more I have investigated the phenomena of 'modern Spiritualism,' and the wonderful complex character of spirit mediumship, the more clearly I have been enabled to comprehend how exactly its character and phenomena correspond to those which occurred through the ministrations of Jesus of Nazareth and his mediumistic disciples. With a little modification or explanation of the terms used in the New Testament, they are parallel."

The following questions were propounded to the intelligence conducting one of the seances, "How is it that returning spirits are so much given to prophesying future events? Is this knowledge of facts and events that are to be an absolute knowledge? Are there laws governing the succession of circumstances which are inevitably sure in their working, and are there spirits who can read them correctly? If so, how comes so much false prophecy?"

The answer was given in these words:

The old adage that "Coming events cast their shadows before," contains a very great truth. It means this: that all the conditions incident to this material life have first what would be termed a spectral existence in the other life, or, in other words, beyond your sight or knowledge. As your own Emerson says: "Truth is always in the air, and those who are the most susceptible to it get it first." These spectral conditions are always in your midst, and spirits have no difficulty in seeing them, defining them, and tracing them to their ultimates here with you. The reasons why so many mistakes are made are to the reasoning mind very obvious : First—the channels are all more or less imperfect through which they prophesy; second—the conditions which surround the channels are all more or less imperfect, and surely these two circumstances are enough to render unreliable almost every prophecy that is made unto you.

The following illustrates the injudicious tendency of incorrect teachings, and certain mental disturbances.

Q.—Do you not think that a great many mediums have done a great deal of harm among certain classes?

A.—I certainly do, inasmuch as they are unfortunately organized, so that they attract to themselves a class of spiritual teachers who are poorly adapted to give spiritual truth. And again, there are others who throw themselves upon this great rushing tide of spiritual influx before they are half-fledged as mediums, and, therefore, harm ensues.

Q.—Do you think any more are made insane through the means of Spiritualism than by old Theology?

A.—Statistical records show that the number of insane persons who have been made insane by modern Spiritualism are far in the minority when compared with those who have been made insane by popular Christianity. We do not know how these notes will compare when Spiritualism is eighteen hundred and seventy one years old.

Q.—I should judge by the question answered previously, that you do not deny that Spiritualism is injurious to mankind?

A.—Everything—I care not whether the thing be good, very good, or bad, very bad, or ranging between the two—is, to some, a positive evil. Modern Spiritualism proposes to bring more of goodness than evil to humanity. Thus far it has done this, as its record, spiritual and mortal, will show.

Q.—Can truth, under any circumstances be injurious?

A.—Yes it can; because the injurious things, or evil things, of this life are measured by the senses of this life. Therefore, measuring truth by the senses of the mortal life, there are conditions under which it had better be withheld; for if it is expressed it will do harm.

The following passages are quoted from discourses given through a noted trance-speaker.

The question is asked: "Why are the communications of the spirits so vague, and conveyed in so mysterious a manner as to leave doubts, on the mind, of their being genuine?" First, if modern spiritualism be true, and if there is a principle by which those in the spirit-world can communicate with persons on the earth, it is controlled by a fixed and positive law; that law is as certain when applied correctly, and as uncertain when applied incorrectly, as is telegraphic communication between New York and Washington. If a man along any portion of the route cut the wire, your telegraphic message will stop at that point; or, if there is any fault in the operator, your message will be sent incorrectly. It is the same in communications between this and the spirit world. There are lines of thought and feeling;

minds, and tables, and chairs, are but the wires which they use to convey their thoughts. You are at one end of that telegraphic chain, your spirit-friend at the other. If there is no intervening influence, the message will be conveyed; if, in any way, the line of communication is disturbed, the message will be incorrectly given. You call it a lie, and give up Spiritualism. But there are sufficient communications that do come correct, to prove, to any candid mind, that this spiritual communication is an absolute science; and no man of reason or judgment, if there were, in a hundred cases, one that was correct, or one out of every ten, would pretend to say that the other nine proved that it was not a science. It is the natural order of a new science to make mistakes; this is true of the infancy of all sciences. But if, in the tenth time of trying, you succeed, it demonstrates the principle, and ten thousand failures cannot disprove it. And if nine out of every ten mediums give you false communications, and the tenth one gives you a correct one, that proves the principle. If nine out of every ten spirits lie to you, that only proves that those passing from the earth retain something of their earthly character.

"Your father, mother, husband, or wife, or child, may be close beside you, their souls almost throbbing with your own. Yet there is no chain, no medium, no telegraph there. The doors of your external senses shut them out. They may knock at the doors of your mind; you do not receive them. You cry 'Humbug! psychology! mesmerism!' Your friend remains in silence. Again, your spirit-friend may even endeavor to communicate with your mind, without using any such outward means, in a beautiful thought or feeling. But the physical form may be an obstruction to the correct transmission of the communication, in the present imperfect state of the science.

"Out of all the spirits that are accused of lying, probably not one in a hundred does so intentionally. Everything is called a lie which does not precisely, in all its points bear the criticism of those who investigate it. What we call a lie is that which is given with the intention of deceiving. Something given in ignorance is not really a lie. For instance, a man may state, in all sincerity, that the moon is green. Now, probably there is something which causes that man to see the moon in that color. You all say that he is mistaken, you call it a lie, a falsity, a deception ; it is real to him. Now, spirits, employing mediums whose brain is not wholly under their control, are liable to tell you that white things are green, that something occurred which you know did not ; but that does not prove that it is not a spirit ; it does not even prove that it is not your spirit-friend who professes to communicate ; it only proves that they have not perfect control of the medium.

"The time is not far distant, when raps, tippings, writings, and even trance-speaking, or any extraordinary manifestations, will all pass away, and man in the external image of his own divinity will see, and hear, and feel the presence of the angel-world all around him, and your own souls shall not require your external vision, or external feeling, or any of the external senses, to prove to you that spirits and angels are really here.

They shall come to you in the stilly night, with soft and pleasant voices. They shall sing to you the songs of perfect love and peace; and no man will have a doubt. This is our prophecy. How is it to be done? By a gradual and almost imperceptible growth into a more spiritual condition; and, as it is reaching its culminating point, the time may not be as far distant as most people may imagine. Spirituality is far more rapidly growing upon the inhabitants of earth than in any former period of man's history. The slow steps of a world, forever slow in acknowledging the truth, shall accomplish more in the next fifty years than it has done in the last thousand. Yet it will be slow, for it must come step by step, like the wheels of some majestic chariot; the more majestic and grand, the more slow and solemn shall be its approach. It shall not come to you at once, with an overwhelming power, like the day of pentecost, or like the mighty avalanche which at once buries all opposing obstacles; but softly, gently, gradually, like the approach of a genial summer after a dreary winter, when day by day the buds and blossoms put forth, and ere long you reap the fruition of the golden harvest; or, like the quiet repose of slumber, when you sleep you shall not know how you came to sleep.

"We do not suppose that there is any material or external science which can demonstrate modern Spiritualism. Chemistry and geology fail. Mesmerism, psychology, and clairvoyance, are in themselves so mysterious, that we cannot use them for the explanation of another mystery. Ask any man who pretends to be-

lieve in mesmerism, who is a professor of that science,
if he can demonstrate to you what it is. He can not
do it; nor can psychology or clairvoyance be explained.
They all pertain to mind; they are of those mysterious
things which belong to the science of mind; and no
system of mental philosophy can explain it to you.
Mental philosophers treat of the facts when they should
explain the principles. Those who treat of a man's
life, treat simply of what he did, how much he ate and
drank, and what he said, and never of what he thought.
No biographer can tell you what the man thought—the
thought of Washington, or Napoleon, or Webster, or
any great statesman or warrior that has lived. No one
knows what they thought; you only record their ac-
tions, their deeds, their external, physical manifestations, which many times are as much at variance with
the real thoughts of the person as is night with the
light of morning.

"Spirits can not communicate to you positively, and
beyond the power of contradiction. There is no such
thing as having anything beyond the power of contradiction, and especially if that thing be a new one, and
unsanctified by church and state; if the whole world is
warring against it, especially if it interferes with religious creeds and prejudices, something which shall destroy old institutions. You know that mankind have
great affection for old institutions; it is natural to us
all. We all revere aged men, not so much for what
they are—though they may be great even in their second childhood—but we remember what they were: they
are still kind, still gentle, and will presently pass away.

It is a reverence for past greatness and for feebleness. Now, this is so with institutions. Men nourish and cherish them as long as they can, until at last they are obliged to give them up. There may be no positive standard of thought or demonstration, by which any and every person may ascertain if Spiritualism is true. The writings of Andrew Jackson Davis, Professor Hare, and Judge Edmonds, being among the most prominent spiritual works, are said to be standard works among spiritualists. They are not so. Spiritualism has no standard works. Davis, Edmonds, and Hare, relate their own experience. But no two spiritualists can possibly have precisely the same experience; it is as varied as is their existence. Your spiritual communications are not like Professor Hare's; your friend, through whom you have received the demonstration, may not be like his. Consequently, you may not possibly demonstrate it as he has done. You can only investigate Spiritualism in your own way, and arrive at such conclusions as your own reason and judgment shall dictate, and solve that which is mysterious, only by a gradual and successive chain of thought, just as any scientific principles are reasoned out, just as any propositions in mathematics, in chemistry, in geology, are demonstrated; it must be done by a slow process of education, of investigation, of intuition, embodied in an expression of external forms."

From another writer we quote these passages:

"The rule, given in scripture, for trying the mediums for prophecy, is to look to the accomplishment of the

prophecies, and not to the age or country in which the
seers live. 'When a prophet speaketh in the name of
the Lord, if the thing follow not, nor come to pass, that
is the thing which the Lord hath not spoken, but the
prophet hath spoken it presumptuously.' (Deut. xviii.
22.) Swedenborg saw in vision and accurately foretold the precise day of his own decease ; also the very
hour of the decease of Olof Olófsohn : and the happening of many other interesting events. These have
passed into history. Judged by the rule of the Scriptures, Swedenborg was a true seer. By this, the speaker does not mean to assert, that he could foresee all
events, nor that he was free from mistakes. He would
neither be willing to assert nor to admit that, in relation
to any of the prophets, whose writings are recorded in
the Old Testament, He can ascribe omniscience to none
but God."

"In our own time, the death of the late Czar Nicholas,
was foreseen and foretold in this country three months
before the event.   The late war in the Crimea, was
foreseen and foretold in this country eighteen months
before its commencement. 'When the Arctic was destroyed, her disaster was communicated to four different persons, who were unknown to each other, and that,
at the same instant it occurred, and long before the
news reached the shore.' The cases of true prophecy
in this country, within the last eight years, that are
well authenticated, are quite numerous. Judging by
the standard of Jewish and Christian Scriptures in the
light of history, there have been true prophets and seers
in the different ages and countries of the world, to whom

some things of the future have been made known; and we have them among us still.

"This is precisely what we ought to expect. The Divine law is not changed. The mode of Divine communication is not altered. Paul, writing to his Corinthian brethren, while giving rules for the perpetual guidance of Christians, says: 'Follow after charity, and desire spiritual gifts, but rather that ye may prophesy.'

"We are informed that a Dutch Ambassador told the King of Siam, that in his country, in cold weather, the water was so hard that it would bear an elephant, if he were there. The king replied, 'Hitherto I have believed the strange things you have told me, because I looked upon you as a sober, fair man; but now I am sure you lie.'

"The fact transcended his philosophy. In like manner when the wonderful things of the Scriptures were presented to the mind of David Hume, they transcended his philosophy, and so he rejected them as fabulous. He did not stop to consider, that there might be other laws of nature with which he was unacquainted, and so he rejected the evidence of the facts. Under like circumstances weak and superstitious minds at once arrive at the conclusion, that the laws of God are reversed; that the events are supernatural—miraculous.

But the true Spiritualist or Christian philosopher will receive the facts, if the evidence be amply sufficient to prove them. He is aware how little he knows of the Divine laws. If he knows of no laws by which such phenomena can be produced, he will not infer that the universe has got out of order, that the laws of God are reversed, nor that the facts occur contrary to those laws.   He will reasonably suppose that there may be, and probably are, other laws, with which he is unacquainted, and patiently wait till he discovers them.

"The present age of Spiritualism is nothing less than a full return to the ancient faith of the Church, and a complete revival of the doctrines of Christianity.   There have been mediums for spiritual intercourse in all, or nearly all, the ages of our race.   During the gross materialism and infidelity of past ages, mediums without the pale of the church were persecuted and hung. And, in the fierceness of their rage, the infidels of the seventeenth century, under the assumed garb of Christianity, persecuted unto death by false accusation, many who were not mediums at all.   Among the ancients, aside from the mediums mentioned in the Jewish and Christian Scriptures, Socrates stands most prominent. He asserted, that for many years he was accompanied by a demon, guardian spirit, or angel, who, whenever he was tempted to do anything wrong cautioned him against it.

"On the 13th of August, 1800, in the State of Maine, a spirit went in company with Mrs. Butler and forty seven other persons about half a mile.   Rev. Abraham Cummings, who was uncle to the late Dr. Asa Cummings, wrote a history of the appearence of this spirit, and published it in 1826.   He took and printed the testimony of thirty one witnesses, who had seen or conversed with the spirit in the year 1800.   Mr. Cummings, in his narrative, says :   ' With all these witnesses I am intimately acquainted.   I took these testimonies from

their lips, for the most part, separately.' After giving
the testimony, Mr. Cummings says: 'The above
witnesses are exhibited not for the want of more (for
more than a hundred have seen the spectre, or have
heard her words,) but because repetition is tedious.'
The testimony, part or all of it, was taken in the year
1800. One witness, Dorcas Johnson, speaking of the
manifestation on the 13th of August, says: 'There I
heard and saw the spectre. Her voice was distinct from
any other, and her music the most delightful that I ever
heard. When she walked with us she moved without
stepping. And when we arrived at the house, by direction of the spectre, given to my brother, James
Springer, and by him to the company in our hearing,
we opened to the right and left, so that the spectre and
Mrs. Butler passed together between our ranks. Then
she vanished from my view, and I saw her no more.'
The testimony of others is equally explicit.

Of the distinguished Sweedish seer, concerning whom
we shall further remark in treating of various religious
organizations, he says :

"Among modern mediums the most prominent of all
stands Emanuel Swedenborg. He stands prominent
on account of his eminence and high position as a man
of learning and science ; also because he was in contact
or daily intercourse with the spiritual world for twenty
eight years, and also on account of the mass and value
of the spiritual communications which he committed to
writing, amounting to about thirty printed volumes.
But very few have yet received the doctrines taught by
or through him, or even read his works. The world

was so steeped in materialism and infidelity that his doctrines have been generally rejected without examination.
By self-sufficient and dogmatical persons, he has been
denounced as an insane man.

"To say nothing of other countries, in this country
alone at the present time, the mediums cannot number
less than one hundred thousand. Among the believers
are included Judges, Senators, Orators, Clergymen,
Poets, Mathematicians, Chemists, and Philosophers.
All these are denounced as insane by the whole hosts of
infidels. Why should we be supprised at this? When
Paul gave an account of the spiritual manifestations that
he witnessed on his way to Damascus, to Festus and
Agrippa, Festus charged him with insanity.

"There is no doubt that murderers, drunkards and
harlots may become mediums for evil spirits, as readily
as moral men and Christians can become mediums for
good spirits. Every man, whether in the material or
spiritual world, is naturally attracted to the society of
others who are like him. * * David was a polygamist,
an adulterer, and a murderer. Solomon was a sensual-
ist, an adulterer, and a polygamist. Does any one deny
that they were mediums for spiritual intercourse? Mary
Magdalene has been by many supposed to have been a
harlot. She was a medium for spiritual communications. Seven evil spirits took possession of her and
made themselves manifest by communications. Why
should not evil spirits, or the spirits of evil men do the
same thing now?

The same writer after enumerating many of the phenomena already cited, says that spirits "can and do,

with or without the hands of the medium prick off music unknown to all in the family, and that whether the medium is a musician or not; that they open the spiritual hearing of suitable mediums, and utter spiritual words, and make them audible to such mediums, which words cannot be heard by others, though present; that they produce the odic or spiritual light, and make it manifest to all present; that they intervene for the cure of diseases, and in rare instances produce the human voice.

"The performers, who do these things, claim to be the spirits of deceased persons. They identify themselves in the most unmistakable manner, by exhibiting their spiritual forms to seeing mediums (sometimes many mediums seeing the same spiritual form at the same time;) by writing their own handwriting; by relating facts in their history long since forgotten by all present, and other facts that none present ever knew; by recitals of poetry, which they were accustomed to repeat, when living in the material body, and sometimes by taking possession of the medium, and exhibiting in pantomime the motions and habits of body, to which they were accustomed while living here; and sometimes the motions and habits of persons that were insane; and sometimes speaking through the organs of the medium in a voice to imitate their own natural voice before death. To most of these facts we have millions of living witnesses. We have seen and observed them ourselves. To use the words of Jesus, 'We speak that we do know, and testify that we have seen; and ye receive not our witness.' (John iii. 11.)

"Religious teachers ought to know, that practical psychology or mesmerism is the actual communion between two spirits, while both are in the body, that ordinary experiments in mesmerism require two parties, a subject or medium and an operator ; that the operator establishes the spiritual communication by means of his will ; and that, consequently, if his soul and spirit survive the process of death, no good reason can be assigned why the operator in mesmerism should not retain all his mesmeric power, and even find it increased, by throwing off his external body. This is what we find to be the fact ; and this is the way, in which the phenomena of spiritualism are produced.

"But no operator in mesmerism, while in the material body, has been able to produce any of the higher phenomena of spiritualism. The operator in mesmerism, is able to throw his subject or medium into a trance ; to control him in most cases at will ; to deceive his senses ; to present to him imaginary pictures, and induce him to receive them as real. But, so far as we can learn, no operator in ordinary mesmerism, from the beginning of the world, has ever been able to produce a real rap without contact ; to move a table without contact ; to induce the medium to speak or write in any language which was alike unknown to the medium and the operator ; or to conceal present material objects from the vision of all others present, while the subject or medium is permitted to see them. These and many others of the phenomena of Spiritualism are a higher branch of the art, which the operator in Mesmerism, cannot produce by the power of his will, until after he passes into the spiritual world."

"The operator in mesmerism, when he is freed from his external body, and becomes a free spirit, if he can find a medium through whose organization he can freely work, and upon which he can act as a lever by his mesmeric or will power, can produce the raps, move the table, and take up the pen and write in the same manner as the speaker can, by the power of his will through his own organism. He can write through the hand of the medium or without it, in any language which he understands in the same manner he formerly could through his own bodily organs. He can enter into the medium, and expresss himself and speak in any language which he understands, provided he has perfect control of his subject, in the same manner as the speaker can through his own organs. In order to obtain spiritual manifestations, it is never necessary to have any mesmeric operator present. When such operators, with a strong will, are present, they have power in some degree to counteract the will of a spiritual operator. But the finest spiritual manifestations are obtained, when only one, two, or three are present, and when all present are mediums.

"But if all the spiritual manifestations of the present day are produced by mesmeric operation in the body, then no doubt all those recorded in the Scriptures were produced in the same way; for they appear to be entirely similar. If piano fortes are now taken up from the floor by ordinary mesmerism, and without contact, then the walls of Jericho were pulled down by the same means. If writing without the medium's hand is now produced by human magnetism, or ordinary mesmerism,

then the writing in Belshazzar's palace was produced in
the same manner. If spiritual hands are all now produced by ordinary mesmerism, then the hand seen by
Belshazzar was produced in the same way. If the ward
of the lock is thrown back, and the bolted door opened
by ordinary mesmerism in this age, then Peter was
brought out of prison by the same means.

"If the spiritual mediums, in all cases, now see the
spiritual forms of their deceased friends by ordinary
magnetism, then all the manifestations of the forms of
Jesus to his disciples were produced in the same manner. If spiritual mediums in all cases hear spiritual
sounds by ordinary mesmerism in these days, then the
disciples heard the voice of Jesus after his death in the
same way. Then we have no reliable evidence that
Jesus ever rose out of the dead. And so I might say
of all the spiritual manifestations recorded in the scriptures. Then is our faith in vain, and Christianity a
fable.

"Mesmerism is only one branch of the infinite system
of spiritualism. Mesmerism is only confined to that intercourse which may be established between two human
spirits, while both still reside in their human bodies.
Spiritualism regards all that intercourse which exists or
may be established between any two spirits in the Universe, whether they are both human spirits or not,
whether they are both equally elevated, or whether one
is the Deity, and the other one of the lowest spirits that
have been organized by his power. Spiritualism ex-
plains the origin of the doctrine of the transmigration of
souls ; it shows the mode in which nearly every system

of idolatry was introduced into the world ; it is a key to unlock all the dark volumes of ancient history and mythology, and furnishes a scientific basis for all true religion.

ADDITIONAL FACTS.

On page 113 and subsequently, mention has been made of some remarkable examples of various phases of physical mediumship. It was thought sufficient to satisfy the average of inquirers, if we should devote that amount of space to this particular department of manifestations. Inasmuch however, as names have been mentioned in connection with that phase of mediumship, it may appear invidious if other names, equally prominent, should be omitted, especially as the facts developed through them have excited considerable interest in the public mind, and are referred to as an almost indispensable portion of the evidence which has been brought to the attention of the public. We therefore here present some additional items.

The astonishing manifestations through Mr. Home have gained a world-wide fame. According to the positive testimony of prominent literary persons in England, only a few months ago, he was removed bodily through the window of a room in which the party were assembled, into the outer air, and thence into the window of another room, at a distance of seventy feet from the ground.

Elongation of the body by several inches is a wonderful circumstance vouched for by many witnesses. And not less remarkable, the drawing of hot coals from the fire by the hand, unprotected by interposing material, without the ordinary effect of burning.

The manifestations through the Misses Fox are equally celebrated, having been long known throughout the extent of America as the pioneers of the extensive and more modern spiritual movement. Commencing with the simple form of raps or "knockings" as they were called, the members of the family were seriously annoyed with the noisy demonstrations going on in their house independently of their will power, and in spite of it. The manifestations went on through various gradations to some of the higher forms of development. Spirits have shown themselves visibly for years past in their presence. While sitting with one of them, now Mrs. Underhill, a lady seated in a chair was taken up in our presence without visible contact some distance from the floor, and in the light.

William Fitzgibbon, a lecturer on od force and psychology, about six years ago engaged the services of the various physical mediums who from time to time went to Brooklyn N. Y.; among whom were Miss Jennie Lord, the Eddy family, and Mrs. Ferris. These were all at his residence at one time. The manifestations were so powerful that Mr. F., who had given offence to the spirits, was obliged to seek the protection of the company in the room. He was a man of positive will, and if he could not have his demand complied with, would swear at them. The result was they became an-

gry, which was manifested to such an extent that it was
feared they would damage the house. They broke loose
the chandelier as he was passing under it, and struck
him on the head with such force as to cut a large gash.
He became so much alarmed that he dared not get into
the cabinet which was used for the exhibition of their
power. At one time while he was in the cabinet they
took off his boots and struck him repeatedly and severely with them on the head. Others who got into the
cabinet at the time were not treated roughly, showing
discrimination in the treatment of friends and enemies,
and sufficient self-respect to protect themselves against
abuse. A company of persons about ten in number,
residing in New York, hearing of the powerful demonstrations which had been made, went to the house and
remained until past midnight. By agreement the mediums were sent into the uppermost story of the house,
and the company commenced an examination of the entire premises, taking the cellar first, and ascending flight
by flight to the top. They fastened the windows in
each apartment first, then locked the doors and took the
keys with them. Each one had a lighted taper. On
reaching the upper part of the house they extinguished
their lights and were in total darkness. No sooner was
this done than there came the sound of slamming doors,
the opening and shutting of which could be heard by
all. Lights were again procured and the doors examined. All were found fastened as when they had left
them. The lights were again extinguished, and immediately a loud concussion was heard like the firing of a
cannon, which shook the house. Lights were again

struck, and all the doors found fast as before. There was no possibility of deception.

The manifestations produced through the brothers Davenport, and through Mr. William Fay who travels with them, are genuine and of an astounding character.

Strange occurrences took place through the person of Mr. Dyer in the south east part of Philadelphia, at the residence of his son-in-law. Mr. D. was an aged man, and was taken care of by an unmarried daughter. About twenty years before his exit from this world he was holding a conversation with his brother upon bible questions, both being of the Methodist persuasion. The gifts were spoken of, and Mr. D. said he desired to have the gift of seeing in retrospect the lives of those who came into his presence. His desire was gratified, and he became obliged to tell persons of their faults, when he met them. This continued so persistently that it became offensive to him, and he at length said, "I remember the very time and place when I made that request. Now I have got more than I desired, and wish the gift could be removed from me." At that hour he was taken sick, and thenceforward was unable to work. His body become distorted, the spine assuming a curve like the letter S, from which he never recovered. Subsequently he said "I am satisfied that if I had not found fault with the gift, and it had remained with me, I should never have suffered as I have for fifteen years." A few years before his departure to spirit life bells were rung in the house without hands, similar to the occurrences at Dr. Phelps' residence. The servants while at their domestic work were disturbed. When making bread, the tray would be pulled out of their hands, and food in the cellar would be placed in each corner. The girls got frightened and left. A bell hanger was employed to replace the broken wires. The family were alarmed and sent for the son-in-law, who was travelling in the West on business, to return. The damage done to the property amounted to three hundred dollars.

One morning the old gentleman called his daughter to him, and said that they should not be troubled any more, as he had prayed all night, and a voice had come to him saying that from that time the disturbances would cease. They did cease.

Mr. D. felt confident that these disturbances were caused by unruly spirits. The gift of psychometry came back to him at one time. Once a young minisister called upon him, feeling it his duty to converse with him about his renunciation of methodistic doctrines. The minister requested permission to pray, which was assented to. After rising from his knees, the old gentleman took his visitor by the hand, saying "I have a little advice to give you. You have a secret vice, which, if you do not refrain from will be the means of seriously injuring your health." The young man blushed, and left, and although invited, never called upon the venerable brother again.

The wonderful manifestations which occurred at the house of Rev. Dr. Phelps at Stratford, Conn., some years ago, created considerable excitement in the public mind, which was embarrassing and annoying to the reverend gentleman and his family. One fact is observable in the history of the manifestations there; the doctor was never, so far as we are aware, charged with imposture in connection with them. Doubtless he felt, in common with those who have had to be the victims of suspicion, the disagreeable position in which he was placed, in consequence of that general suspicion. He challenged the strictest investigation, even to the extent of offering his house and all that it contained, to any one who could detect a natural cause for the disturbances. He thus wrote in relation to them, "I have seen things in motion more than a thousand times, and in most cases when no visible power existed by which the motion could be produced. There have been broken from my windows seventy one panes of glass, more than thirty of which I have seen break with my own eyes. I have seen objects such as brushes, tumblers, candlesticks, snuffers, etc., which but a few minutes before I knew to be at rest, fly against the glass and dash it to pieces, when it was utterly impossible from the direction in which they moved, that any visible power should have caused the motion. As to the reality of these facts, they can be proved by testimony a hundred fold greater than is ordinarily required in our Courts of Justice, in cases of life and death." Dr. P's property was destroyed to the amount of thousands of dollars by the violence of these physical demonstrations. Vast numbers of persons from Bridgeport and adjoining towns visited the scene, and became eye-witness of the repetition of the strange occurrences.

It must be remembered that the religious denominational duties of Dr. P. led him in a direction entirely opposite to the encouragement of such things, or their acceptance, or even the acknowledgment of their truth when they cannot be prevented. Yet with these facts occurring in this family is it not remarkable that the son, now a Professor in the Theological Seminary at Andover should make an open attack upon Spiritualism, attributing all its manifestations, as have been seen in the first division of this book, to Satanic agency? Its lessons have, however, not been altogether lost, inasmuch as their effect is seen in the spiritualistic tone of " Gates Ajar" and "Hedged In," books from the pen of the Professor's accomplished and spiritually minded daughter.

More recently, the events at the house of the Cashier of the Fitchburg Bank were of a startling character, among which was the moving of large soap stone slabs, without physical contact, an account of which was published in the Atlantic Monthly for August 1868. Persons of scientific acquirements were called in to witness them, and the contributor of the article very candidly urged upon persons of such pretensions, to give the subject an investigation.

Dr. Henry Slade of New York, and Peter West are also mediums through whom remarkable phenomena have been developed, as great numbers can testify. A slate is written upon without the physical contact of human hands. We have sat in the light with some ten other persons, when the slate has been held up by the medium above his head, with a small piece of pencil upon it, so short that it could not be grasped by a man's fingers, and verses and communications would be written all over the slate, there being no possible opportu-

nity of deception. This has also been done upon and
under the table. The hand writing was sometimes so
delicate as to be far beyond the chirographic skill of the
mediums.

The facts concerning the cabinet manifestations of the
Eddy family, concerning the mediumship of Mr. Reed,
the physical occurrences through Mrs. Ferris, and those
which have been seen in the presence of the Bangs family, Mrs. Maud Lord, Mrs. Cutter and the Walker
family, are indeed marvellous, but we should occupy
too much space to enumerate them in detail.

A spirit hand has taken our memorandum book and
watch from our pocket—we say spirit hand, because it
was impossible at the time, and in the place where it
occurred for it to have been accomplished by the hand
of any person in the flesh. The touch was different
from the tangible feel of fleshly hands.

Before concluding this account of the varied physical
manifestations, it is in a measure necessary to mention
the astounding events which have occurred at Moravia
in the state of N. Y. Many visitors were attracted
there at the beginning, and others have followed, from
an anxious desire to know the facts for themselves,
down to the present time. Among these are parties
well known in literary and scientific circles. We sub-
join a statement from Mr. William White of Boston.
The most candid statement written by an unbeliever is
the report of a correspondent of the N. Y. Sun, to which
reference may be made.

Mr. Bigelow of Boston recognized Mr. Tufts, his
father-in-law. Mrs. H. F. M. Brown and many others

recognized their friends, who gave them the most satisfactory tests.

The mode of manifestation being given in the passages quoted from Mr. White, we need not anticipate it. These phenomena have been promised, and there can be no doubt that more of the same evidence will be given, realizing the long cherished hope of anxious friends.

Mr. White of the Banner, writes " At one seance, a small hand patted Dr. Storer upon the knee, and a voice, in a low whisper, called, 'Father, father,' and gave the full name of his little son, who has been in spirit-life fourteen years. A voice, evidently that of a man, saluted us as 'Bro. White,' in a loud whisper—the value of both these incidents being enhanced by the fact that our names had been carefully kept from the knowledge of the medium.

" In the second part of the seance, the lamp being lit and the medium shut into the cabinet, faces appeared at the square aperture in the partition, and in two instances out of the fifteen or twenty which we saw, we were both simultaneously impressed with the resemblance of faces to those of persons whom we knew. One was of dark complexion, full beard and mustache, and certainly looked like Charles H. Crowell, late associated with us in this office. He did not speak, but made several efforts to present his features at different angles, and when asked if we were correct in our recognition, bowed an affirmative. The other was a venerable countenance, presenting hair of the whiteness of wool, the white beard trimmed short, and the features sufficiently distinct in color and outline to suggest the honored name and presence of the truly revered John Pierpont. He, too, responded in the affirmative, when his name was suggested, but it seemed impossible for him to remain long enough at the aperture to make the recognition positive and beyond doubt. Our anxiety to accomplish this, seeming to thwart the conditions, Mr. Keeler suggested that something lively should be played on the piano—perhaps some dancing tune—when a voice, appearing to proceed from the dimly-seen form within the cabinet, and apparently about a foot from the window, uttered a remonstrance in low but firm and distinct tones : ' No, my friends, those tunes will call around you spirits of a lower class. This is a serious subject.' Hands were frequently seen, in two instances holding out well formed flowers. Quite a lengthy talk was addressed to us, purporting to come from Dr. Baker, formerly of Owasco, who is a frequent participator in these circles. He it was who, through the trumpet, stated that he could promise us, from positive knowledge, that manifestations similar to the present would become general all over the world."

A few further facts concerning spirit likenesses are subjoined :

"Some months ago, Mr. J. E. Warner, a photographer, of Fall River, was called by some parties who lived in Cherry street to take some pictures of a deceased child. The latter was placed in a chair, and over it was arranged an arch of roses, with one sprig hanging down from the centre. As we are informed by one who declared himself an eye-witness, several pictures were taken ; and in the sixth, partly obscuring the pendant sprig, appeared, clearly defined, the face of the child's mother, who has been dead several years. The statement comes with the assurance that there was no chicanery in the matter ; and it is said the case, well authenticated, has created considerable local excitement."

George S. Shaw says : "Last Sunday I was called out to take a picture of a deceased child. I made five pictures, and in the fifth appeared the shape of a face just above the child's head. There was a wreath of roses and leaves over the child's head, and the face seemed to be looking out from the leaves down at the child. It has created considerable excitement here. The child's mother died last winter, and people that were acquainted with her say that it is her face."

The Orleans American, printed in Albion, N. Y., publishes the following statement in its issue of June 22 : 1871.

"I had a daughter born in England, and died there in 1844, at the age of fifteen, and Mr. Milleson, of New York, now stopping at South Barre, New York, a spirit-artist for the departed, has drawn a life-like picture of said daughter, and presented it to me without my knowing it was to be done, and without any knowledge on his part that I ever had such a daughter. I am sure it is a true likeness of my child. HANNAH COTWELL."

The beautiful crayon drawing of the *Spirit Bride* executed in the highest style of art, ornamenting the wall in the rear of the platform in the Banner Free Circle Room is worthy of mention. It was drawn by

Mr. E. Howard Doane, while under perfect control of the spirits, and would do honor to the pencil of the most famous.

If it is true that photographic likenesses can be projected upon a metallic or glass plate, is there any difficulty in believing that Jesus was able to show himself to Mary Madgalene and some of his disciples?

Jesus doubtless understood the law involved in the transfiguration, and the danger attending it, when as in John xx. 17, he appeared to Mary and said " Touch me not, for I am not yet ascended to my Father ; but go to my brethren and say unto them, I ascend unto my Father and your Father, and to my God and your God." This indicates that he did not claim for himself what the Christian theologians claim for him.

Its probable effect upon the medium is explained by the extreme sensitiveness which is often observed when under control. Health and life itself is sometimes endangered by sudden interruptions, in so apparently unimportant a circumstance as another person entering the room at such a time. The precipitation of instruments when floating about in the atmosphere on a light being suddenly kindled, as already mentioned, is another example of the folly of destroying suitable conditions.

Last autumn manifestations were reported to have occurred in Plymouth Church through the mediumship of one of the lady reporters.—" one of two or three ladies who sit at a table in front of the platform at Mr. Beecher's church, and take notes of his sermons for the

Monday morning papers. For several Sundays past the influence has accompanied her to the church, and has manifested itself by shaking the table, slightly tipping it, confusing the ' copy,' and, altogether, giving the lady who reports for the New York Herald and the other fair reporters spasms of fright, lest the manifestations should become palpable to the congregation."

SPIRITUALISM AT THE METHODIST CAMP MEETINGS.

The following facts were communicated to the Banner concerning the Hamilton Camp Meeting from a gentleman who was an eye witness of what he related.

"Among those attending on the day of his visit, it was the lot of our friend to encounter several who, though church members, were also chosen instruments for the exhibition of spirit power. One lady who had a cottage on the ground, and whose husband had recently passed on, said to him that last year her husband was with her in the form, and that she knew he was with her in spirit at this camp meeting, for he demonstrated his presence to her the first night she came there. She had told her minister of the fact.

"Another lady to whom he was introduced, said, ' you have two spirits near you,' and proceeded to give their names correctly, thus proving the identity of those gone before who were present. He also saw a well defined case of spirit healing. The harmony among those present was deep and abiding. All had met for one purpose—the saving (?) of souls; no other issue was to be discussed—no opposition allowed—therefore the facilities for spirit control among those susceptible, were excellent. But one speaker for each service was allowed, all the rest being occupied in forming a circle—whereunto all were called to assemble—around the speaker's stand. Here sinners were exhorted to come forward for their own sakes, or those desiring prayers for others in whom they were interested, and all was done to create passivity and readiness to receive—conditions which the Spiritualist understands to be so necessary for successful manifestations or for healing purposes. To the mind of the visitor it was rather amusing to hear the frantic pleadings of those officiating for sinners to come forward, when at the same time it was stated : 'We are all miserable sinners.' As for the results of these Methodist circles, one case copied from the Boston Herald's report of the meeting on the day when our informant attended, will give a good idea :

"'At the prayer-meeting immediately following one of the sermons on Wednesday, Aug. 23d, there was a peculiar manifestation, formerly of more frequent occurrence than of late years. A man, while kneeling at the altar, was held for over an hour in a trance, apparently cognizant of all that was going on around him, but utterly incapable of movement. To many it was a convincing proof that God was present in power, while others regarded it with feelings of curiosity and misbelief. Whatever was the nature of the 'trance,' the man caused considerable excitement for a while, a large crowd pressing around to get a glimpse of the subject.'

"If this 'trance' indeed showed the presence of God

or the 'Holy Ghost,' it was strange that so much fear about the matter should have existed, and such profuse efforts have been put forth to 'rub out' the good they have done by all their prayers and exhortations—severe and continued chafing of his person having been made use of before the man returned to a normal condition. Our informant is of the opinion that any spiritual healer could have brought the man out of the trance in less than five minutes. He has known of several cases of insanity which were caused by such strong psychological influence as this being thrown upon a subject, and no one being near who understood how to throw it off. Many cases which would have proved fatal to the mind of the sufferer, have been cured by the exercise of power sufficient to break the spell, by some person acquainted with the law of conditions. Detriment from the use of this power arises chiefly from ignorance of the laws governing it. Spiritualists in their treatment of this power, ascribe it to the laws of Nature, and not to any favorable conditions arising from their 'conversion' to or acceptance of any particular religious faith. The exhibitions of its existence are in no wise dependent upon the moral character of the person influenced.

"Not long since, an old gentleman, we are informed, was 'converted' in the town of Hampton, N. H., and was very anxious that a neighbor of his should also experience religion. While praying for the above object in a 'circle' as above described, he suddenly sprang over four seats, and seizing his unrepentant friend, commenced pounding him vigorously, accompanying his flagellations with exclamations like the following:

'You old sinner, you ought to have been converted years ago.' His victim was released from his grasp, and he sent to the insane asylum, where he died, a raving maniac, in eight days, and the revival was broken up."

In continuance of this subject we would refer to the files of the Troy (N. Y.) Daily Whig, for July wherein is contained an account under the caption of "The National Camp Meeting at Round Lake," the sub-heads of which are: "Wonderful Experiences"—"People Going to Another World"—"What They See There"—"How They Are Received"—"Trances"—"Visions," etc. The whole article, (two columns long) which was written in a liberal spirit of criticism, abounds in such statements as these:

"The ground all day has resounded with songs and shouts and vigorous lamentations. People fall over at the meetings, and are stilled by a trance influence for hours. At the services Sunday evening, Miss Laura Seward, of New York City, was overcome, and fell into a trance and remained in that condition until morning. Hardly had she recovered, when she was up again seized with the influence and fell back upon the floor. A large crowd of people gathered about the tent to view the statuesque form of the unconscious lady * * * Upon coming to consciousness a second time, she related a wonderful experience.

"Of course, as all messages coming through a medium are (like light) colored by the channel through which they flow, so the revelations of the Methodist brethren and sisters are clothed in the garb of scriptural language and imagery—or ignorance, as the case may be—even to the assertion of one good brother that the streets that are slippery with gold, the harps that are of the unalloyed metal, and the gowns that are of the costilest fabrics will not be for the ones who indulge in croquet.

"A few Spiritualist media, who understand the powers of control so lavishly put forth at these camps, would have no trouble—if they were allowed—in showing to the partially developed subjects of the Methodist praying circles, that the power which wrought in Jesus and his disciples in the dusty highways of Palestine, lives and works to-day, for the enfranchisment and elevation of the whole human race."

PRESENTIMENT—DREAMING—PROPHECY.

We do not propose to treat of the topics in this subdivision in a philosophical way, but to classify under it a series of facts bearing upon the general subjects, and to content ourselves with the narration ; simply interspersing such comments as may suggest themselves.

PRESENTIMENT.

"This word—which Webster defines as 'an antecedent impression or conviction of something unpleasant or distressing'—is beginning to figure largely in the press of to-day. Hardly can a paper be taken up, no

matter from what section of the country it may emanate,
which does not give in its columns 'local' or 'miscella-
neous' articles headed like the following: 'Strange
presentiment' 'singular fulfilment of a presentiment,'
etc., etc.   Though in past years these 'shadows' have
been sometimes 'cast before' upon the minds of those
receptive enough to detect them, yet it has been re-
served for the civilizing influences of the present age to
offer to the spirit-world the faculty of impressibility in
a fuller and broader sense than before.   It is indeed
doubtful if among the victims of any recent accident of
any magnitude, there has not been some individual
strongly impressed with a sense of his impending doom.
At least such seems the case, judging from the number-
less paragraphed assurances of the fact which we perceive soon after duly vouched for by 'one of our most
respectable citizens.'

"Not long since, the Boston Herald published an
account of the death at his post of James Percival,
brakeman on the Maine Central train which went through
a broken bridge.   A week previous he said to one of
the employes on the train that 'they would not run together much longer,' and even specified the nature of
the accident whereby he should meet his death; which
forecasting, subsequent events proved correct.

"An Eastern exchange alluding to a recent accident
at a neighboring saw-mill—in Damariscotta—whereby
one of the operatives lost his life, says that a sister of
his, employed in a cotton-mill at Augusta, on the day
previous became strongly impressed with the certainty
that her brother was about to meet a violent death, and

was so affected that she left the factory and continued in an almost distracted state of mind throughout the night. The next day a messenger drove up to bring the tidings of his death. The young lady saw him approaching, and recognizing him as one of her neighbors in Damariscotta, anticipated his sad message by exclaiming 'He is dead.'

" Still another instance comes to our knowledge in the case of Frank St Clair, a carpenter by trade—now lying a cripple at the Naval Hospital, Chelsea. This person, a native of Boston, enlisted in the navy during February last, was attached to the receiving ship, and from her drafted as fireman on board U. S. steamer ' Worcester,' bound to France with provisions for the suffering people. As soon as he heard that he was to go on that ship, he was strongly impressed that something disastrous was about to happen to her, and he made every effort to obtain his discharge, or at least become attached to some other vessel. Not succeeding, he was obliged to put to sea, and while passing Deer Island, he is represented as having told a fellow-fireman that something would certainly happen to them, and he would gladly leave the ship and go on shore among the convicts, so deep was his despondency. A few days afterward the bursting of a boiler on board killed several persons, and badly scalded others, among them Mr. St. Clair, who was so severely injured that it is doubtful if he ever regains the use of his hands.

"The mass of mankind will in time learn the importance of heeding these impressions, indices as they are upon the barometer of the spiritual being, of the coming cyclone of disaster. Till then, the lesson must be repeated over and over again."

A Philadelphia paper vouches for the truth of the following story :

A few months ago a gentleman died, leaving a considerable fortune to be shared among his heirs. During life the deceased had been on the most intimate terms with a friend, whose interest in him and his family was not of such a character as to be severed by the hand of death. It had been the general understanding for several years that this friend had been designated in the will of the deceased as his executor. The subject had frequently been broached between them, and invariably the deceased had asserted that he had made a will, disposing of his property in a way in which he desired it to be distributed, and that his friend had been named in the document as his executor.

When, however, a search was made for the will, no traces of it could be found. Every nook and corner of the house into which such document would be likely to creep, was peered into with the same unsuccessful result. In this state of the case, by the general desire of the relatives of the deceased, his friend took out letters of administration, and proceeded to wind up the affairs of the estate in the way provided for by the law in cases where persons die intestate. The house in which the deceased had lived was repaired, and put in such order as to render the widow and her children comfortable, and other important measures were taken by the administrator at his discretion.

Meanwhile, the search for the missing will continued, under the belief that it would yet be found, since the deceased had so frequently declared that he had prepared such a document. The administrator, engrossed with the cares of the estate, naturally devoted much thought to it during his unemployed moments, the subject of the missing will, on such occasions, always coming uppermost in his mind. One night, not long since, it engaged his sleeping as well as his waking hours. The semblance of his dead friend entered his bed chamber, and accosted him in the familiar tones.

"You are spending a great deal of money on my house," exclaimed the spectre.

"Yes, but not more than I would on my own house under similar circumstances," was the response; the dreamer actually rising up in bed at sight of his spectral visitor.

"You are spending a great deal more of my money than I ever did for such a purpose," continued the spectre, with a touch of rebuke in his ghostly voice.

"Not more than the case demands," was the rejoinder. "You are a dead man now, and have nothing to do with the business. It's my affair, and I shall do as I think proper."

The dreamer, as well as the visitor, was getting slightly warmed as the dispute progressed.

"I am come to tell you that you have not thoroughly searched for my will," rejoined the spectre. "In it you will find just what I wish done with my money."

"Your will!" laughed the dreamer. "We have searched high and low for it, and it can't be found.

Why did you hide it away if you wished us to follow its instructions ?"

"Look you!" cried the spectre, slipping up to the bedside and resting his ghostly form upon the covering; "your search for the will has been very careless.   In the fourth story back room of my house you will find an old bureau.   Have you looked into it?"

"No," responded the dreamer; "I have seen no such bureau."

"In the top drawer of this old bureau," continued the spectre, "there is a package of old letters.   Open the bundle; the will is in the middle of it."

With that the spectre bent forward, as if to touch the dreamer, who sprang in terror from the bed, and was awakened by the shock, to find himself standing in the middle of the room.

On the following day the administrator related his vision to the members of his family, and again at his place of business he ran over the occurrence, but gave it no serious thought for a moment.   In the evening he called upon the widow on a matter of business, and after that was transacted, related to her his singular dream of the preceding night.

"I had forgotten all about it," said the widow; "but there is an old bureau in the lumber room up in the garret.   But my husband would not have placed anything of value there for safe-keeping."

This ended the conversation, and the administrator journeyed homeward.   He had just thrown himself in his easy chair before the fire, in slippers and dressing gown, when there came a violent pulling at the door bell. In another moment the widow was ushered into the parlor. She was laboring under considerable excitement, and held a folded paper in her hand.

"Here is the missing will!" she exclaimed, thrusting the long-sought document into the hands of her astonished friend.

"Where did you find it?" he inquired.

"Just where my husband told you he had placed it, in your dream last night. I ran up stairs as soon as you left the house, and I found the package of old letters in the top drawer of the bureau, and there was the will, right in the middle of it!"

Such is the singular vision and its strict fulfilment. We have told "a plain, unvarnished tale," without essential omissions, and without any fanciful embellishments, the only thing to be added is the fact that the administrator knew nothing of the existence of this old bureau until the widow recalled to mind that there was such an article of furniture in the house; and that he was the first time made aware that there was in the house a bundle of old letters which he had not examined, when the missing will was placed in his hands.

We clip the following important statement from the Wakefield (Mass.) Banner of Oct. 28th, 1871 :

Mr. Editor— Permit me to lay before your readers a true statement of 'the dream or presentiment, or whatever it was,' that warned us of the fire which occurred at the Eaton place. About three o'clock that morning I was awakened by my spirit friends, as I often am. I arose, lighted my lamp, walked about my room and went back to bed. I was wide awake. I put out the lamp. A voice spoke to me and said, 'Mark now an entirely new influence that comes to you.' Soon I saw, or rather experienced a vision. I was in the midst of a fire, in which one man seemed to be prominent. All the accompaniments were there—the noise, confusion, smoke, etc. When I came to a normal state, I at once distinctly recognized the vision as given by my spirit friends, but thought it was to show me their power in displaying the scenes at Chicago. I lay there thinking about it when I heard the word 'futile' spoken. I did not then know its purport; but soon another vision opened before me. I caught the words 'famine' and 'shelter,' and knew that an effort was being made to impress me with the condition of the people of Chicago. This vision faded away without producing any of the effects of a reality. The voice spoke again : 'This vision fails to you ; it is the only way we can teach you.' After awhile I fell partly asleep, and was awakened by an unpleasant dream. Immediately they spoke to me and said, 'Get right out of bed and don't light the lamp.' I started to obey, and felt a strong impulse to go down stairs in the dark. A second thought, and I lighted the lamp and lay there wondering, and a little vexed that my spirit friends should allow me to be so disturbed. In about ten minutes, I heard a cracking noise like pine wood burning. I spoke to my husband, and he found, on going down stairs, the closet in flames. This account illustrates some of the means that our loved ones on the other shore use, to show us their contant love and care. [This communication written with such evident candor and particularity of detail is signed SARAH K. HART.]

Scribner's Monthly for Nov. 1871 contains a thrilling account of terrible suffering endured by Mr. Truman C. Evarts, the contributor of the article, while on an exploring expedition to the source of the Yellowstone River in August previous. After wandering in the wild passes of the Rocky Mountains, for thirty seven days he was finally rescued by a spirit guide, and returned to civilization in a half-starved condition. The following paragraphs are extracted from the publication above named.

" While I was thus considering whether to remain and search for a passage" [i.e., over the Madison range of mountains, into the valley beyond, where he hoped to find settlers,] " or return to the Yellowstone, I experienced one of those strange hallucinations which many of my friends have misnamed insanity, but which to me was Providence. An old clerical friend, for whose character and counsel I had always cherished a peculiar regard, in some unaccountable manner seemed to be standing before me, charged with advice which would relieve my perplexity. I seemed to hear him say, as if in a voice and with the manner of authority :

'Go back immediately, as rapidly as your strength will permit. There is no food here, and the idea of your scaling these rocks is madness.'

'Doctor,' I rejoined, 'the distance is too great. I cannot live to travel it.'

'Say not so. Your life depends upon the effort. Return at once. Start now, lest your resolution falter. Travel as far and as fast as possible—it is your only chance.'

'Doctor, I am rejoiced to meet you in this hour of distress, but doubt the wisdom of your council. I am within seventy miles of Virginia. Just over these rocks, a few miles away, I shall find friends. My shoes are nearly worn out, my clothes are in tatters, and my strength is almost overcome. As a last trial, it seems to me I can but attempt to scale this mountain or perish in the effort, if God so wills.'

'Don't think of it. Your power of endurance will carry you through. I will accompany you. Put your trust in heaven. Help yourself, and God will help you.'

Overcome by these and other persuasions, and delighted with the idea of having a travelling companion, I plodded my way over the route I had come. * * * When I resumed my journey the next day the sun was just rising. Whenever I was disposed, as was often the case, to question the wisdom of the change of routes, my old friend appeared to be near with words of encouragement, but his reticence on other subjects both surprised and annoyed me."

At last, becoming completely worn out with fatigue and hunger, the conviction that death was near took possession of his mind. He continues :

"Once only the thought flashed across my mind that I should be saved, and I seemed to hear a whispered command to 'Struggle on.' Groping along the side of a hill, I became suddenly sensible of a sharp reflection, as of burnished steel. Looking up through half-eyes, two rough but kindly faces met my gaze."

These were two mountaineers who had been sent out to search for the lost man, and he was rescued at last, at the very extreme of exhaustion.

DETECTION OF CRIME.

The cases last narrated illustrate firm impressions made upon the mind both in presentiment and dreams. It is sometimes difficult to distinguish the one from the other. The following facts were developed through clairvoyance, and are derived from the same agency, although differing in its modus operandi from the others.

Some twelve years ago a young man left the town of R—, Vt., for the West, with the intention of making it his home. After selecting a farm he returned East for the funds necessary for its purchase—some fourteen hundred dollars. On his way back he made use of the railroad cars and stage coaches as far as public conveyance would carry him, and then was obliged to take private conveyance, or travel on foot to the location selected. He promised to write to his brother, who was left at home, as soon as he arrived, but that relative not hearing from him at the expiration of three weeks, became anxious as to his safety, and yielding to the desires of some of the friends, visited a person in the town who possessed the gift of "clear seeing," to consult with her as to the fate of his missing brother. This lady, who was a member of the Methodist church and did not believe in Spiritualism, notwithstanding her mediumship, became unconsciously entranced, and while in that state described the road as far as the cars and coach went, and then pictured the absent brother's taking passage in a wagon with three other persons, and the nature of the route, which was somewhat aside from the regular roads through a piece of woods. She said they killed him about the centre of the two mile journey through these woods, and threw his body between two fallen hemlock trees, and that a lock of his hair was now frozen into the ice where the body lay over one night. She said next day his body was thrown into a pond near by.

The remaining brother was so well satisfied in his mind as to the truth of something very serious having happened, that he determined to make the journey of some twelve hundred miles to ascertain the full nature of what had taken place. On arriving, he found everything as had been described. At the end of the public conveyance he hired a man to take him to the spot, and to his astonishment found the lock of his brother's hair as before mentioned. Having secured it, he went to look for the pond, and found its bottom to be covered with deep mud, in which it was impossible to reach the body. So perfect, however, was the description given him by the clairvoyant of the parties who wrought the deed, that he recognized the men as soon as he saw them. On his complaint they were arrested, and one of their number turning State's evidence, they were convicted, and sentenced to State Prison for life for the crime. One of the men has since died ; the other still remains in prison.

The brother of the murdered man, the lady and many others acquainted with the facts, are still living witnesses to the truth of clairvoyance, in which they firmly believe. I am acquainted with the lady. Gaining a knowledge of these facts some time since, I thought they should be made public, as additional proofs with which to convince the minds of the skeptical. Here was a revelation made by a person who did not believe in Spiritualism, to parties mostly Methodists.

Another case almost as wonderful as the above occurred nearly at the same time : A robbery was committed in a small village in the vicinity, and it was thought advisable to send for this medium and see if she could not detect the thief. She obeyed the summons, and was placed in a room in the hotel whither by common consent all the people came and passed before her, each taking her hand, that she might find the guilty one ; and at last one person, who had always stood well in the estimation of the community, was accused by her as he was passing. She said : "You took the goods." He tried to ridicule the assertion, but she, under a powerful influence, seized hold of him and told him if he did not own the theft, she would detain him till he did. He finally confessed, and the goods were restored. Several other cases of a like nature have occurred in her experience. Clairvoyance is revealing the thoughts of many hearts, and murderers, robbers and hypocrites tremble at its revelation.

VERIFICATION OF DREAMS.

Accounts of fore-warning by impressions made on the mind in dreams abound in tradition, and are not unfrequently recorded as matters of veritable history. Jacob, according to Jewish history, was thus fore-warned, and had his dreams realized. Pharaoh dreamed of circumstances which he could not understand, and Joseph was called upon to act as interpreter. These are familiar to every reader of the Hebrew scriptures.

But startling events occurring in our own times, come to us with equal, or even greater force, because well authenticated, the proof of their fulfilment being easily accessible; in some cases by reference to living witnesses.

Unpublished cases are familiar to thousands who have heard the narration of circumstances from persons who have been themselves the recipients of the fore-warning, and have been witnesses to the succeeding events which constituted the corresponding fulfilment.

A few cases are subjoined:

The springing of a leak and the loss of Schooner Sachem of this port, occasioned by her sinking on Georges, Sept. 8th, was attended by a singular circumstance, which we hereby publish, assuring our readers that it is correct in every particular, and will be fully substantiated by the master of the vessel, Capt. J. Wenzell, from whose log book we gleaned the particulars:

The vessel left Brown's Bank on the 7th of September at 9 P. M. for Georges, with a fresh N. W. breeze,

At midnight, the steward, John Nelson, arose from his berth, and going aft where the skipper was, remarked in an agitated voice, his whole appearance indicating great fear :

"Skipper, we are soon to have a severe gale of wind, or something else of a dangerous nature is going to overtake the vessel, and we had better make land if we can, or at least keep clear of Georges, so as not to have it so rough when the danger comes."

Capt. Wenzell asked him what made him think so, as everything was clear at the time, and there was no apprehensions of trouble or danger.

Nelson replied, "I have been dreaming, and twice before I have had the same kinds of dreams when at sea, and both times have had narrow chances of being saved. The first time we were run into the day following the dream, and left in a sinking condition. With great efforts in bailing and pumping we reached the coast of Norway. The other time we experienced a terrible gale, had our sails blown away, and the vessel, half full of water, ran before it under bare poles, until we met the northeast trade winds, when we patched her up and made out to get her into Havana."

He then told the purport of the dreams, which were of females dressed in white, either standing in the rain, or near a waterfall, or attempting to cross a brook. The figures in each dream were the same, but the surroundings somewhat different.

The steward was a reliable man, and was so much in earnest that the captain, although seeing no signs of a gale of wind, and not inclined to be superstitious, con-

cluded it best to be on his guard, and charged the man
forward to keep a strict watch.

The wind was now increasing, with a heavy sea rising, and at about half past one A. M. the vessel was
about five miles from Georges banks. She was hove to
under a close reefed foresail, and they were furling the
balance reef, when a white light was observed to leeward, supposed to be on board a fisherman lying at anchor. Suddenly one of the crew sang out from the
forecastle, "The vessel is filling with water!" Telling
him not to alarm the men, the Captain went down and
found six inches of water on the floor. The pumps
were immediately manned, and bailing with buckets
commenced, after which the Captain went sounding
around in the hold to find the leak, but the vessel was
rolling so hard, and the water made so much noise
among the barrels and in the ice-house, that it was impossible to hear anything else. It was thought that the
leak was under the port bow, and the vessel was wore
round and hove to on the other tack, in hopes to bring
the leak out of the water. The steward was told to get
some provisions and see that the boat was ready to
launch at a moment's notice. It was now blowing a
strong breeze from the northward, with a heavy sea.
They spoke schooner Pescador and told them their condition. With all their pumping and bailing they could
not gain on the leak, and the crew were determined not
to remain on board another night. The tide swept
them down to leeward of the Pescador, and efforts were
made to speak her again, but they could not reach her.
Their movements were seen on board the Pescador, and

upon asking them to send their boat to take them off, they did so at once. When they left the Sachem the water was eighteen inches above the forecastle floor. At two P. M. she rolled over on her side, raised herself once, then plunged under head foremost, the master and crew feeling thankful to God that they had escaped and were safely landed on board the good schooner Pescador.

These are the facts, and our readers can account for the dreams and the disasters in any manner that best pleases them. We publish the statement, because we consider it somewhat remarkable that the dreams should be the harbingers of disaster on three occasions.—*Cape Ann Register.*

"During the past month Samuel Gorden of Tuftonboro, N. H., missed a fine large colt, 2 years old, which was found in a deep valley in the pasture, dead. Mr. G. supposed he died from some natural cause. But that night his wife dreamed that the colt was shot, that she saw the individual raise the rifle and fire the fatal shot. Her husband put no confidence in the dream, but to satisfy the importunity of his wife he called some of the neighbors to his assistance and made an examination and found it even as the wife said. The ball entered just below the eye, passed through the head and down the windpipe, lodging in the lungs."

A story went the rounds of the papers some time ago under the head of "The value of a dream," which as published in the Hartford Times of a recent date, runs as follows :

"One of our most prominent and wealthy citizens had purchased a sightly piece of land outside the city, but within the town limits, and the purchaser was troubled somewhat because he had been told that he could not get water, owing to the elevated postition of his land, without digging further Chinaward than any one would be likely to undertake. As we said, this troubled him. He wanted a well on his place, and, although a man of great energy—one who never allowed any obstacle, no matter how great, to turn him from his path—he hesitated long before undertaking his task. The thought of excavating for a well through half a mile, more or less, of solid rock was enough to deter the stoutest heart. At this juncture, before he had resolved upon anything definite, he dreamed that he had set a gang of men to digging for a well on a certain (to his mind) well-defined spot, and that after digging a few feet, beore the rock was reached, water flowed in abundance. The gentleman, though not a bit superstitious, and holding dreams as lightly as anybody, was more impressed with his sleeping vision than he would have cared to acknowledge. At first he would have scouted the idea of treating the subject seriously enough to put a spade into the earth at the spot indicated in his dream ; but, do what he would, he could not dismiss the dream from his mind, and finally resolved to test it, but without any real belief that his dream would be verified. He set his men to work, and, strange to relate, after digging fifteen feet, water abundantly flowed, and thus the dream fully came to pass. We have seen the well with our own eyes, and the dreamer, who is a gentleman of undoubted veracity, assures us that our story is true."

It is well known that the Wesley family were for a considerable time visited by unseen intelligences, who made known their presence by well marked physical manifestations. One of them was also a dreamer, and the following story is prefaced by the narrator thus :

We would advise those who are sorely troubled and vexed in spirit, lest peradventure they have not found the true Church, to read the following vision of the celebrated Wesley, who at the time was seriously troubled in regard to the disposition of the various sects, and the chances of each in reference to future happiness and punishment. A dream, one night transported him in its uncertain wandering to the gates of hell. "Are there any Roman Catholics here?" asked Wesley, thoughtfully. "Yes." "Any Presbyterians?" "Yes" again was the rejoinder. "Any Baptists?" "Yes" "Any Methodists?" by the way of a clincher, asked the pious Wesley, "Yes," to his great indignation was answered.

In the mystic ways of dreams, by a sudden transition he stood before the gates of heaven. Improving his opportunity he again inquired : "Are there any Roman Catholics here?" "No," was the reply, "Any Presbyterians?" "No." "Any Baptists?" "No, Sir." "Any Methodists?" "No." "Well then, he asked, lost in wonder, "who are they inside?" "Christians," was the jubilant answer.

SPIRITUALISM IN COURT.

In the summer of 1868 a Spiritualist Camp Meeting was held in the immediate vicinity of Boston. Mr. and Mrs. Feitel were among the attendants thereof. They returned to Boston by a horse railroad car on Sunday, when a serious accident occurred. In the catastrophe Mrs. F. was injured, and it was supposed, for life. A claim for damages having been set up and refused by the company owning the road, suit was entered for the recovery of the amount claimed. The following extracts from the report of the trial will be read with interest by all who have any regard for freedom of opinion in religious matters.

Able counsel was engaged by the respective parties in controversy, viz: Mr. Somerby for the plaintiffs, and Mr. Sweetser for the defendants. The main question involved was whether a meeting of Spiritualists held on Sunday could be considered a religious meeting : if not it was an infringement of the law.

The argument was entered upon by the lawyers for the plaintiffs striving to establish their case, and the lawyers for the horse railroad company claiming that Mrs. Feitel and husband were travelling—contrary to the statutes in such cases made and provided—on Sunday ; that they had been attending a place of public amusement, and that she was injured on her return, and so were not within the law, and could not recover damages. The defence also endeavored to prove that Mrs.

Feitel had a tendency to paralysis, and had had one shock (or more) of it previous to the accident. On the morning in question the first witness sworn was Charles C. Dudley, who was summoned by the defence to prove the advertisement in the Banner of Light, of the camp meeting ; cross-examined, he proved to be a strong witness for the plaintiffs, as he was on the car, and testified that, while going at the rate of some six miles an hour, the car suddenly stopped as if it had struck a stone wall, and then fell, (the forward end) he thought, some eighteen inches, throwing the passengers in a heap together. Himself and wife were strangers to all in the car.

Witness Charles A. Whitmore was then sworn for the defence to prove the character of Laura V. Ellis's manifestations— which were advertised in the Banner of Light as a part of the camp meeting services. His testimony was received after some objections on the part of the plaintiffs' counsel. The witness testified to the various phenomena which generally occur at her seances, and which are too well known to our readers to need explanation here. He could not tell who untied her, but no one was with her in the cabinet. Cross-examined, he thought that the order preserved at the tent was good—that the people, about fifty in number, were quiet and very respectable. Being asked if he thought the manifestations in the tent might be looked upon as a religious ceremony, he replied that Mr Ellis said he gave the broadest liberty in accounting for the phenomena—persons might decide for themselves how they were done. Witness said there was nothing done differently in the tent than if it were a religious ceremony, which Mr. and Miss Ellis and some of the audience conscientiously believed in.   Just as any denomination —Protestant or Catholic—might hold its meetings after a peculiar form so he thought the exercises in the tent passed off.

To offset the testimony of several medical gentlemen for the plaintiff—who had said, to their minds, the accident was sufficient to have produced the paralysis claimed—Drs. Alton Ellis, of Boston, and Gilman Kimball, of Lowell, both of whom had given much attention to the subject of paralysis, were introduced by the defence, and testified in the main that the shock of the accident—in their several opinions—was not sufficient, of itself, to produce the result claimed—the incurable paralyzation of the lady's lower limbs.   To them there must be something else in the history of the case to bring about so serious a result.

Dr. H. B. Storer was then called, and after some preliminary interrogatories were put, the examination proceeded as follows :

Somerby—Do you believe these things as a matter of conscience?

Storer—Yes, sir.

Somerby—You being chairman, was there anything done at the meeting except such as might have occurred in any religious assemblage?

Storer—No, sir.

Somerby—It has been said by some witnesses that there was praying and singing and hallooing after this manner.

Storer—There was not quite so much shouting as is generally heard at camp meetings. Our meetings were very orderly and still.

Sweetser—How could you call the "spirits" to order?

Storer—By disturbing the conditions, and thus preventing further manifestations.

Sweetser—What do you mean? How could you disturb the conditions?

Storer—By expressing dissent at the proceedings and by requesting them to stop. I should appeal to them just as to a person in the body.

John Wetherbee, a prominent Spiritualist, was then summoned to give what facts he might know concerning the religious character of the meeting. In answer to opening interrogatories he gave his name, and said his business was that of a broker.

Somerby—Were you present at the afternoon services held at this Spiritualist camp meeting in 1868?

Wetherbee—I was.

Somerby—You will tell the jury if there was any disturbance there.

Wetherbee—There was not.

Somerby—State, as far as you know, whether or not the physical manifestations spoken of, by Miss Ellis, were parts of the religious exercises.

Wetherbee—It is a part of my belief.

Sweetser.—You say, according to your belief, the exercises were of a devotional character. What do you mean?

Wetherbee—I believe in Spiritualism—in whose in-

terests the meetings were held—in spirits, and, consequently, in Laura Ellis.

Sweetser—You say you believe in Miss Ellis. What
do you mean by that?

Wetherbee—She gets into a cabinet, and is tied or
untied by an unseen power—some power outside of herself—and that power I call spirits—disembodied human beings.

Sweetser—So they can take a ring from her finger
and put it on her nose !

Wetherbee—Yes.

Somerby—You call that power "the spirits" ?

Wetherbee—Yes, sir.

Somerby—Do you believe in God.

Wetherbee—Yes, sir ; and worship him, I hope.

Counsel for the defence considered the following a
point in argument.

Spiritualism was a something not very well defined
as yet, and he thought but a few believed in it. There
didn't seem to be anything about it that was real. To
believe that men have conversed with spirits he thought
was foolish, and the matter purporting to come from
these spirits is the sheerest nonsense in the world. He
referred facetiously to the tying, untying and ring feats
of Miss Ellis. Nobody could understand it—he could
not see any use in it. He thought there were many
among the Spiritualists who disbelieved in God, the
Bible, or in anything. He believed we should "support religion in some form, and not the class which has
the Banner of Light for an exponent."

G. A. Somerby then took up his argument for the plaintiffs, from which we give the extracts below. After referring to the claim in the case for damages sustained, and his conviction that the learned gentleman who had just addresssed them for the defence had not met the points he had raised for the plaintiffs, said :

"It is certainly plain to my mind that this woman was clearly within the law; that she was doing that which she had a right to be doing upon the Sabbath day in Massachusetts ; that she had a right to be upon the cars that day for the purpose ; that she did all that she could to take care of herself; that the company were negligent, and by that negligence she is permanently injured. I wish to discuss this case carefully, and it becomes necessary for me to consider whether or no this woman had a right to be there on that day. Let us see. For the first time in my experience, I have occasion to discuss a man's religion—a woman's religious opinion. I have got to look and see what she believes. * * * *

When I talk about a man's religious opinion, I talk about something that is free as air. The great and crowning feature which distinguishes Massachusetts from the old countries is, that here a man may have any religious opinion, and no man may sneer at it. There is no law by which we can try the belief of any individual. Every man's religion in Massachusetts is respected, and no court, no man or collection of men has a right to hold it up to ridicule. Any other doctrine would dwarf a man's religious faculties, and tear down precisely what all the creeds are seeking to uphold. If a man and woman believe in God as the Supreme Being ; if

they go further, and believe that God is a revelator,
and that these spiritual manifestations are permitted by
him, or are according to his will, I pretend to say—as
a debater, not as a theologian—that they believe in just
what the others do ; the only difference is in degree.
Why, is not the bottom of all beliefs a faith in the immortality of the human soul? Is it not that a man believes he shall live hereafter, and shall see his father
and mother and children, wife and friends forever? Do
you not all believe this [addressing the jury,] however
widely your creeds may differ? All denominations are
teaching this underlying truth, whatever else may be
contained in their tenets ; and yet this Spiritualist denomination has been held up to be sneered at because
its followers go further than the others.

Reference has been made by the learned gentleman
on the other side to the vagueness and mystery attending
the spiritualistic manifestations ; but are there not things
just as mysterious in the teachings of the other sects?
Who can, for instance, describe the process attending
the transubstantiation? It is not a matter of demonstration, but a matter of belief of any religious denomination—and what a multitude we have!—from the
strongest to the weakest—the Catholic, the Orthodox,
the Swedenborgian, the Shakers or the Spiritualists—
all are entitled to respect, all are alike in Massachusetts,
because the words of the constitution are that a man's
religious belief shall be protected.

No man has a right to sneer about what he does not
understand. Suppose I was pleading for the Catholic
religion to-day—who should explain all about its cere-

monics? Should I, or any one else, say it is not true
because I cannot describe all its mysteries? I must be
governed by the fact—Do they, its professed followers,
believe it? Do they act as if they do? Suppose I
take the Swedenborgian—a doctrine harder to understand, even, than the Spiritualist. Its followers believe
in it, as a matter of conscience, and cherish a belief in
departed spirits, as do the Spiritualists. Go into a
Swedenborgian family, and see the empty chair kept in
its place, in remembrance of him or her whose bodily
presence shall fill it no more! I cite these examples
and make these remarks as explanatory that any man
has a right to stand on and by his religious belief.
Who shall judge when a man is honest and when he is
not? Who is endowed with that power which shall enable him to tell, when a man swears that he believes,
that he swears falsely? Who shall condemn or ridicule
that which is not to be explained? There is not a blade
of grass that waves upon the bosom of the earth, not a
revolution of our planet around the sun, not a ray of
light that illuminates the otherwise darkened air, the
mystery of whose being or occurrence can be explained.
What is the power which carries about these bodies of
ours? No man can tell. All Christians together believe in the immortality of the soul. They believe that
soul exists. The body falls away—the spirit remains;
and is it a strange thing to believe that that soul which
thinks and reasons and feels can communicate with
earthly clay? Why, gentlemen, I venture to say—I
don't care what your religious tenets—that I do not
think there is a man of you who did not believe, when

his mother or his children left him, that they were near him in spirit; that there is not one of you who is not often impressed to do this thing or to avoid that, and cannot tell how or why.

I stand here to defend no religious doctrine, but to show that these parties, as Spiritualists, believe in their religion—are conscientious in it; that their doctrine, by examination, is found to be kindred to other religious systems, though wider in degree; and that they have a right to believe in it.   Suppose all this had taken place in a church.   Suppose she had attended a service such as is agreeed to upon all hands---heard singing, by a choir, of devotional hymns, listened to prayers and preaching, and then, returning home, had met with this injury.   But the meeting she did attend, and from which she was returning, was devotional; its whole aspect was such.   Is there any line of discrimination to be drawn in free Massachusetts against her any more than against a Swedenborgian, an Orthodox, a Methodist, or a Roman Catholic?   No !---because it was with her a matter of conscience, and she was then and there worshipping God according to the dictates of that conscience.   Men have no right to arraign her.   If it be a matter of conscience, I claim she had a right so to do ---a right to worship God as she chose to believe * *

If the parties then and there assembled—right or wrong—believed that these manifestations came from spirits, they and she had a right to say by their presence, " We believe in the immortality of the soul; we believe in this communion of friends who have left us. We may be wrong, but we believe !"   They may not be able to demonstrate it fully ; but are the other Christian denominations better off ? Suppose you ask a man to define the Trinity. Multitudes of good men have affected to believe it, but how shall it be described? And yet all who desire have a right to believe therein. If these people believed, that is all that is required. It is not a question as to how absurd or otherwise any religious system may be to an unbeliever—its integrity is guaranteed by the constitution. A Quaker, in his gray garb, entering a Roman Catholic church, may think its elaborate services mere form, without a heart in them ; and a Catholic beholding the Shakers as they dance on Sunday around the room, each sex separated, might consider the exhibition immeasurably profane or indescribably ludicrous. But the question in both cases is, Do they—the worshippers—believe. in what they are doing ? They disturb nobody. Therefore I say, without standing out for Spiritualism or any other religious system, but as an American citizen standing upon the law and the constitution, that, if a man believes in Spiritualism, I care not what the form, he has a right to be defended."

The advocate then proceeded to speak of the claims of his clients to be believers in Spiritualism as a matter of conscience, and desired to know if anything in evidence had transpired to show that they had not told the truth. On the Sunday in question, Mrs. Feitel attended the Spiritualist Sabbath school in Charlestown —in which, previous to her confinement, she was a teacher—and then visited Boston with her husband (who was a practical chemist, engaged in making vincgar), to see that matters at his store were all right which was necessary, as much loss of material might occur if the processes did not go on properly. They then went together to the camp meeting grounds in Malden. After attending the general exercises there, they went directly back to Malden, waited for a chance in the cars, and, finding it, started for home. The lady had started for and had attended the camp meeting just as she would have done the regular meeting of her society, or just as any man would have gone to his church. She attended---so she claimed---the camp meeting for purposes of worship; and when the services were over, she took the best way to get home which offered itself. Was she not to be defended in this, her just rights in the matter? In proof that camp or field meetings for religious purposes were recognized as proper to be held by the laws of Massachusetts, Mr. Somerby read from Sec. 22, Chap. 16th, of the General Statutes.

It was evident, to his mind, that Mrs. Feitel, when she attended this legalized order of meetings, was just as much within the protection of the law as if she had gone out of her house to the hall where she generally attended. As regarded what had been said in ridicule of the spiritual belief, it must be remembered that Spiritualism was a new matter; and, like all new movements, many things would be done at the first of it which would not be done at the last of it. The question for the jury was, to consider the motives of the plaintiffs in attending the meeting, and whether if, on the 5th of September, 1868, Mrs. Feitel, in going to a place where her regular society and many Spiritualists of other towns had gone, did anything worse than if she had attended a Methodist camp meeting.

Mr. Somerby thought the statement that liquor was sold on the ground, contrary to the rules of the committee, ought not to prejudice the mind of any gentleman against the meeting, and especially not against the lady, who attended it in good faith. What was there, he asked, in this woman's going to that meeting and returning, that you would not have done if you had believed just as she did? He could not sympathize with what had been said about the announcement that, at a certain time, spiritual manifestations would be given by Miss Ellis. I don't laugh at such things because I don't believe them. I have no right to do it. Mr. John Wetherbee, a stock broker, and a man well known in financial circles, had said, "I believe these things as a matter of religion ;" and so had Dr. Storer, who was a man of intelligence. Who should challenge their conscientious belief? Could any one tell him why religious services just as orderly and decorous as in a temple could not occur under the green leaves and amid the waving grasses of a cool retreat in summer? He could see no force in the attempted defence set up by the railroad corporation, that they were running illegally on that day, and that therefore the plaintiffs were also in the wrong. The defence had not succeeded in establishing that the plaintiffs went for wrong purposes, or that they did not go to the meeting as a matter of conscience ; and he could not see where his clients failed to comply with the provisions of the Sunday law, which said :

"Whoever travels on the Lord's Day, except from necessity or charity, shall be punished by fine not exceeding ten dollars for each offence."

I cannot see any word here about going to church. I claim that the constitution, as it stands in Massachusetts, is beyond all law; the law proceeds and flows from it.

Judge Wells—How far do you say that a man may travel to church on Sunday?

Somerby—As far as he desires to. I know of no yardstick by which to measure the distance. I know of no law by which a man must go to any particular town to meeting, any more than to any particular church. If there was no church of his persuasion in the town where he resided—what then? Suppose we go back to the original Puritan times : suppose a Catholic wished to attend church, and there was none except by going to Worcester, for instance ; is there any anything in the law of Massachusetts to prevent his riding there, and driving back the same day, if he could? These matters of conscience existed before the Constitution was framed, and are recognized by it. They do not depend upon law at all, but are fundamental. The Legislature could not pass any law contrary to the provisions of the Constitution. Hear the declarations of the Massachusetts Bill of Rights :

1. All men are born free and equal, and have certain natural, essential and inalienable rights ; among which may be reckoned the right of enjoying and defending their lives and liberties ; that of acquiring, pos-

sessing and protecting property; in fine, that of seeking and obtaining their safety and happiness.

2. It is the right, as well as the duty of all men in society publicly and at stated seasons to worship the Supreme Being, the great Creator and Preserver of the Universe. And no subject shall be hurt, molested or restrained in his personal liberty or estate, for worshiping God in the manner and season most agreeable to the dictates of his own conscience; or for his religious professions or sentiments; provided he doth not disturb the public peace, or obstruct others in their religious worship."

And article third of the same instrument has been amended so as to read as follows:

"As the happiness of a people, and the good order and the preservation of civil government, essentially depend upon piety, religion and morality; and as those cannot be generally diffused through a community but by the institution of the public worship of God, and of public instruction in piety, religion and morality: Therefore * * * the people of this Commonwealth have a right to invest their Legislature with power to author-ize and require, and the Legislature shall from time to time authorize and require the several towns, parishes, precincts and other bodies politic or religious societies, to make suitable provision at their own expense for the institution of the public worship of God.

* * * * * * * *

And every denomination of Christians, demeaning themselves peaceably, and as good subjects of the Commonwealth, shall be equally under the protection of the law; and no subordination of any one sect or denomination to another shall ever be established by law."

I claim, from this, that it is fundamental that a man's worshipping God as he pleases, does not depend upon legislation, but as long as a man keeps himself inside the Constitution—no matter what his religious tenets— and does not disturb others, so long he is within the protection of the law.

At the conclusion of the arguments of respective counsel for the parties in controversy, the Judge gave a very lucid charge to the jury, of which the following is a synopsis.

The plaintiff claimed that she was travelling to and from a religious meeting, and according to her religious belief. The matter depended upon the character of the meeting to which she was going. The statute reads:

" Whoever keeps open his shop, warehouse or work-house, or does any manner of labor, business or work, except work of necessity and charity, or is present at any dancing or public diversion, show or entertainment, or takes part in any sport, game or play, on the Lord's Day, shall be punished by a fine not exceeding ten dollars for every offence."

If therefore, the meeting in Malden was of this character—a show, public diversion, entertainment or play —then travel to it would be illegal. It is true, said the Judge, that religious worship and religious belief are not defined by the constitution, and no man is limited at all in his religious belief, nor in his right to worship according to his own belief: and no one can say, because he dislikes or disbelieves in the manner of exhibiting this belief, or the form of any particular religious worship, that it does not come within the constitutional rights of another who does believe it to follow it. But, in order that it shall have this character of religious worship, it must be shown that the parties regard it to be a religious matter.

There is one feature of the meeting to which I ought perhaps to call your attention : In the advertisement published beforehand was a notice of Laura V. Ellis, and at the meeting itself it was announced that she would exhibit certain manifestations in a tent close by, admission to which was twenty five cents. And you have here heard the character of those manifestations. I think the facts are such that I can instruct you that that exhibition in that tent, for the purpose of gain—to which there was a charge of twenty five cents for admission—was a show ; and that all persons attending it, or knowing to it, could be punished according to the stature. And if she [Mrs. Feitel] went out to attend that show, then her purpose was not a legal one. If upon the whole evidence, you are satisfied that it was a show or entertainment, and not for religious worship, then it was a meeting by an attendance on which she was not entitled to recover.

The case was then given to the jury, who, after due deliberation, returned a verdict of $5,000 [the original claim being $15,000] damages in favor of Albert J. and Mrs. Feitel.

The interest in this case centers in the fact that by a

judicial decision, a liberal construction is given to the
Statute of Massachusetts, concerning the right of every
man and woman to conduct or attend religious worship,
on Sunday, according to the dictates of their own conscience ; and the fact is also settled that under the Constitution, spiritualists can enjoy the liberty of holding
their meetings on that day, equally with their orthodox
neighbors.

We insert here also an account of another case of
Spiritualism in Court, in which the question of the legal responsibility of mediumistic healers for alleged
mal-practice in that capacity was in dispute.

"On Friday June 23d, in the Superior Civil Court
for Plymouth County, Mass., held at Plymouth, the
case of Luther T. Phillips vs. William Chandler came
up.   This was an action brought by the plaintiff to recover for injuries received from an unskilful surgical
operation performed by the defendant.   The defendant
is a well-known Spiritualist doctor residing in Kingston,
and it was contended by the defence that he can neither
read nor write, and is entirely ignorant of medicine,
that he never pretended to have skill of himself, and
that his patrons well knew that his treatment was wholly
dependent upon abnormal influences while in a trance
condition, and that there was no responsibility beyond
the acting in good faith to obtain the abnormal influence.

The court (Judge Reed) ruled that where a party
holds himself out as a Spiritualist doctor, he is only
held to use the ordinary reasonable means to procure
the attendance of spirits at the time and place of the

treatment—or that if the party so holding himself out to treat disease takes the ordinary means in use with such person to induce the attendance of spirits, he is not liable for want of skill while so treating his patients.

The case was submitted to the jury upon the question whether the defendant treated the plaintiff while in the condition he contracted to be in, and if not, whether the plaintiff suffered injury from that treatment, and to what extent. They rendered a verdict for the defendant."

The particulars of the case are not given, but the term surgical is doubtless used in a technical sense, for strong as the faith of any one may be in the power exercised through what is here called a Spiritualist doctor, it is not probable that the patient would risk the use of instruments in his hands. There are adventurers travelling about, presumptuous enough to boast of surgical skill employed when under control, ready to perform difficult operations, but their pretensions are heralded in the most audacious style of unprincipled charlatans. They have brought disgrace upon the cause of Spiritualism, wherever they have travelled.

There must be good evidence of acquired knowledge and manual dexterity, to command the implicit confidence of the patient, at any time, before he can safely place trust in the surgeon; and the injunction against surrendering reason to blind faith, certainly applies in cases where the knife is pretentiously seized by ignorant hands, to the imminent danger of life and limb. The intelligent surgeon may, however, be aided by spirit power.

WHAT GOOD HAS SPIRITUALISM DONE?

This question is often asked by those who are skeptical as to the truth of spiritual phenomena, as well as by those who no longer deny, but who nevertheless doubt the practical value of the revelations.   The first answer suggested, is that it gives the most satisfactory proof of the immortality of the human soul, which can be derived from no other source.

But there are other practical results more directly cognizable by the senses, many of which have been heretofore adverted to.   Among these, and by no means the least important is the cure of disease.   The gift of healing, it is contended by this doubting class was vouchsafed only to certain favored ones who lived in the apostolic times, since which it has ceased to exist.   The following cases are cited to show that it exists among us at the present day.

CASES ILLUSTRATING THE CURE OF DISEASE BY SPIRIT POWER.

The first case is related by a young lady who was herself the recipient of the healing power, after suffering seriously from the effects of an injury of one of her limbs, inflicted through the carelessness of a companion, producing what seemed to result at length in permanent inability to use the limb, and in its progress involving the spine. We have omitted some unimportant details, otherwise giving the language of the writer.

INJURY OF THE LEFT KNEE-JOINT.

Some six years ago, while attending school in Lowell, Mass., I fell down stairs through the carelessness of a schoolmate, injuring myself considerably. Since then I have been troubled at times with my spine and left knee.

About a year since my general health failed me also. I began to suffer again with the pain in my spine, which grew worse and worse until it was almost unendurable. I received treatment from one of the best physicians in Boston Highlands (as I then resided in Boston,) but was not benefitted. He then advised me to go away from the salt water. I immediately went to Danville, New Hampshire, where I had the advice of other physicians. They all agreed in saying it must be moved. In the course of a few weeks my left knee became very painful, and swelled a great deal, but the pain in my back was somewhat relieved. In a very short time after leaving Boston I was unable to walk without the help of a crutch. For the last seven months I have suffered intensely, being obliged to recline a great part of the time. [She then had recourse to a prominent healer, who said "I am going to cure you," and after five minutes manipulation, she was able to walk. She continues the narrative ;]

I went back to the reception room, and in a few minutes saw one of my skeptical friends coming in. I walked across the room to meet him, saying. "What do you think of it?" He was so much surprised to see me walking that for several seconds he made no reply. At last he said: "Well, well, I do not know what to think of it! You do not walk much as you did yesterday!" An old gentleman (who by the way was an Episcopal clergyman,) who had not seen less than eighty winters came tremblingly to the door, and in a broken voice said, "Who did this? who performed this cure?" addressing the Doctor. "God did it." "Yes, I know he did, as he does everything that is good. But who was the instrument?" "I was the instrument," replied the Doctor. "But by what power do you claim to do these things?" "By the same power that Christ did—by the power of God." "But do you not think that borders a little on blasphemy?" said the old gentleman, who had advanced further and further into the room, until at last he sank into a chair. "No," said the Doctor, "for Christ said, 'The works that I do ye shall do also, and greater, because I go to the Father: and these are the signs which do follow them that believe; they shall lay hands on the sick and they shall recover.' I am a practical Christian; the churches—they are all idolatrous. Did you ever hear of a minister laying his hand on any of his sick parishioners and healing them? I heal the sick in the same manner as Jesus did, and I am not afraid or ashamed to own it." "But Jesus was the son of God?" "I claim to be the son of God. We are all sons of God," replied the doctor. "Didn't you ever think you was the son of God?" "No." "Well, it is time you did, with your head already covered with grey hairs." "Jesus and the apostles healed without coming in contact with the sick," said the old gentleman. "So do I sometimes." "Well, here, cure this limb," at the same time holding his limb out toward the doctor, who was sitting at the opposite side of the room. "I can't." "You are honest. Why not?" "Because of your unbelief. Jesus and the apostles could not do many wonderful works in a certain city, because of the unbelief of the people."

A LADY RESTORED AFTER BEING PRONOUNCED BY HER PHYSICIAN HOPELESS.

A correspondent communicates the following :

"Some fourteen years ago, Mrs. Conant was giving sittings at the National House, Boston. I was then stopping at the New England House. A sea captain was boarding there with his wife. She was taken very sick; her doctor had no hopes of her recovery, and her sister was summoned from New York City to see her before the change called death took place. She was a Baptist in belief; therefore the divine from Tremont Temple (Kalloch) was called to pray with her.

Meeting the captain, and hearing how dangerously ill his wife was, I broached the subject of Spiritualism to him gently, (he being a stranger) and advised him to call on Mrs. Conant—who was controlled by Dr. Kitredge—and see if he could not give some assistance to the sick one. He said he did not know anything about such things, but was willing to try anything, as he had no hopes of her recovering. I told him I would go with him to see her. We met her, and I asked if she could examine a patient at a distance. She replied that she did not know what could be done, but she would give a seance and see. She then passed into a trance, when Dr. Kittredge came, and I asked him if he would go to the New England House and examine a patient, not stating who it was, or what the trouble. The doctor asked the number of the room. The captain gave it. All was silent for five minutes, when the doctor spoke and stated who he found in the room, and just the condition of the patient, and said that the attending doctor did not understand the case, and that if he (the captain) would go to her room and make passes over her head and rub her, he thought she could be saved from the change. The captain followed the advice of the spirit, Dr. Kittredge, and in a few weeks' time his wife was sitting by his side at the dinner-table with myself opposite, and I know I did not 'see through a glass darkly,' but 'face to face.'"

INSANITY.

A case came under our personal observation about twelve years ago. One of our well-to-do, influential Boston merchants, who had previously become convinced of the truth of Spiritualism, called upon a medium, through whom his brother-in-law and his mother manifested their presence, describing the condition of his sister who was then an inmate of the McLean Asylum, in Somerville, and whose mental disease, as stated by the Superintendent, had a suicidal tendency in as dangerous a degree as any patient then under his charge. These spirit relatives begged that she should be taken out of the institution, and placed under magnetic treatment, aided by spirit influence, promising benefit if not a cure from that course.

The gentleman having so much confidence in this promise, and aware that the medium had no knowledge of the case, except that derived through the spirit friends, followed the advice given.   He first made arrangements for the medium to accompany him as a friend, on a visit to his sister.   Then he was again importuned in the same way to remove her to a temporary boarding place where the desired means of relief could be employed.

Having acceded to the urgent solicitation, the patient was met by several mediums, and from thence removed to a more permanent place where a number of mediums resided, and the proposed remedial influence tested. The result was restoration to soundness of mind, which has continued to this day.   For six years past the lady has had charge of her daughter's twin children.

It may be stated that the cause of the insanity in this case was religious excitement, the patient entertaining the idea that she had committed "the unpardonable sin." It is alluded to in Mr. R. D. Owen's late work—The Debatable Land, p. 523.

There was a gradual improvment in both the bodily and mental condition, from the time she was subjected to the change of treatment.   The patient enjoyed the spirit control, and often asked the spirits to come and converse with her through the medium.

RHEUMATISM AND CANCER.

Hon. Neal Dow in an article entitled "What is it?" communicated to the *Congregationalist* of Jan'y 25 1872—a weekly religious newspaper published in the interest of the denomination known by that name, relates a conversation held between a friend of his and a magnetizer, whom he designates Dr. Blank, concerning two cures effected by the vital magnetic process. He quotes the celebrated passage from Shakspeare, "There are more things in Heaven and earth than are dreamed of in our philosophy," closing his paper with a repetition of the opening question, and adding "Can the doctors tell?" The first case was one of Cancer and the second one of Sciatica, a severe form of Rheumatism. We give the substance, reversing the order by inserting first a letter under date of Oct. 1869, addressed to the magnetizer, by the friend alluded to, on whose person the cure was performed. Mr. D's estimate of his friend is given in the first two paragraphs of his article, which we copy from the Congregationalist.

"A few weeks ago, being in an eastern city, I called on an old and valued friend living there, and in course of our talk, I asked him about his wife, who had been cured of cancer, and wished to know all about it from him, as I had heard the story many times from other parties, and so he proceeded to tell me.

I may premise that my friend is a most intelligent man, not at all given to new things because they are new, nor lightly esteeming old things because they are old; there is not among my circle of friends a man of sounder sense, or better judgment, or more reliable; nor one whose advice would be more eagerly sought by his friends in circumstances to need counsel. Well, my friend proceeded in his story which concerned matters transpiring two or three years ago.

The letter alluded to is in these words:

Dear Sir,— I send you a few words of cheer, on account of the remarkable cure you have effected in me. May God bless you always, wherever you may be. About the first of June, I was prostrated with Rheumatism, and after suffering terribly for more than three months without obtaining any permanent relief, I saw your advertisement in the Portland Daily Press, and without any faith in your mode of treatment myself, was induced by my wife to call on you as a last resort. I was on two crutches, and could not walk a step without them. I had not slept any the previous night, and was in intense pain in my right leg.

After one treatment by you of about twenty minutes the pain left me entirely and has never returned.

I threw my crutches away and have not been on them since.

I write this to you, without any solicitation on your part, in order that you may be encouraged to continue to exercise the mysterious power of healing the sick. Hoping your patients may have as much reason to rejoice in your great success as I have.

Yours truly.

The particulars of the other case were published in the Banner of Light over a year ago. The patient who was afflicted with the cancer was the wife of the writer of the preceding letter.

The facts are stated as follows :

Dr. Blank informs us that a few months ago, a lady called on him in a sorrowful state of mind, informing him that a professor of one of our medical institutions as well as her family physician, had informed her that she had a cancer which would prove fatal, if not removed before the expiration of two weeks.

On her way from the professor to the doctor she had consulted with a clairvoyant physician, who declared that the knife must not be used, but that the trouble could be cured without such harsh means. The doctor gave her a magnetic treatment, and then went with her to some persons who made cancer a speciality, and their opinion was that the disease could be cured. This encouraged her to risk the "new mode" of treatment, but, in obedience to the prejudices of her friends who were not acquainted with, but much opposed to the magnetic process, she declined risking so dangerous a case with any one save a regular physician. The next day after Dr. Blank's treatment he met her, and she reported her case improving, and also said that she knew of an experienced physician who possessed the power, and had made a cure for a friend of hers, and that she had decided to place herself under his care on her friends account. She was under this doctor's treatment by the laying on of hands for a month, and was cured. She visited the Professor who had advised the use of the knife, and he was very much surprised at the result.

Dr. Blank says he desired the facts known, as the lady is not a Spiritualist, but, with her husband is an active church member, and reliable.

INJURY FROM A FALL.

Hon. G. W. Woodman, in Army and Navy Hall, Portland, on Sunday, Nov. 19th, gave an account of the wonderful restoration by aid of the spirits, of Mr. N. M. Woodman of that city, who was very badly injured by falling twenty-three feet through the scuttles of his store. A synopsis of his statement appeared the next day in the Portland papers, and the Boston Journal's correspondent furnished that paper with a brief account.

The full particulars of this case appeared in the Banner of Light, June 3d 1871, furnished by J. B. Hall Esq., of that city. The parties are all highly respectable, and have many friends in Boston, where, as well as in Portland, much interest is felt, as the case is one of unquestionable spirit power.

In the "Vital Magnetic Cure" we have explained the gift of healing more at length, together with the law of electric, magnetic, and spirit-forces affecting human life, and their application in the cure of disease ; and in Evans' "Mental Cure" the psychological method of treatment is clearly and intelligently stated, which supercedes the necessity of dwelling upon those topics here.

According to our observation the practice of using opiates for the relief of patients suffering from severe pain, has been increasing of late, which seems to us entirely wrong in many cases. Persons becoming accustomed to such medicines require more and more in quantity to produce the same effect. As it loses its effect the system becomes deadened by its use. We remember well being called to see a patient who had used Morphine to excess, and we had been in the room but a few minutes when we felt drowsy by taking on the condition of the patient. Does not common sense and reason show that such conditions work against Nature? On the other hand does not magnetism assist Nature to harmonize and vitalize, and thereby eradicate disease? We doubt the propriety of such excessive use of opiates in cases of sickness, and it seems to us that the most essential thing thought of by regular practitioners is to relieve, not remove the cause of the disease. When magnetism is better understood, less of opiates will be used.

Before closing the evidence derived from the exercise of the healing power, it is proper in this connection to insert an answer to a question relative to

THE ALLEGED CUPIDITY OF HEALERS.

We have already alluded to the charge, but as this opinion was sought from a higher intelligence, we quote it from the Banner.

"We find healing mediums making fifteen and twenty dollars per day. Is this not an abuse of the power which they receive from the spirit-land? The prices charged for a few minutes' time place this heavenly blessing beyond the reach of the poor.

"ANS.—You have a saying amongst you that contains much wisdom. It is this : " The love of money is the root of evil." These media, being susceptible to the influence from the higher life, are also susceptible to the conditions of this life ; and when once they become mediums used publicly and privately by the world at large, their needs are largely increased. As all their strength, all their life physical is used up by another —what you may be pleased to call a divine calling—they have no possible chance of obtaining that which meets the necessities of this life in any other way than by setting a price upon their mediumship. So I shall not presume to condemn them ; for, in all human probability were I a mortal, and should I stand as they stand, I should do as they do, because they are held in the inexorable clutch of a power outside of themselves, and because most of them are thrown under influences belonging to this life that have a tendency to lead them downward instead of upward—have a tendency to develop all the lower conditions of their natures—the love of money, the love of power, of place, of fame, of all that this world holds great and good. But while you Spiritualists complain because this condition of things exists because of high prices charged by your media, you should not forget that you have something of a duty to perform toward them. It seems to me to be this : by your good deeds, by your prayers, by your sympathy, to lead them out of this condition, and to assist them to a more spiritual one.   Instruct them to obtain their livelihood from the rich, and not from the poor.   That is God's justice.   I know it is not man justice, but it is Divine justice, and ever should be exercised by mortal media. Most of them are not so thoroughly developed that their guardian spirits can instruct them in these things as they would wish to.   They make attempts in that direction, but they are but attempts, for the medium's spirit immediately meets them with opposition ; the question is settled at once—they are obliged to retire. There are exceptions ; there are some who are willing to receive advice from their guardian spirits—who are willing to abide by it ; but they are the fortunate class of media.   Let it be your duty, oh Spiritualists, to ele- vate your media, to sustain them by your sympathy, your prayers, and just, good lives ; and by-and-by they will rise out of this low, material condition, where their guardian angels can control them, and deal justly with the public through them.

THE DUPLEX CHARACTER OF OPPOSING TESTIMONY.

In estimating the moral value of the testimony given for or against any cause, it is but just and fair that their antecedents, the consistency or inconsistency of their testimony, the spirit in which they utter it, should all be considered. This is the practice among intelligent jurors in common affairs. No one who is honest, and upright, although mistaken, need fear to have his evidence fairly weighed in the balance of justice.

It is well to criticise some of the testimony which has been quoted against Spiritualism, in order to ascertain how far such testimony militates against the claim that it has its foundation in truth. Some of them may be quoted against themselves. No one has vociferated more fiercely in terms of denunciation than Mr. Knapp, yet he has acknowledged the truth of the phenomena, not however with candor, as will be seen by the facts given in the California letter subjoined. The moral impression he has made upon the community may be inferred from remarks which we extract from a Boston newspaper.

"The Elder is evidently getting mad, and unless he is soothed and conciliated may yet be drawn into the use of language which will be unbecoming in "a man of God" and inconsistent for a professed follower of "the meek and lowly Jesus," who taught that we should "bless

those who curse us," and "do good to those who de-
spitefully use us and persecute us."

The following from a correspondent of the Banner,
contains a more reliable statement of the physical manifestations occurring in presence of the reviler.

LETTER FROM CALIFORNIA.

I have been reading Elder Knapp's statement to a
Boston audience of his experience with what he calls the
devil's demonstrations at the house of Thomas Hook, at
Stockton, Cal.   Without any desire to contradict the
Elder, or to say that he has mis-stated or omitted any
important fact concerning the affair, I will, briefly as
possible, relate what was stated to me by Mr. Hook in
person.   I have known Mr. Hook for about sixteen
years, and Mrs. Hook when she was Mrs. Greenfield.
I also had some acquaintance with Mr. Greenfield in his
life-time.

A short time after these demonstrations had ceased,
I met Mr. Hook in the city of Stockton, and, by his
solicitation, I went to his residence to hear his story of
the affair and to see the result of the demonstrations.
He showed me a box of broken dishes, vases and spittoons, that he said had been dashed from shelves, tables,
etc., and broken as I saw them.   After the water sprinkling on the bed of the child had ceased, the little girl
(medium, an adopted daughter of the family) saw two
men in her room, and described them so accurately that
Mrs. Hook at once recognized her former husband, Mr.

Greenfield, and Mr. Hook a deceased uncle, neither of whom had the child ever seen in their life-time. Each of them gave his name, which confirmed them in the belief that the girl really saw what she pretended to see. Mr. Hook was then sheriff of San Joaquin County, and Mr. Gates spoken of by the Elder was clerk of the county. On being questioned, these spirits stated to these gentlemen that an indictment for the crime of murder against a prominent man of the county would be stolen unless it was removed from the files of the clerk's office. It was so removed; and in a few evenings after, the office was broken into, and the entire files of indictments were rumaged and scattered over the office. So much for the Elder's devil. Several other things were done concerning that affair, but not worth relating here.

When the Elder arrived, he was invited to the house of Mrs. Hook, who was a member of the Baptist Church. The Elder proclaimed, with a confident air, that it was the devil making the disturbance, and he could lay him by prayer; but before the Elder had fairly got up steam, things began to fly about the house, and kept up such a clatter that the Elder soon weakened; and, just as he was on the eve of winding up, a spittoon started (without hands) from an adjoining room, and landed on the floor close to the Elder, and flew into several pieces. This was too much for the Elder. He cut short the "Amen," and left the house in hot haste. So much for the Elder's success in laying the devil.

Many strange things happened at the house of these

parties that I cannot relate. I may mention one or two singular occurrences : one was the carrying by unseen hands, in open daylight, a large, heavy platter of beef from the well-house into the front yard, a distance of twenty paces, and then dropping it. At another time —and I think Elder Knapp was present—when the table was being set with dishes, knives and forks, the plates commenced to slide along on the table and hop up on each other, the cups and saucers followed suit, until all the dishes were closely piled on the centre of the table. The corners of the tablecloth were then gathered up, as if by the human hand, and brought together, and the whole carried out of the house on the veranda and dropped.

Mr. Greenfield, the deceased husband of Mrs. Hook, was for a good many years a Baptist preacher ; but, from some cause, he became dissatisfied or disgusted with the profession, and retired from the pulpit. Mrs. Hook related to me the conduct of the reputed spirit of Mr. Greenfield, who, it appears, was the principal actor in smashing things about the house, and who was a man of violent temper, and what occurred during these demonstrations was exactly characteristic of him when in anger. These exhibitions of temper were common while he was a preacher of the gospel. This is one of Elder Knapp's devils. What a compliment to his deceased brother !

I do not know that I violate the confidence of Mrs. H. by stating these last-mentioned facts, as she freely and voluntarily made the statement here related. Nor would I slander the deceased ; but, on the contrary, I will state that he was much respected in Stockton, and was understood to be a good moral man, and at one time a Justice of the Peace. I state the facts as related to me by one who knew him best, to show how silly is the devilish conjecture of the Elder. If he really did turn devil at death, the Elder will find him a congenial companion when he gets over the river; for who so loves to roll the word "devil" under his tongue, as a sweet morsel, as this same Elder?—who so familiar with the "devilish" doings of the "devil" as Elder Knapp? Did he ever speak in public ten minutes without referring in some way to his old companion and wayfaring traveller? He says "the devil had an eye on him, and knew he was coming to California." Certainly; and didn't the Elder send him ahead as a missionary to open the way for his "hell-fire" and "devil's" doctrine?—and didn't the Elder make use of this story in his own way, all over the State, to scare children, women and soft-headed men? There can be no doubt of the intimacy of the Elder and the "old deceiver," since they go hand in hand; and in part consideration of the old fellow's services, he makes him more powerful than the Almighty, and tickles his vanity by making his hearers believe that he is omnipotent and omnipresent, and can influence man where God and the powers of heaven have no earthly show.　　　　　　　　　　R. B. H.

A confusion of names having made an erroneous impression on the minds of persons abroad, in regard to the identity of Mr. Hatch, who was the victim of scurrilous abuse from the "Elder," we here make the explanation. The person spoken of in the scandalous lecture delivered in Tremont Temple during the revival melee, is not the Hatch who was once an advocate of Spiritualism, and who figured in the farcical proceedings in Cooper Institute; but a respectable Unitarian Minister doing city missionary work, who courageously stood at the door distributing religious tracts to counteract the effect of the peculiar religious teaching which formed the substance of the lecture, and similar harangues.

The abusive language and slanderous charges brought out a defence from a number of Spiritualists who had been blessed with the "gifts" and their friends, who addressed letters of reproof to the evil-tongued revivalist, calling his attention to the libellous character of the falsehoods, for which he could be held amenable. But he probably thought that discretion was the better part of valor, and has retired to the security of his farm, where he can enjoy the pecuniary profit of his vulgarity.

So also is it with Mr. Fulton. The bitterness of his hostility against the cause and its adherents over-reaches its mark, destroying his influence, when addressing candid persons who fail to see the application of his evil reproaches. They attribute it to bigotry, and are led to inquire for themselves, rather than driven away from an investigation.

He has a sister in the spirit-world, who recently sent him the following message, at one of the Banner of Light Circles:

"I am here to request a favor of my brother, Rev. Justin D. Fulton, preaching in Tremont Temple in your city. It is this: that he will give the people his

views concerning the twelfth chapter of First Corinthians.

I know he has.no faith in the return of the spirit, but
I also know he will have, for there are hidden springs
in his being, which, when they gush forth, will bear
him on to spiritual knowledge whether he will or no.

I shall not be weary though he repulses me again and
again. If I feel that it is my duty under God to return,
I shall do so, trusting the consequences with that God
who watches over me, and watches over him. I am
Clara Fulton Pope."

What of Dr. Hammond, who has written a book
against Spiritualism, denying the facts which his fellow-
opponents have been compelled to acknowledge. A severe but just criticism upon the demerits of the book by
the pen of a competent reviewer was published some
months ago. A flat denial of these facts is as absurd
now as it would be to tell every man and woman he
should meet that they had totally lost the senses of sight
and hearing.

It will be remembered that this same Dr. Hammond
during the late civil war, through the influence of some
well meaning citizens, who are now ashamed of their
recommendation, received the appointment of Surgeon
General of the U. S. Taking advantage of his official
position to accomplish selfish ends, he was arrested and
brought before a Court-martial on charges involving
reputation for truth, honesty and fair dealing. The trial lasted nearly four months, and resulted in peremptory
dismissal from office, and irretrievable disgrace. It

pained the heart of our late good President to be compelled to issue the following official order.

"The record, proceedings, findings and sentence of the Court in the foregoing case are approved, and it is ordered that Brigadier General William A. Hammond, Surgeon general of the U. S. Army, be dismissed from the service, and be forever disqualified from holding any office of honor or trust under the government of the United States."

A. LINCOLN.

August 18, 1864.

This erudite gentleman is represented as saying that the movement of tables and chairs is against the force of gravity, and due to hallucination, legerdemain, and fraud. Commenting upon this, one of the ablest writers exclaims "Oh, science! science! do let us retain some little confidence in common sense, which has long been teaching that whenever we moved our chairs and table with our physical hands, we did it 'against the force of gravity.' It seems, then, if common sense be right and Dr. Hammond right, that every time we ever sat down to our dinner table, our chair was moved up to it by either hallucination, legerdemain or actual fraud. Though we are three score and eight, we are not yet so old as to discard truths and facts because they are new to us."

Some of the opponents who have exhibited themselves as exposers have two faces, either of which they turn to the gaze of the public as caprice suits them, or rather as their improvised audiences are willing to pay for.

Among such are Bly, Von Vleck, H. Melville Fay, and similar double dealers. Having mediumistic powers, they are at one time holding seances, at another getting up a show, and denouncing mediumship as imposture, apparently oblivious to the fact that both classes of listeners can readily detect the imposters.

Bly was controlled by the spirit of his uncle, a noted blind phrenologist, to examine phrenological characteristics, and did it in a perfectly satisfactory manner. But as the old gentleman was one of the earlier and honest Spiritualists, he must have felt ashamed of the tricky side of his protege.

Barnum, the notorious expositor and practitioner of humbugs consorted with Von Vleck to make a show of Spiritualism at his museum.

One of the latest of these feats was performed in a Methodist meeting by a person who had been an advocate of Spiritualism for years and had given tests of spirit identity before associations of Spiritualists, then turning Methodist took the same method of proving that what she had previously done was false ; yet though this new departure was stimulated by the cheap charge of fifteen cents a head, there were but few hearers. Catch-penny traps are not always profitable to the vendor, even if he includes his principles in the sale.

Thomas L. Harris has pursued an erratic course, upon which we find the following criticism published : "A friend who has recently visited this eccentric genius at his community home near Buffalo did not form a more favorable opinion of him and his present enterprize than we did of his Mountain Cove movement, many years ago, which went up soon for want of funds and faith, both of which are abundant in his present experiment.

The rich vein of poetry which formerly ran through him to enrich the early spiritual papers is entirely exhausted, or is perverted into a sewer for the waste waters of Christian bigotry, of which he seems now to have a remarkable share. The stream of eloquence too, that in the early days of Spiritualism, thrilled so many hearts, has turned into a channel little better or more profitable to the race than that of any bigoted sectarian. We are sorry for Bro. Harris, but not for his earthly period, as the wealth he has secured will enable him to procure earthly comforts; but the richer treasures of the other life, which he has lost by his course, will cause him many years of regret and sorrow. He seems to have been too weak a vessel to contain the new wine, or else he had not got all the old theology out before the spirits poured in the new, but retained ' enough to spoil the pure Spiritual Philosophy, causing it to sour in his brain. We thought him a little crazy in the Mountain Cove movement, but as he partially recovered from that, we had hopes of his entire recovery; but he could not bear the flattery and praise which his inspiration and eloquence drew around him, and he soon began to suspect himself to be an "especial messenger of the Lord," superior to his fellow-men.

For all useful purposes to the race, Bro. Harris seems entirely lost, having crawled into a community shell, where he deals out the orders of Christ to the family, and supposes, or makes them believe, he is the medium of direct communication with that part of the

Godhead which on earth was, and is, the Christ. It would seem, at this day, that no sane man or woman could fall in such blind superstition as that of Bro. Harris and John Noyes of Oneida, and several others, more or less distinguished; but we are still more surprised at any families who possessed wealth, and the means of education which it brings, who should be so deluded as to follow after such fanaticisms. Yet this is the history of the race. There have ever been some to fall into every new scheme of salvation and redemption, and wealth is not always security against ignorance and delusion.

Elsewhere we have mentioned Rev H. W. Beecher in connection with this subject.

Although Mr. B. does not openly advocate Spiritualism, he recognizes the value of the services of clairvoyant healers, and is not ashamed to employ them in his family, nor to recommend the vital magnetic force as a healing power to his friends. It is a current report that in his society there are many avowed believers, and that responses are given to his teachings by raps and other demonstrations.

In conducting a funeral service recently, Mr. B. urged the mourners to rejoice in the accomplished victory of the departed; to thank God for what work he had done so well, for its great results and for the noble, manly, sweet Christian demonstrations of a useful life, and not to think of him hereafter as one reposing beneath the grass and the flowers, but rather listening for a voice from the angel, as they looked at the grave, saying to them "He is not here, he is risen."

Rev. G. H. Hepworth is strongly mediumistic, and perhaps is not fully accountable for all his acts and words. His mother enjoyed spirit-communication with his father for many years previous to her exit from earth-life, and Mr. H. has often been heard to express his belief that his father did really communicate with his idolized mother. The last time we saw her, she was playing the piano, and at the same time improvising a communication to us. She kept up spiritual circles, and her friends enjoyed spiritual communication through her organization as well as through others: and after her departure, Mr. H. kept the rooms open for that purpose in remembrance of her. It is very questionable whether he will enjoy with equal satisfaction the fruits of his late summersault.

In a funeral sermon, after Mr. Hepworth had cited cases of mediumship in the Scriptures, the case of Joan of Arc, Socrates, Luther, Swedenborg and Indian medicine men, he remarked, "I have been greatly interested in the new sect or denomination that has come into existence in the last few years. Its members call themselves Spiritualists. Fifteen years ago they were laughed at, now who laughs at them? Then, few had ever heard of such a system of doctrines, now they number their converts by the millions, and these converts belong to all classes of society, from the poorest to the richest and most learned. They have thirty journals devoted to the propagation of their faith. They have a library of five hundred volumes advocating their sectarianism.

"The moment your eye glances over these figures, you

ask, why is this? The answer is plain; first because the doctrine of communion has put off its oppressive robes of selfishness and personal aggrandizement, and put on the white garments of good news to the world; and second, because nothing is more evident to my mind than that the world longs to believe and needs to believe something of the sort; it is essential to our religious well-being.

"The very minute that terrible desolation enters a house and robs the family of a loved member, leaving as a memento of the past only the vacant chair, the holiest part of our human nature looks up to Heaven with a dim vague expectation, with a belief that has never taken a definite shape, perhaps that though we cannot see them, they do see and know us."

SEANCES—CONDITIONS, AND RULES FOR THEIR GOVERNMENT.

The word *seance*, borrowed from the French, means simply a sitting or session. It has in a great measure superceded the more homely word *circle*.

In visiting a place where a circle is to be held, the inquirer, it is supposed, has a definite object in view, whatever that may be. Whether he will be successful or not, depends partly upon the motive which prompts him, and partly upon circumstances not altogether within his power to control. Both are involved in conditions necessary to success, and these conditions are now so well understood from long experience and observation, that specific rules have been deduced for the government of the sitters.

In the first place it is essential that harmony should prevail among all the persons in the company, and a willingness to receive whatever may be given in the way of manifestations, each one being willing to yield in a state of passivity, for the time being to any influence which may be attempted to be exercised over them by the invisible power.

The manifestations may be either physical or mental; it is seldom that both kinds occur at the same time. Where a variety of well developed mediums are present, this may occur. If the seeker is about to visit a place where the physical only are known to occur, and is at the same time opposed to them, he should remain away, as his presence would disturb the harmony, thereby destroying the conditions, and probably entirely prevent thereby the expected result. The medium who is susceptible to the control of a spirit who has passed beyond the veil, is in the same degree controllable by the psychological power of a positive will, exercised by a spirit yet in human form; so that nothing can be expected beyond what emanates from the controlling mind. It is unwise therefore to encourage skeptics to attend a circle when their will is more positive than the spirit mind which usually controls that circle. Candor, fairness, and a passive state of will on the part of such investigators are pre-requisites. It is of less consequence, when the controlling power of the spirit is known to be positive, and almost indomitable.

This is the case with many of those who produce the physical manifestations.

He who has reached a fore-gone conclusion on any subject, is not in a proper state of mind to investigate. The truth is not in him, neither does he desire it. The Scripture enjoins seekers after truth in the words "seek and ye shall find ; knock and it shall be opened unto you." Determined opposition is at once perceived by the sensitive medium, although not a word may have been said. Persons carry with them the record of their life indelibly impressed, and the medium is enabled to see their interior condition. Facts of whatever nature, social or moral, political or commercial, are reflected as if in a mirror. Those who have enjoyed the smiles of fortune, and lived in ease and comfort, as well as those who have had to struggle for bread in the battle of life, have brought before them their personal history and experience, which startles their inner consciousness just as was experienced by the Jewish woman at the well, quoted in another place. Secret doings are brought to light. It is not surprising that the dishonest merchant, the falsifier, and the evil doer in any sphere of life should become alarmed at the display of such a panorama before him. Discretion is used as to the revelation of the facts shown to the medium. If they affect his moral status, they are shown to him as an affectionate parent would chide and guide to happier conditions, his erring child ; otherwise they are as confidential as in ordinary intercourse in private life. A case of this kind came under our observation about three years ago. A young man who was a stranger in this section of country visited a lady who had this remarkable power well developed. She was engaged with a room full of company and could not immediately give him a sitting, but was impelled to tell him in presence of her other visitors that he had been associating with an ill-disposed companion, describing the young man thus designated, his habits, and the manner he had employed to entice her visitor to places which were unsuited to his unfoldment, and to fit him for a higher plane of life. She added " There is a lady who is in the form, that you have neglected— you have not done right in the case." The visitor acknowledged the truth of the statement, confessing that the young man alluded to had done as was described, and that he had neglected to write to his mother for two years. We heard the entire conversation, and was struck with the candid acknowledgement of the visitor. So also have we known many persons who had been living a degraded and miserable life saved by a similar interposition of either father or mother, brother or sister.

For those who are not familiar with spirit manifestations, a few practical rules are necessary to be observed.

1. The seeker should first go alone, and sit with the medium in the same way as if asking counsel of a physician or a lawyer. By this means the medium avoids commingling the magnetic spheres, as would be the case. if a third person were present. Friends often wish to accompany the inquirer to gratify curiosity, harmless in itself, but acting as a disturbing element under such circumstances, and preventing clear communications. The same applies to the healing process, as may be seen

by reference to the pages of "Vital Magnetic Cure."

2. Sit in a passive condition, waiting patiently for whatever the spirit sees fit to communicate, which will be given as the need may be, whether of a material or spiritual nature, and not necessarily as the inquirer may desire.

3. The medium should take no thought of what may be said, or consider whether it will please or displease, but speak as the impulse is given, provided he or she is sufficiently developed to feel confidence in the gifts that have been bestowed. Many feel a lack of this confidence, and allow themselves to fall into an anxious state of mind, lest they should fail to give satisfaction to their patrons. This should be avoided by all, whatever the phase of mediumship—speaking, writing, healing, or giving tests in any way. Let the gifts be exercised naturally, without restraint. Many go to consult mediums for the material benefit they can derive. It is not wise to run to them for advice upon every trivial thing, for upon most of earthly affairs we know sufficiently well of ourselves, and can gain no additional light by seeking in that way. We lose our own identity by so doing, and diminish our influence and usefulness. Would information be asked of persons in earth-life, upon all points which we refer to those in spirit-life? We think not, and it is not to be supposed that those who have gone to a higher sphere can be interested in minor affairs, which we can just as well settle for ourselves. Some seek advice solely for the purpose of accumulating wealth. The better spirits decline such advice, as not being conductive to the highest enjoyment of this life.

They know that hoarding is a propensity very difficult to out-grow, after leaving the body. The plans of
such are, therefore, generally thwarted, and after a few
lessons they gain wisdom, and begin to look upon Spiritualism more for the good they can do through its teachings, than to gratify selfishness.

4. How to form a circle. Let as many investigators
who are harmonious and likely to attract similar influences, as it is desired to bring together, be seated at a
convenient distance from each other, joining hands.
It is generally better to place positive and negative persons alternately. Sometimes the sexes are thus seated
—a male and a female alternately, but there are many
positive females, and negative males. If a person in the
circle has been developed in such a manner as to be able
to analyze the chemical forces of the various persons in
the company, they can by that means be arranged so as
to secure the best manifestations. After sitting quietly
for a short time, some susceptible person may suggest a
change of position, to facilitate the object. This being
done, and all quiet as before, the magnetic forces will
be harmonized : then the hands should be separated.
The influence will be concentrated on the medium.

If a developed medium be present, the spirit will ar-
range the seating of the compnay ; but if the object of
the session is development, the rules given should be followed.

We have long since ceased to sit in circles. They
are useful in attracting power to a sensitive ; but a few
friends whose magnetism is adapted to each other, or
even one magnetizer with suitable adaptation being pres-

ent will do as much for a partially developed medium
as can be gained by sitting in a circle for some length
of time.   Our best mediums never could or would sit
in promiscous circles, but were developed in a quiet
way alone, or with a few special friends present, or
through a severe sickness.   One thus developed is more
independent than those developed by circles, furthermore
the latter require for a long time the sustaining power
of the circle, in order to accomplish much.

Most mediumistic persons who are frail and delicate
are cured of disease and developed by magnetic treatment.   It is not advisable to push forward the devel-
oping process by such means more rapidly than they
grow interiorly.   It is better that development should
take place first interiorly, then exteriorly; for thereby
there is a protection against influences that are injurious
to many negative mediums.

No two are affected alike, consequently no rule can
be invariable to bring about a good development spiritually.   But we can say to the mediumistic live right,
and aspire to the society of good angels, and they will
surely unfold you in their own good time.

The promiscous circle among Spiritualists has been
superceded by the parlor seance, where not much regard is paid to the arrangement of the persons convened.
There is generally present, a well developed medium
who can enter a room full of company promiscously assembled, if necessary, and exercise the gift of speaking
or any other phase without embarassment.   Those who
desire tests, employ a medium for that purpose; if
teaching is wanted, one is selected who has been devel-

oped on that plane, and so of physical manifestations of whatever kind. If the spirits see a medium whose faculties they desire to exercise, they will make it known ; then the person indicated must meet them with a willingness to be controlled, by remaining passive, before harmony can be established, and the effort rendered successful.

Physical phenomena convince those who are materialistic, and exacting in reference to tangible proofs. With the progressed, they have had their day, but that day for the masses is not yet over. They have been of immense service as the harbinger of truth in the form of mental manifestations. Many materialists have been convinced thereby of the existence of an invisible, but intelligent power, and of the immortality of man.

The truth and good resulting has not however been unmixed, because of the palming off of imitations with the exhibition of genuine phenomena. In some cases the medium has not been to blame. Some spirits after going out from the earthly form have been the occasion of charges of deception against innocent mediums. If they can do a good act, they have the power to do its opposite, as when they exercised the faculty of will while they were inhabitants of earth. If investigators would take this fact into consideration, they would not fear spirits after, more than they had done before their change from one sphere to the other.

A word more to mediums. If they will live according to the teachings of spirits from the higher spheres, they will soon become of themselves a power to control spirits on a lower plane than themselves ; and there is no need to fear injury from those of higher planes. It is only those who have not yet grown up to the level of our condition of life that can tempt us into downward paths. Those who are superior to us in wisdom and goodness will rejoice to meet our aspirations, elevating us to the joys of a higher and purer life.

There is a peculiar phase of mediumship to which no allusion has been made, and which has proved a stumbling block to beginners. Mediums often see and decribe spirits still living in the earthly form, giving their names, and the particular circumstances occurring at the time of the clairvoyant view, personifying them so that they can be recognized, although many miles away. "What a story they tell me," says the skeptic, "they give me the name of a friend still living. It is a delusion!" A medium is controlled for some years, it may be, receiving advice and information, and at last finds that the alleged spirit is still in the earth form.

This presents a question difficult to solve. The only explanation which occurs to us is that a spirit has assumed the name of the friend, as is done in earth-life, where a person falsely represents another, deceiving as it were, "the very elect." This is done sometimes, apparently, without their being conscious of it.

A curious phenomenon seen at both public and private circles is worthy of record, although already known to Spiritualists, viz: the sudden appearance of the name of a spirit in raised letters on the arm of the medium. This has been done repeatedly in the persons of Charles Foster, Mrs. Friend, and Mr. Colchester; thus identifying a departed friend of some one present. In one

instance, in the case of Mr. F. a pistol was marked on
the arm in addition, and it proved that it was by a pistol shot that the communicating spirit was transferred
from material to spirit-life.   We have had sittings with
all three, and received the same proof, twice after writing names on paper and rolling into pellets ; once without writing, and in no case where the spirit was known
to the medium.

MISCELLANEOUS FACTS IN SPIRITUAL EXPERIENCE.

Many facts occur in the lives of individuals which are
of general interest, and should extend beyond the limited
sphere in which they originate.   A few items of a mis-
cellaneous character, belonging to Spiritualistic experience, but which cannot be conveniently classified, are
here collated.

As we come into our world without our knowledge
or consent, welcome or unwelcome, and have duties imposed upon us as soon as we arrive at an age of responsibility, it behooves us to learn all we can of the laws
which govern life's phenomena, while on our earthly
pilgrimage.   We often hear persons who are called
Christians say "there are many things we do not understand, and God, for a wise purpose has withheld the
knowledge of them from us ; and the seeming mysteries will at the last day be solved." But it affords no
consolation to a thinking being to sit down, without at

least trying to understand all that concerns him. Spiritualism, if true, is part of the decree of life, which must be accepted, as is the fact of the sun, moon and stars, and the effects of electric, magnetic and spiritual forces.

We have quoted the discovery of crime through a medium. A case in point occurred in Boston. A young man, belonging to the Baptist church whose pastor is one of the bitterest opposers of Spiritualism was in the employ of a member of another evangelical church. A person with mediumistic power, but not a professional medium, called at the office of the employer, and although not seeing the young man said "You have a young man at work for you who has an old head on young shoulders," describing him so accurately that he was easily distinguished from others in the establishment, and advised his being watched. In a short time he was caught stealing forty dollars. The employer sent for his minister who came with a deacon, and advised that the culprit be kept, or he would go to hell. "Perhaps you will change your opinion by talking with him" said the employer. They took the young man into an upper chamber, and asked him to kneel down and pray, but he refused. They then came down and told the employer that he had already gone to hell, and they thought nothing more could be done for him. He had also appropriated to his own use money belonging to the Sunday school connected with the church. We were present when the spirit through the medium gave the caution. We believe the money was subsequently returned, and through this check on his dishonest practices, he was saved from a dishonorable course in earth-life, and unhappy experience in the future.

Spiritualists are by their enemies charged with lawlessness. We would not shield a wrong-doer from the consequences of evil deeds. It would be useless to attempt it, for the transgressor of law cannot evade its penalty under any circumstances. Neither would we recriminate, but there are facts enough to show that religious pretensions are not proof of virtue and honesty. Jesus said that none were perfect—"no, not one." We knew a methodist minister who had preached for years, and afterwards entered into mercantile business. Almost his first act was to prepare for failure by transferring his property, and the end soon came. There was clear evidence of dishonesty, yet some who had been swindled joined with others to aid him in contending by law with those who had been fortunate enough to see through the operations of the reverend merchant, and secured the payment of their claims.

Another reverend of the Baptist persuasion was employed during the week in an office where money was received, and sums were missed. The proprietor suspecting him of appropriating the funds to his own use, took proper measures and caught him. The case was not prosecuted, but submitted to the arbitration of three persons, one a minister, another a merchant, both gone to the spirit-world, and ourself. The decision was that the money should be refunded, and the embezzler leave the city, and try to be "converted." At the trial he presented numerous letters written "by the love of Jesus" &c. Some years afterwards we heard him preach in New York on "Christ and him crucified." We thought if he could only save men from stealing. we would not put a stone in his way, and left him undisturbed.

It happens sometimes that persons receive a statement through one medium, which afterwards appears to be corroborated through another. But this is not always proof. We have known some to be attended by a spirit or a band of spirits, who on coming in presence of a sensitive, would get a mere repetition of what had been said before. It is the same statement whether true or false, from the same controlling power, and not one a corroboration of the other.

The question is sometimes asked why some good, reliable mediums are always poor, while others no more sincere or reliable are liberally rewarded. The following answer to such a question asked by a person styling himself an earnest seeker after truth, from one of the higher intelligences gives an explanation.

A.—This earnest seeker after truth is as ignorant of the true philosophy of Spiritualism—of spiritual manifestations—as are the majority of these seekers, whether earnest, honest, or otherwise. They can't seem to rid themselves of the idea that the spirit-world is inhabited only by the pure and the good, when the fact is, it is inhabited by all classes of intelligence. The evil, the undeveloped spirit has just as much power, and, under many circumstances, more power to return than has the just, the well-developed spirit.

It should be understood that there is a law of chemical forces underlying all physical life, and acting through

physical life.   Jesus understood this when he said that
the poor should lose even that they had, but the rich
should continue to gain riches.   Now, it is a well understood scientific fact with us, that they who are able
to attract to themselves the riches of this world have
the attracting chemical power in their own physical composition, and they will be rich, in spire of all adverse
circumstances.   The poor have not this attracting power, and they will be poor, in spite of all fortunate circumstances.   The old adage, "Like attracts like," is
divinely and humanly true.   Those persons who are
poor, who are poorly supplied with the comforts of this
world, if they attract any spirits to them, it is likely to
be a class that correspond with them in physical condition, such as are unable to lead them into wealth.
There are various degrees of this chemical force, this
power of attracting wealth.   Some persons possess it
in a great degree.   Your countryman, George Pea-
body, possessed it to a very large extent.   He could
gain wealth almost with the turning of his hand.   Others possess it to a less extent.   Each one gains wealth
according to the attractive power that exists within his
own physical composition.   This is a scientific fact,
recognized in our life, which, by-and-by, the scientists
of earth will take up and prove.   Until then, it must
remain as a mere assertion on our part.   This "earnest
seeker after truth" tells us that he has a belief in an all-
wise and good God.   A belief in a good and perfect
God inspires faith in the manifestations of God in every
thing by which we are surrounded, in the inner or the
outer life.   If God takes note of and cares for the fall-

ing sparrow, to my mind, he will not forget to care for his poor as well as his rich. Jesus said to some of his friends, "The poor you will have with you always"— a sublime prophecy of the condition of Nature. There will always be poor; not that the earth does not furnish enough for all, but that the all-wise Spirit of Life, in organizing and making up these physical constitutions, has made them all to differ. The differences so existing, in some lead to poverty, in others lead to wealth; but the certainty of happiness at some condition of being the soul always understands. It is not the inner life that makes complaint against its Maker, but it is the outer life—the part that has been educated in the ignorance and folly of this life; while in the soul-life of every individual there is trust in God.

The radicalism of some of our speaking mediums is occasionally objected to, even by reformers. But we think it is good in its order, as the pioneer work. The heavy plough which tears up sods and roots is necessary to break up new ground for improved culture; then the seed can be sown for a better growth, and thus is preptation made for progress onward in this life, and its continuance in the next. In this work each should do his part: nor can every hindrance be at once removed; for all change and permanent growth is gradual. Some advise the entire rooting out of tares while the wheat is growing; but there is danger of both being destroyed together. The developed should assist the undeveloped to a higher and better condition of life, and when the sifting comes, there will be less of chaff to separate. The barrier of exclusiveness is not needed.   Truth and right will at last prevail.

Philanthrophic mediums would be glad to be in a condition to give seances free.   Some are so sensitive that when money is mentioned as a compensation, they shrink from it, and were it not that their necessities compel them to receive it, they would work for the cause with much more force and efficiency.   If they could be furnished with good dwellings and supported as teachers of Theology are, so as to be free from pecuniary trouble, the communications would be clearer and unmixed with individualisms.   Those with whom wealth is not the first object, will doubtless enjoy a higher reward in spirit-life.

It would be but just that a reasonable per centage of sitters should be allowed by the prosperous mediums an opportunity to receive communications from spirit friends free, as is the practice among physicians.   Unfortunate persons, even of liberal culture, who are destitute of pecuniary means, are deterred from seeking a message, for want of the two dollar fee.

Doubtless the record of individual earth life will be taken as the standard of merit or demerit in the future life, and that will determine each one's place in the order of progression.   Every act is daguerreotyped, and may be read with as much ease by the developed spirit, as if in a printed book, and sometimes this can be done by spirits in the earth form.   If this be true, oh Hypocrite ! what is your position ?

There is some intrinsic goodness in human nature, hence although bigotry stalks abroad, it is not every minister who is intolerant. We once heard a methodist minister in a western city say, after receiving magnetic treatment, that it would pay his society to employ a magnetizer to magnetize him, as they would get better sermons thereby. He called on the magnetizer the following day, and the subject of Spiritualism being mentioned, a lady present remarked that she had become convinced that her daughter then in the spirit world, could, when conditions were favorable, come back and communicate with her. She was a member of an evangelical church, and had some fear of endangering her standing therein. The language and sentiments of the communications were of such a high spiritual tone that the minister became quite interested, remarking "If that is Spiritualism let me have more of it, and if the church to which you belong objects to your remaining, for believing in such teachings, you can find a home in my church." Great numbers are precisely in this embarrassing position. Prejudice is so strong that they are afraid to express their convictions freely.

Still, liberty of conscience is gaining ground. Ministers called evangelical, sometimes preach as good spiritual discourses as we have heard from those who are the open advocates of Spiritualism. We have heard one of them say "We pity the soul that joins the church under religious excitement, as in revival meetings," and another when giving an invitation to partake of the "Lord's supper" remark that it was for those who felt the need of it, but as for himself, he considered it only a means to an end, and had outgrown it as a command.

Others are leading their congregations out of empty
forms into substance, and they embrace the spiritualistic
faith as rapidly as they are prepared to receive it. These
teachers think that by giving them food adapted to their
wants, they are accomplishing a greater work than if
they preached the whole truth. Each must be his own
judge of such matters. There is more proneness to
error in believing too much than too little.

True Spiritualists as a general fact, do not care so
much for money as for truth. Jesus taught simplicity
in dress, diet, and all external, worldly things. He
knew that money was good only for the supply of the
necessary means of support. Did he ever receive money for magnetic treatment? He worked for nothing
except what he had gained in spirit. He of course was
supported in his mission free of expense. His precept
was "As ye have freely received, freely give."

But it is not the part of wisdom to follow literally the
advice that we should take no thought for the morrow.
Mediums are not passed over Railroads free or at half-
fare, as are all grades of clergymen. They must pay
hotel bills and other unavoidable expenses; hence if
they have no fixed salary, and give their time to the
service, they must take fees, or give up the work.
Modest and unassuming ones have suffered by neglecting
to require reasonable compensation. What can a spirit from the land where material needs are no longer felt,
accomplish through a medium whose nervous system is
harrassed by anxiety to obtain means wherewith to pay
high rent, and indispensable food and raiment? Religious teachers, placed over churches have generally been

cared for, in these respects, and are at ease, which enables them to follow any line of thought untrammelled.

The wealthy Spiritualists have it in their power to do good by enabling mediums in needy circumstances to employ their gifts with much greater efficiency, by building hospitals for the sick in mind and soul, and asylums for other sufferers, as well as in other practical ways. If they could be aroused to active benevolence, using their surplus means for such noble ends, they would not lose their reward.

In regard to the grade of spirits which are attracted to investigators, we are satisfied that it depends very much upon themselves. If they have good aspirations they will attract to them spirits of an elevated order, and will progress to higher, happier and holier conditions. If they cater to the grosser and undeveloped spirits, allowing their organization to be used for base purposes, they will be degraded to a lower level, and are in danger of sinking, by perverse habits, to the depths of infamy. The law governing these things need not be mistaken, for it is uniform in its application and invariable.

There has been an indisposition on the part of scientific men to engage in the discussion of Spiritualism. This is due in part probably to the materialistic tendencies of some branches of Natural Science. Learning was for a long time under the exclusive control of the church, and even now there is a strong disposition on the part of theologians to control the institutions of learning, and the methods of culture. One extreme begets another, and when it comes to a choice between bowing to the authority of the church in matters of science, or rejecting her dictum altogether, the liberal-minded investigator discards her claims. Something is to be attributed to the misappropriation of terms, and the disposition to under-value attainments in science, on the part of many Spiritualists. Extravagance of assumption and the dragging in of side issues have driven away some who would have willingly inquired further. But religious bigotry has had more to do with it than any thing else.

It has however been admitted within the domain of science, and good, able and honest men have risked their reputation and pecuniary means in its investigation, and after arriving at favorable conclusions, by engaging in its advocacy.

When a person who has been distinguished in any way, speaks a strong word against Spiritualism, it is quoted by the stand-stills in triumph. They do not stop to consider the motive that has prompted it, so as to estimate fairly its value, which might result in its being worth nothing. At best it could but show that people differ ; as we might quote on the other side such names as Judge Edmonds, the jurist and advocate, Robert Dale Owen, the philosopher, statesman and diplomatist, Gov. Talmadge, Dr. John Piermont, the sage, poet and divine, Epes Sargent, Prof. Mapes, Elizabeth Barrett Browning, William and Mary Howitt, Baron Von Reichenbach, Mr. and Mrs. S. C. Hall, Anna Cora Mowatt, with a vast host of others, quite as distinguished.

Added to these names, we now have that of Von Fichte, the German philosopher, son of the celebrated author, and the compeer of Kant. The following copy of his letter is worth preserving.

My Dear Sir: Accept my warmest thanks for Hare's work, which, had you not sent it to me, would probably have escaped my notice. I made myself acquainted with its contents without delay, and can state the following as being my present impression in relation thereto.

As to its revelations concerning the world beyond, they seem to me to be of the highest importance, because they not only, at least for the most part harmonize with those which have been given by other spiritual seers, but because they are intrinsically reasonable, God-worthy and truly cheering. I myself have the greater reason to think them valuable, as they essentially agree with the principles of my own psychological investigation, which is entirely independent of them. I refer to that which is really essential and decisive, laying aside a great deal that is unessential in these "revelations," (such as the demonstration of the existence of spiritual spheres which are said to surround our planet, &c.) which may, I fear, furnish abundant material for doubt and ridicule to those who are unfavorably disposed.

As to my present position with regard to "Spiritualism," I had an opportunity last year of becoming acquainted with its phenomena and testing them repeatedly. This was through my personal acquaintance with Baron Guldenstubbe and his sister, who spent the winter of 1869-1870 at Stuttgardt, and who honored me with their full confidence. I have come to the conclusion that it is absolutely impossible to account for these phenomena, save by assuming the action of a superhuman influence; but that deception, credulous acceptance of worthless things, false interpretation of incidental matter—in a word, subjective admixtures are not wanting; on the contrary, that they often play a principal part, which obscures the value of the whole thing. In short, there is a great deal of chaff, and but little genuine grain in the thing, so that I have often become weary of attending such experiments, or of causing them to be made, although two excellent mediums were at my disposal after the departure of Guldenstubbe. I feel, however, deeply interested in the cause, for I am by no means unaware of its high importance, both in a religious and social point of view. I shall therefore be grateful to you if you will continue your communications, and I assure you and your worthy friend, Counselor Aksakow, of my most grateful appreciation of the indefatigable zeal with which you so perseveringly devote your powers to that cause.

Yours, with high respect,

J. H. VON FICHTE.

To Mr. Gregor Constantin Wittig, Breslau.

[Concerning the spheres above mentioned, the following extract from a communication may be regarded as a comment.]

The spirit-world is not in the form of a belt, but of a sphere; a spiritual planet in all respects, save spirituality, like your own. And yet you have the spirit-world amongst you—spirits who have never left the earth.

Millions of them are your guests daily. They live
here; they have their dwellings here; their attractions
are here; this is to them their spirit-world, and the first
sphere which every spirit occupies for a longer or short-
er time after death.

As a further indication of progress, it may not be
amiss to state that interesting accounts have been given
by three of the lecturers on Spiritualism within the last
year, of its spread in England, France, Italy, and some
parts of Asia, accompanied with names of prominent
persons who have ascertained the truth of its revelations
for themselves.

THE DOUBLE.

The "Double" is a curious spiritual phenomenon which
has recently attracted renewed attention. It consists of
the apparent presence of a person at a particular spot,
when it is known that that person was in another place
at the same moment of time. According to the testimony of patients who have undergone magnetic treatment, it is not an uncommon occurrence for them to see
their magnetizer, although many miles away, as distinctly as if he was present bodily. At the same time they
feel the effect of magnetization as perceptibly as if they
were touched by him. This takes place more readily
when the chain of sympathy is connected by a letter, or
any material substance. There is an account of cases
of this kind in the Banner of Light of Jany. 20. 1872.

When two persons are in rapport, the electric, magnetic or spiritual forces operate, and conditions being favorable, spirits still in earth-life, can visit others and produce effects as plainly as if they were tangible, and in the same way as they are produced by disembodied spirits. This has come within our own experience. There may be truth in the vulgar adage that "the devil is always near when he is spoken of." The spiritualistic presence of any one, in the body or out, may so impress the mind of some one concerned, as if present in the body, and clairvoyance affords confirmation.

An interesting fact is related concerning this phenomenon, in the personal experience of the late President Lincoln. Previous to the assassination, happening to look in a mirror, he saw not only the reflection of his own person, but a second object precisely similar. It struck him as ominous of some impending evil; yet he had no fear, and although a spiritualist, and having remarked at the time that he should not live to serve out his term of office; and notwithstanding his being forewarned by letters from mediums who had seen in prophetic vision some such terrible catastrophe, he took no precautionary measures for his own safety.

While alluding to Mr. L., we may further remark that he frequently held circles at the presidential mansion. Among the facts which occurred during his investigation was a remarkable test given him in New York. Visiting one of the test mediums, the spirit of a friend who had been sick in Illinois was announced. He said it could not be his friend, as he had but recently left him improving. On reaching his hotel, however, he received a telegram announcing the person's decease corresponding with the time of the manifestation.

Mr. Anderson, the spirit-artist, was employed by Mr. L. to draw or paint a picture. The artist was impelled to make a drawing of an Urn, tipped over on its side, which he said was all he could get, nor did he understand its meaning. It was construed to be a symbol of mourning.

The great conflagration at Chicago was prophesied by several mediums, some of whom were arrested on a charge of fortune-telling, and made to suffer persecution, because it was given them to foresee that which was so fearfully verified.

Louis Napoleon is said to have been similarly forewarned, and protected himself by the use of a bullet-proof breast-plate, which proved effectual when attacked.

Queen Victoria is a constant recipient of consolation from the spirit-world, through a medium in her household. Her excellent husband, the justly esteemed Prince Albert who communicates with her, was an earnest inquirer and a believer when here.

THE DARWINIAN THEORY.

Since the Mosaic account of creation has proved unsatisfactory to reason and common sense, the theory propounded by Darwin as to the origin of species has aroused a lively interest in thinking minds. It is a difficult subject, and requires more study than the majority of people can give to it. Indeed all such abstruse

themes will probably remain unsettled until the finite
mind can grasp the infinite. We are, however, much in-
debted to scientific students for the steps of progress
which have been taken.   History teaches us nothing beyond the fact that man in shape and intelligence was always very much as he is now, and what existed farther
back is only conjecture. It is interesting and instructive
to speculate about it, and sometimes the active thought of
a single human intellect makes an obscure subject plain.
We can with some degree of profit be witnesses of the
controversy going on between active and cultivated
minds, capable of discussing it.   The question whether
the egg or the chick, the seed or the plant was the first
in order of existence may sometime be solved, and so
whether such a change can be effected by culture in the
course of time, as to constitute new species.

With the highest culture thus far, distinct lines remain.   The sour crab may become a fine apple, but a
turnip remains specific.   Hybrids go no further than
the first step.   A horse cannot become a man, but it is
not impossible that the first bifurcation of the primitive
vertebrate may, by progressive development in one of
the two branches, carried to its ultimate, produce a
change no less wonderful in the origination of species.

RE-INCARNATION.

Another theory, still more curious has been advocated
by Allan Kardec and others, somewhat to the dismay
of the mass of Spiritualists, viz : that embraced in the

doctrine of re-incarnation. They teach that a spirit as an individual does not complete its term of life with what is ordinarily understood in physical birth, death, and entrance on spirit-life ; but that after a time, which may extend to thousands of years, it re-enters a body in embryo, living another ordinary term of human life in the body of the new infant through all the stages of growth to adult life, and perhaps old age, in a manner akin to the transfer of the soul from inferior animals to human beings according to the ancient doctrine of metempsychosis.

Believers in the teachings of Spiritualism do not doubt that some spirits are attracted to mortals in the infantile stage of life, becoming their guardians and continuing to act as such through earth-life. But this is simply control by another distinct and separate spirit, and not permanent possession of the new organization. Spirits, whether recently disembodied or those who have left the earth hundreds of years ago, as Jesus, Socrates, Demosthenes and many others come and communicate with individuals through suitable mediums ; but if they are thus controlling independently, they cannot at the same time be living another individual earthly life. There is a temporary incarnation of a spirit in taking possession of a body, and through it living out its incomplete life, being attracted to that body through peculiar chemical forces, gratifying its appetites, enjoying its pleasures and suffering disappointments : the person being conscious of such possession, and to some extent sympathising with that control by virtue of the similarity of chemical forces, feeling and acting in some measure like the controlling spirit. It is what is called obsession or possession, be it good or bad.

But imagine an exquisite musician, finely organized and cultivated, with intensely delicate touch, returning to earth, taking on infantile conditions again, being trained for and living a hard, practical, unartistic life during his second incarnation, completing it, passing on and returning again, seeking another embodiment in infantile conditions—not finding circumstances favorable, roams about, and so comes back three or four times in as many or fewer generations. The imagination may cause a person to personate anything. We knew a man who thought he was the embodiment of Jesus, yet was a frequenter of bar-rooms, and a smoker and chewer of tobacco, habits which we could not think Jesus indulged in while on earth, nor that he would be attracted to any one who gave way to their indulgence.

An elderly woman imagined herself to be the old "harlot" of the Bible, and conducted as that character might be supposed to act on earth. She believed that the representation of prophecy and its fulfilment was to be made through her, and that she must therefore act as she did. She had lived a respectable life, and hence was to be pitied and ought to have been cared for in some good psychopathic institution such as has been proposed by Prof. Mead. Such cases bear evidence of an unbalanced state of mind, and should be treated as such. If spirits come to do harm, they should be taught better, and treated as if they were yet in earth-form ; and the person approached by such a spirit, with temptation to evil, should summon courage to resist, saying "Get thee behind me, and lead me not into wrong-doing."

We can account for the peculiarities of many positive women and negative men, by their susceptibility to positive or negative spirits, who are attracted to them, some doubtless going back to ante-natal conditions through psychological power.

The doctrine of re-incarnation deprives us of our individuality, making us mere fragments, never complete, and destroys the hope of the future as effectually as if we were to lose our faith in immortality.

OBSESSION.

This subject has been treated of in "Vital Magnetic Cure." It is only necessary now to cite a few cases in illustration, and to add a word or two in support of the fact that obsession is a verity. There seems to be occasion for this, inasmuch as in a recent work it has been denied.

The difficulty in conceiving of such a condition as obsession arises from the idea of a special devil which entered into all the theological systems, now one after another passing away. The conduct of the person so afflicted was demoniac, as described in the New Testament, and as is often seen in cases occurring in our own time.

But it is a simple matter after all. Obsession, or as it is otherwise expressed, possession, is simply spirit control of a particular kind, and more persistently continued than control in general. Control is possession for the time being, and in this sense all mediumship is possession more or less complete. Its synonym (obsession) is more particularly associated with the demoniac idea, and therefore offensive : obsession then differs from other cases of control in quality and duration. A bad or undeveloped spirit holds the unfortunate person by a firm grasp, makes him conduct himself like one violently insane, and is indisposed to give up to the control.

In the biography of J. M. Peebles, there is an interesting account of a case and its cure ; and similar cases may be found in Mrs. Hardinge-Britten's Book.

The following occurred under our own observation. A man of considerable susceptibility to spirit-influence became a healing medium, but was unwilling to admit that Spiritualism had any thing to do with it. He wished to remain in the church to which he belonged, thinking that he could use the spiritual forces at the same time. Not long after he ran into the "affinity" channel, and was soon unbalanced. He resolved to go west, the second wife trying, but ineffectually, to dissuade him from it. She accompanied him to South Framingham, returning by next train, and leaving him to pursue his journey. Arriving in Brooklyn, his conduct was so strange as to attract public attention, an account of which was given in the papers. He wanted to hire the Police Station House for healing purposes, telling the officers that he had performed so many cures in Boston that the doctors were after him, and the New York doctors were working with them to kill him ; and that if he could get possession of the Station, he would send for Mr. Beecher and several other prominent persons, which would enable him to get up conditions to overpower the physicians. At his own earnest request, they took him to Court to see the Judge, who being occupied, he had to wait his opportunity. In a few minutes he ran down the street towards New York, where he was taken charge of and sent to an insane asylum. It seems to us that in his attempt to ride two horses, as the expression is, he was thrown. What he needed was magnetism to equalize the internal forces, and quiet him, which his wife succeeded in doing as soon as she arrived, taking him to Boston, where he was restored to his usual health.

We knew a lady who resided in Irving Place, New York, in affluent circumstances. She was of positive temperament. Becoming convinced of the truth of spirit communion, she visited a lady medium to whom she gave pecuniary aid, although strongly opposed by her husband. After his decease, trouble arose in the settlement of his affairs. She was his second wife, and had a legal interest in the property. An influence operating on her partially developed condition prompted her to commit acts of extravagance and indelicacy, disrobing herself at her window, and in other ways acting in a manner entirely opposite to her natural character. Spiritualistic friends who had her in charge never doubted her being acted upon by undeveloped spirits. She was always positive, and resisted magnetic treatment, seeming herself to know the law which governs, it making it necessary for a very powerful influence to be exerted to subdue her positive will. Her relatives and supposed friends placed her in an insane asylum in Massachusetts, where she probably is to-day. We believe such cases can be cured by adapted magnetism. Was she to blame? Jesus did not ask his patients why they were in such conditions as he found them, but used his strong psychological power to cure them. The spirit or spirits departed instantly. It is useless to use harsh treatment, and worse than useless to cry "humbug," for the unfriendly spirit cannot be exorcised by such means. When the affliction comes home to any one, by his relative or friend being thus attacked, which all are liable to, he regards the case very differently. The case must be dealt with in moderation, not ignoring the presence of the controlling spirits nor provoking wrath, but reasoning, appealing for the right, and using the counteracting power within reach.

Jesus recognized obsession, as we have seen. The cases he treated resembled insanity. The resemblance, occurring in connection with public interest awakened concerning Spiritualism, has given rise to the statement that the latter causes insanity. But is there any one thing, good or bad which when carried to excess, will not cause it? Various causes have been enumerated, which produce it, as disappointed love, domestic trouble, religious excitement, intemperance, and many others. We are informed by a recognized expert, who has made the subject a life study, that religious excitement stands second in the list of causes. The mind already disordered may be agitated by Spiritualism, when the community generally are interested in it, as it may by any other subject, but in such cases it is not a cause, but an incident. The main question, after obsession has been proved to exist, is how to effect a cure.

THE DREAD FUTURE.

The following is a synopsis of a funeral address, extracted from the Louisville Courier-Journal :

Philosophically speaking, there is no death—only change onward and upward forever. It is evidently impossible to find absolute rest in the universe. Motion is everywhere ; and change, by methods inverse and diverse, is a fixed law, ever evolving the more etherealized forms of life. Leaves are now falling from the maple, the oak and the elm ; friends are falling—all of your eyes have wept and hearts ached ere the present occasion. How true that man, the earthly man, "dieth and wasteth away."

Winter dies in northern latitudes that spring may carpet the earth in grasses and grains ; and man the immortal of man—that is, spirit—disenthralled from the physical organization, may traverse space and pass on in its path of destiny toward perfection.

Being knows no destruction. Annihilation is a meaningless term. The conservation of forces demonstrates this position. It is physically impossible for something to become nothing—all that was is, and eternally will be. Death, so called, is no enemy, but, natural and beautiful, it must precede immortal life, as must the acorn the oak, or the bud the opening flower. Stars that fade from our skies fade to illumine other portions of the sidereal heavens, and friends—our cherished friends that pass on through the valley of shadows, go to people the love-lands of immortality. They take with them consciousness, reason, memory, and their souls' holiest affections. Pure love is immortal. This true—our dear departed loving us still—they delight to project their thoughts earthward ; delight to impress us with the increasing beauties of their progressive existence ; delight in becoming to us what the facts of the nineteenth century demonstrate, the actuality of ministering spirits.

Churchmen joining hands with deists and atheists in denying present inspirations, revelations and communications from the spirit-world, generally entertain erroneous conceptions of death, speaking of it as a "tyrant," as "the king of terrors," and picturing it as a grim, bony skeleton, with scythe mercilessly mowing down humanity. And then, to intensify the horror, they will join in the Christian hymn, beginning with the words

"Hark ! from the tombs a doleful sound, &c."

Such hymns, with the accompanying theological dogmas—the resurrection of the body, the day of judgment and future endless hell torments— are the pitiable remnants of an imported paganism. The preaching of these and other unreasonable chimerical doctrines is filling the country with a scoffing infidelity.

To Spiritualists death is birth—the second birth into a higher state of existence. The body returns to earth, to reappear again only in grasses, flowers and forests. As well ask the oak to return to its acorn, the winged bird to return to the nest and re-inhabit the shell, as to ask an immortalized spirit to return to some gloomy graveyard and take on the dead, material body. "Flesh and blood cannot inherit the kingdom of God;" Paul further said, "We sow not the body which shall be." The body which shall be is the "spiritual body," and essential spirit is the life, the conscious intelligence of this spiritual body connecting mortals with immortals, and angels with God, who alone hath underived immortality.

All the popular religions of the day rest upon traditions. Spiritualism alone rests upon the basic foundation of present, tangible facts. It is the living witness of the future existence. Considered historically, it unites the past and present. Referring to the Bibles of all nations—and especially the Old and New Testaments—we see that immortalized beings held conscious communion with mortals for some four thousand years.

The following incident affords a beautiful illustration of spiritual re-union.

"I was greatly pleased," says Dr. Thomson "with an incident a mother gave me the other day. A child lay dying. Feeling unusual sensations, she said, 'Mamma, what is the matter with me?'

Mother.—'My child, you are dying.'

Child.—'Well mamma, what is dying?'

Mother.—'To you, dear it is going to heaven.'

Child.—'Where is heaven?'

Mother.—'It is where God is, and the angels, and the good men made perfect.'

Child.—'But, mamma, I am not acquainted with any of those, and do not like to go alone; won't you go with me?'

Mother.—'O,. Mary, I cannot. God has called you only ; not me, now.'

Turning to the father, she asked the same question. Then piteously to each of her brothers and sisters, she repeated the same interrogatory, and received the same response. She then fell into a gentle slumber, from which she awoke in a transport of joy, saying : 'You need not go with me ; I can go alone. I have been there, and grandmamma is there, and grandpapa is there, and Aunt Martha.'"

THE CO-RELATION OF SPIRITUAL AND PSYCHOLOGICAL PHENOMENA.

Magnetism, mesmerism, psychology and spiritualism sometimes get confounded. With the exception of the first, we consider them the same, with this exception : spiritualism deals with disembodied spirits, mesmerism and psychology with spirits either in or out of the body. We may liken magnetism and electricity to the ocean ; spiritualism, mesmerism and psychology as vessels sailing upon it. Both are essential to each other when sailing is to be done, but differ in quality and use. Spirits use magnetism and electricity as the vessel does water : as the captain directs the sailing, so the spirits control the minds of individuals.

Many persons possess this power ; some have exhibited it in public, of whom Sunderland, Grimes, Cutter, Stearns and Cadwell may be named. The object of most has been to amuse rather than instruct the public ;

and this they do by showing in a humorous manner, the control, more or less complete, which they have over the will and other mental faculties. This mode is not without its uses, though it would be better to consider at the same time, its relations to mental philosophy. Nearly all persons are familiar with the remarkable phenomena shown at one or other of these exhibitions.

Mesmerists are undoubtedly assisted by invisible spirits. They effect temporarily a complete subjugation of the will of the "subject," and are able to control the more susceptible ones at subsequent times with great facility; making them act as automatons reflecting the will of the operator.

It is a power that may be used for good or evil purposes—good in the hands of well disposed persons, evil if employed by the unprincipled and selfish. It exists in some in a remarkable degree. An example is found in St. Louis in the person of a man of eccentric habits. Many persons coming into his presence are immediately brought completely under his will, acting precisely as he desires. He lives a singular life; does not wash his person, comb his hair or sweep his rooms. It is said that he occupies one of two rooms alternately; remaining six months in one, then removing to the other, and returning in six months to the first, without cleansing either. Some of the most positive mediums on visiting him have been compelled to kneel at his feet. He does not claim to be a Spiritualist. The power thus displayed through this uncouth character is, however, the same. Each person attracts spirits of a peculiar kind, as a general rule, adapted to his own magnetism, wants or desires.   He may be elevated by holy aspirations, or sink below the level of pure morality to a state of almost hopeless degradation.   With himself rests the moral responsibility.

Congenital deformity is often the result of ante-natal impressions made upon the nervous system of the mother, who receives a shock from the sudden presentation of a revolting spectacle before her, influencing the development of the embryo.   In the case of extremely sensitive, mediumistic women, it may be classed among psychological phenomena.

The planchette excited the marvellousness of great numbers for a time, and is still an object of curiosity among those who have not paid attention to the facts of Spiritualism.   It is simply an indicator of mediumship, enabling the spirit to move the muscles of the arm for writing, with greater facility than the arm itself unsupported, and hence manifestations can be produced with less controlling power than is ordinarily required.   As to the truthfulness of the communications, they are precisely the same as those produced by other modes of control.

This, and the publication of such books as "Gates ajar" and "Hedged in," are steps of progress towards Spiritualism, directing the mind to its higher truths and philosophy.

ORGANIZATION.

Spiritualists have generally lacked cohesiveness ; consequently they have never been able to unite, with a concentration of energy upon practical plans of reform. Coming out from all sorts of religious organizations, where they had been constantly trammelled by creeds, and restricted in the expression of opinion and freedom of action, their emancipation from the thraldom and restraint of authority has had a tendency to set some afloat on the sea of life without anchor. Others who have embraced the faith were always free, and their habits of independence have in a measure disqualified them for co-operation.

Numerous attempts have been made at different times to effect an organization, both local and general, which have thus far been unsuccessful. They have gone through the ordinary formalities necessary to assume an orderly shape, declaring principle, adopting a preamble and resolutions, and not the least important, appointing officers ; have moved on zealously in their way, but their active existence has lasted for a short time only. For some reason or other, the interest felt in the movement has abated, no useful purpose has been accomplished, and their constitution, declaration or whatever formed the bond of union has become a dead letter. We have long been convinced that it is impracticable to attempt to unite upon any compact plan, such as those which bind together, and render so formidable for oppression, some of the religious organizations. A movement of this kind does not seem to be any part of the mission of Spiritualism; but its plan is to operate by natural methods, without sudden convulsions, its principles and gospel being made to penetrate the minds and hearts of the entire human family, in and out of specific organizations, silently but effectually, as the leaven is gradually infused through the mass.

A legal organization for receiving and dispensing bequests according to the will of the giver, to collect and disburse funds for charitable and educational purposes, is necessary and proper.

An agreement is had among all the Spiritualists in the nation upon the one grand fact of spirit communion; but beyond this, it has been the general understanding, that they should agree to disagree.

Upon questions of general politics, they must necessarily differ. Through sectional prejudice, they were found to differ upon points of national policy, even when the life of the nation was in danger. Upon other issues, such as woman suffrage, the social question (so called,) labor reform and like topics, they cannot altogether agree. Each party may be as sincere as the other; and recognizing the right of individual opinion, each must pay proper respect to the candid opinions of the other, and thus their respective methods of reform may be divergent, though the expectation may be that they will all reach the same result.

In practical works of humanity, it is desirable that there should be decided unanimity and hearty co-operation; but here there is also diversity of opinion as to details.

Where an organization has been entered into for the reform of a public evil, irrespective of creed, Spiritualists may co-operate with such organization without bringing it into spiritualistic movements as a side issue.

Some organizations called spiritualistic have not fairly represented either the cause or its believers and advocates. Thus at the late national convention, so little was said about Spiritualism, and so much upon other subjects, that a stranger reading one part of the proceedings would have supposed it to be a body of persons convened for the purpose of holding a discussion in the interests of woman suffrage; and reading another would have thought it a medical convention, little dreaming that the beautiful philosophy of Spiritualism was the ostensible attraction which had brought the speakers together.

We are of opinion that if conventions were discontinued, and the money expended upon them, devoted to the publication and distribution of liberal tracts, broadcast over the land, much more good would be done. Schemes to gratify personal ambition should not be tolerated among Spiritualists who endeavor zealously to discourage and defeat it among others. A united effort in proper directions would tend more rapidly to establish Spiritualism as the Universal Religion of the whole human family.

CIVIL AND SOCIAL RIGHTS.

EQUAL RIGHTS AND WOMAN SUFFRAGE.

There are several practical questions involving human rights, which ought not to be passed over, inasmuch as Spiritualism teaches practical duties, and its whole tendency is to the amelioration of the condition of the human race. It denies the right of any one to exercise absolute authority over another, but that equality of rights is inherent, and therefore should be maintained. Equality of rights embraces the exercise of suffrage by woman as well as man.

One of the main arguments adduced against allowing women the exercise of the elective franchise has been based upon the opposition of Paul to woman's independence. But the signs of the times indicate a liberalizing influence at work even in the churches in this direction. In the columns of the "Congregationalist" of Jany 25, 1871, a letter appeared in favor of this movement, from a lady, whose object was to show that the harsh expressions of Paul applied only to the ignorant women of his time. This explanation if accepted by the followers of Paul, will remove an obstacle that has been formidable, because the prejudice has been so extensively rooted. Women in the churches will by this change feel free to accept any position, and act in any capacity for which their talents and acquirements have rendered them capable.

Where they have had a fair opportunity, their capability to fill places of trust and responsibility has been proved. Certain occupations are better suited to the female sex, while others are to males ; but no exact line can be drawn. Fragility of constitution in men, and robustness in women, make exceptions to the rule, as it applies to manual labor. Statesmanship has not been regarded as a function of women, at least by ambitious politicians, yet many of them are in every way fitted for such a sphere. Certain branches of mercantile and mechanical business can be carried on by women, though generally they are men's work. But the whole subject is now so familiar to the public mind, that we need not occupy space by repeating the arguments that have been brought forward in a discussion that has been exhaustive.

Equality of rights is a principle of justice, and should be accorded to all without opposition, irrespective of sex, color or race. "Taxation without representation" was complained of in revolutionary times, and is equally unjust to-day. Equal privileges as a principle, is defended in the Constitution, but by a want of consistency, limited in its application.

Qualification in the exercise of the elective franchise has not been required in any reasonable manner. A property qualification disfranchises every person who has been unfortunate, however capable or patriotic, while every successful knave, albeit an ignoramus or a traitor, is guaranteed the right. If any test at all is adopted, it should be that of intelligence, with reasonable length of residence, in the case of foreigners to give fair opportunity for them to appreciate questions affecting the general welfare.

There is no safe-guard against corruption in politics, but moral training. This is now sadly needed to retrieve the disgrace into which recent terrible revelations in New-York, and elsewhere have precipitated us. Let spiritualists set the example.

FREE LOVE.

This has proved to be a painfully alarming topic, and has brought more reproach upon Spiritualism than any other subject that has been agitated. Spiritualists have been charged with encouraging unbridled license, and teaching it as a right. But it is proper to state in the outset, that whatever meaning may be attached to the expression "Free Love," or whatever perversion of good morals may result from its use or mis-use, Spiritualism is not responsible therefor. It has no more connection with Spiritual Philosophy than with Protestantism or Roman Catholicism, but has sprung up independently of them all.

The charge alluded to, whether true or false, has been extensively made, and has impeded the progress of Spiritualism among the lovers of a pure morality. That it has been practised in its most revolting aspect, by persons known as spiritualists is doubtless true, as has

also been the case among others who have made no pre-
tension to the name. Not only this, but there are persons ranked as Spiritualists who pretend to teach the art
of love; others in cities who so far disregard common
decency as to advertise nostrums called love powders,
making the nefarious traffic a source of gain. With the
morally corrupt, it is an individual affair: and their
culpability is not to be excused or palliated because of
belief in Spiritualism, real or pretended, or of good
standing in church membership.

This is not the occasion for a dissertation on Love,
nor Freedom. Both in their highest sense are admirable
terms. Love is of all the affections, the most elevated,
the purest and the best. Freedom is one of the most
precious of human rights. By a subtle dexterity they
may be combined, making the curious phrase Free Love,
with more than their original meaning, though the com-
bination is claimed to retain only the pure qualities of
both. Whether Love is a sentiment, quality or affection which it is possible to bind, we need not now stop
to consider.

The Free Love which has been thrust upon Spiritualists as a precept is not new, and its practice is by no
means new in the world. Some years ago a couple
went to a western city to propagate the doctrine among
the Spiritualists, with a good deal of pretentiousness.
It was accepted by some unsuspicious, well-meaning
people, but finding that they could not be allowed the
leadership in the movements of Spiritualists, the mis-
sionaries left and at length went over to the Catholic
Church. In their short peregrination however; they did

not fail to sow seed from which bitter fruit was reaped, emphatically to the "disgrace" as a recent writer expresses it, of the cause, to which it had adhered as a parisitic growth.

When a peculiar doctrine is preached to a new audience, it is not unreasonable for the listeners to inquire who preaches it ; for there is sound sense in the old adage that "a man is known by the company he keeps."

We heard a strong advocate of the doctrine, who was formerly a methodist, say that he believed in it to the fullest extent. He claimed to be a leader, is a married man, and it is also well known that he spends but half of his time with his family, and the remainder with his free-love affinities. Being well versed in Bible history, he brings up the practice of King Solomon and David, as examples worthy of imitation.

A person living in New Jersey, but whose base of operations is in New York, who is a firm believer in free-love on the passional order, with but little of the spiritual has great seductive power. His method of charming is as wily as that of the serpent, and his success in carrying out his doctrine so marked that it has been necessary to expose his machinations in the public prints, that the unsophisticated might escape. He boasts of his subtle power. His manner is cool, collected, business-like, and as gentlemanly as if he had been brought up in the best society. His first step is to supply the material wants of each new victim, if in need, and after gaining confidence, the ultimate object is easily accomplished. He then disappears. In one instance we knew of the sad results of a cunningly devised scheme, carried out with as much zeal and apparent sincerity as any true lover could have used in the prosecution of an honorable suit, but too late for retributive justice to be secured. So shrewdly was his scheme managed, that it disarmed suspicion, until the bird had flown, and sadness came over the victim.

Another case may be cited. A music teacher left his wife and two children in the State of New York, in company with a lady of some degree of culture, who had been led to adopt the theory of affinity, and went to the west. After a time he left her for another field of adventure. She followed him. They retraced their steps together as far as the middle station of their wanderings. A child was born, and both abandoned for a new affinity, viz : the sister of the second choice. At first it was avowed that the acquaintance was only of the Platonic kind—love in freedom—between two intellectual friends ; but of course the intimacy increased and intensified, and a child was born ; the first choice (wife) and the second (affinity) being left to shift for themselves. A second, third and fourth child was born of No. 3. All died. In the meantime, the free-lover wrote to the discarded ones, asking them to come and live with him. This being indignantly refused, No. 3. was finally deserted, and went to live in the family of a noted free-lover as a house servant, with all hope of true domestic life blasted.

These are examples of the practice of individuals who were advocates of free-love. One of them, our informant in the case cited states, openly contended for the right of all to follow their instincts, and taught the purity of instinct in the love relation. His practice is all the comment that his theory requires.

Many persons quote passages from the Old Testament, showing the customs which prevailed in the patriarchal age, in justification of their own deeds. But if this is to be the guide, the absolute requirements of the Jewish law, with its pains and penalties is equally binding, and obedience to it should be exacted from them.

In the New Testament, much is said concerning love, the term being used in the sense of charity, and connected with Godliness. Love to God is enjoined, and Paul exhorts his brethren to love one another, and to let brotherly love continue. Love to the neighbor is commanded as a duty. But nowhere is the "free" variety spoken of except in terms of condemnation.

The quality of love depends upon its object, and with reasoning and morally responsible beings, upon the motive which awakens, modifies or chastens it. In refinement and degree it will also correspond with the character of the person cherishing it, from the base, passional, unrestrained animal instinct, to that pure, virtuous attachment, under the control of the intellect and the higher moral sentiments. We have the parental, divided into paternal and maternal, the fraternal, the filial, the love of friends, or friendship, the sensual, selfish or passional, the conjugal, mistaken sometimes for sensual, the love of country or patriotism, the feeling of humanity, or philanthrophy, or love and sympathy for our fellow-beings. But it is difficult to find a logical connection between love in its holiest sense, and freedom, when freedom is made to mean that we may do as we please.

Pure, unselfish love must in its very nature be free and spontaneous. If otherwise, it would cease to exist.

Human nature, notwithstanding its intrinsic goodness, is mingled with imperfection; and to follow instinct is to abandon the controlling power of intellect and morals. Restraint for the limitation of criminal profligacy, (for it cannot be entirely prevented,) by the embodiment of that controlling power in human law, is necessary for the protection of the weak. If all men and women were angels so pure as to be a law unto themselves, there would be no need of restriction in the love relations nor any other. All human laws would cease to be necessary, and would come to an end. Who are so angelic as to be fit for our teachers in such a matter? Are they the modest, unselfish, self-denying, charitable sort of people?

The loose manner in which some of the would-be leaders treat the subject, reminds us of the drifting of a rudderless vessel at sea, without Captain or Pilot.

Take away the marriage code, and the opprobrium which has attached to prostitution goes with it. A writer who appreciates the dangerous tendency of the indiscriminate teaching of this fascinating freedom very properly remarks in a late letter to the R. P. Journal, "I do not believe that anything deserving the name of love ever did, or ever can dictate a marriage, that will be legitimate only for a night. We will have an idea what can, and what does, dictate numerous such marriages, but I cannot attend upon its new baptism, nor consent to this unchristening."

Within the aura which surrounds each individual,

doubtless the subtle attractive power exists. Any one possessing this power in a marked degree, coming in presence of the opposite sex, will wield a perceptible influence, and the other be the subject of that influence.

The negative will to a greater or less extent, be controlled by, and for the time being live in the sphere of the positive, sometimes being spell-bound. The effect may be called psychological, magnetic, spiritual, or as some say elective affinity. It is governed by a law as are other psychic phenomena. The power varies in quality with the individual, and as we have already seen, is potent for good or ill, according to the moral and physical status of its possessor. Like fire, water or electricity, if properly managed, in safe and skilful hands, it will produce good effects. One person will be a willing subject, another cannot resist. We have known persons who could not separate themselves from the sphere of the fascination, until a powerful magnetizer was employed to break the spell, by changing the chemical forces.

The changeling may have as many affinities as he desires, but these are not lasting; they are not conjugal. In time, and the period is generally short, the power diminishes, the attraction ceases, and new subjects are sought. There are, without-doubt, true soul affinities which are lasting; if there were none, the true union of souls, and the domestic happiness resulting would be banished from hearth and home.

MARRIAGE.

It is scarcely possible for a line of demarcation to be drawn between the practical bearings of free-love, just considered, and those of marriage. The same questions apply to both. Some however relate to marriage, which have not been included in the other; but we continue the discussion very much as if all were in common. With the immense experience in the marriage relation, which has been accumulated in the world, it would seem as if no question could have been better settled; yet from the widely divergent opinions to which utterance has been given, based upon the most contradictory testimony, it appears on the other hand, to be one of the most unsettled.

The false aspect in which the subject must necessarily be viewed by parties outside, renders them incompetent to judge of it. Such persons give their opinions, however, with all the assurance of veterans. The happily and unhappily married, the divorced, the absconding, the neglectful, the pure-minded, the sufferers, and even young unmarried women have their advice to give. And this is to be had free, and also for a good fee.

The result of all is that marriage can be made the happiest or the most miserable social condition. It is no new lesson; all young persons, in any degree observant, on the verge of maturity, have learned so much. And so they have hope and precaution about equally balanced.

Nature demands the union of the sexes to carry out her economy, and so the wise and the foolish are ready to make the venture.

Marriage is consummated from a variety of motives, in as many different cases ; from the purest, holiest, and most unselfish, to the meanest. Some are brought about under psychological or magnetic influence, with which conjugal love has nothing to do. This perishes with the decadence of the charm.

One party circumvents the other, practising fraud upon an unsuspecting nature. Among the rich, and in high life, it is not unfrequently a direct bargain and sale of virtue, with as little scruple as can be found in the lowest depths of prostitution. Hence comes the heart-burnings and breakings when the fraud becomes apparent, and the base motive is stripped of its falsity, and laid bare in all its hideousness.

When the motive on the part of both is true and honorable, disappointment is liable to follow, from an exaggeration of the beatific expectations. The man thinks he has secured an angel, which insures a blissful life in the future. The maiden has selected or accepted the choicest of nature's noblemen. Contact with the asperities of life dims the bright prospect, and the less thoughtful and considerate will be tempted to criminate the innocent life partner, and thus bickerings begin. This subject was so ably treated in a recent discourse by Rev. John Weiss, that it ought to be in every one's hands.

Marriage for a home is but a modified commercial transaction ; those of expendency, convenience, or position have less excuse, but have no claim to the sanction of heavenly blessing. If one or other has a prospect of a rich inheritance, and a well developed physique, the prize is eagerly sought.

Parents sometimes become mercenary, and urge marriage upon their children because of its eligibility, although there may be a total want of adaptation between the parties. Where there is a preponderance of one sex in numbers, persons contract marriage more hastily than if the sexes were nearly equal. Girls sometimes accept the first offer, lest they should lose the opportunity.

When the marriage is fruitful, the children form a bond of union, which keeps the parties together, even when serious misunderstandings occur. It cannot be expected that any two persons will be able to see all things alike. Difference of temperament, social training, and religious education, will cause them to look from different standpoints. But where there is a disposition to harmonize, it will prevent bickerings. If such an anomaly could be found as two persons being in all things alike, they would be fossilized and unable to progress, presenting a tedious monotony. Variety gives beauty, as in the varied hues of flowers in a bouquet.

It has been a question whether the sexual relation would continue in the future life. We have heard a person say that he anticipated more then than it was possible to enjoy in this life, in this respect, but to us it indicated his unspiritual character. It is said that in heaven they neither marry, nor are given in marriage.

Spirits may affect those in the earth-form psychologically, by continuing on the earth plane. But it is well
known that in this life, the more spiritually minded a
person is, the less active are the animal instincts. From
this and the fact that the physiological function is no
longer needed, it is reasonable to conclude that the desire ceases. We are never taught that children are born
in spirit life.

With reference to the continuance of marriage in the
future life, we regard it as a unity of spirit, which will
remain perhaps forever, or until outgrown by progression. Spiritual beings are not perfect. The ties which
bind them on earth, cease with earth life. In spirit life,
all are free to select congenial elements and conditions.

It has been asserted that the exercise of the sexual
function is a necessity beyond the propagation of the
species, and that we should learn from animals how to
improve the race. Over-indulgence is detrimental to
health; indeed thousands are constantly being pre-
maturely destroyed by it. Abstemiousness is not incompatible with health, as we see in the life of domestic
animals. Improvement by selection in the propagation
of domestic animals is by direction of the mind of man.
Physiology teaches the laws which should be observed
to secure the highest physical development, and to prevent the transmission of diseased and imperfect qualities.
Not only is the highest health thus attainable, but in the
same ratio, the best moral culture.

The spontaneous attachment which is awakened, may
originate with the female as well as the male. But its
expression by the woman has been very unreasonably

objected to on the ground of indelicacy. When the impulse is sincere, and guided by an honorable motive, and the fortunate object of such affection is an honorable man, worthy of it, we can see no impropriety in her making a proposal of marriage. It will require no more courage on her part than it often does in the case of men. She is intuitive in her nature, and thereby enabled to select a partner in every proper way adapted to her spiritual needs. •

Intuitive perception, psychometry and the opening of spiritual sight, are valuable aids in detecting deception, and want of adaptation, the practical use of which will be perceived in the selection of partners whose conditions are congenial.

In the "Vital Magnetic Cure" this subject is treated of in its psychological and magnetic phases.

The practice of polygamy destroys the equality of the sexes, and affects the rights of unmarried males, who must of necessity remain in celibacy, by the disproportion of women remaining unmarried. If man has a right to a plurality of wives, woman has an equal right to a plurality of husbands.

There are a few questions which, in summing up, each individual may answer.

1. Is not a monogamic marriage the most natural, the happiest, and hence the most desirable condition of social and domestic life?

2. Would parents like their children, of either sex to indulge in promiscuity, before or after marriage, as

some of the bold Free-love advocates teach and practise, with no law for protection or interference?

3. Is there no need of human law to control those who are not developed to such a condition as to be able to control themselves?

4. Why try to reform prostitutes if freedom of the love passion will develop a higher order of morality?

5. Is it not a fact that nearly all of those who advocate the abolition of marriage laws are persons who have been unfortunate in the selection of partners, resulting in domestic unhappiness; and does not the primary cause exist in the individual, rather than in the operation of law?

6. Is not the value of judgment in such persons diminished in the premises, rather than rendered reliable as to what constitutes true sexual union?

7. Do not the mistakes which have occurred show the necessity of a more general diffusion of physiological knowledge, as a means of prevention of future mistakes?

8 Are not self-knowledge and the culture of the higher faculties of the soul indispensable to a correct understanding of the marriage relations?

DIVORCE.

The great prevalence of inharmony in married life has agitated the public mind to a serious extent, and the only remedy for the evil which the majority of minds have considered efficient is divorce. There is a fearful responsibility in resorting to such a radical measure. To justify it, there should be positive proof that the cause is utterly hopeless of compromise and cure.

Incompatibility of temper discovered after marriage, is a cause of a vast amount of domestic unhappiness, whether depending upon difference of temperament, or habitually yielding to outbursts of passion; but if the unfortunate possessor of it is not absolutely insane, and there is a disposition to do right, we question its incurability. A mutual effort to bear and forbear will gradually mould and adapt to each other, dispositions which at first may seem to be incompatible. Depravity must be very great, which would compel a separation, especially where there are children, until every reasonable effort to repair the mischief has been exhausted.

The worst causes of domestic unhappiness are not those enumerated in divorce laws, for the silent sufferer keeps the knowledge of them hidden in his or her sorrowing heart. There are flagrant offenses sufficiently grave, which cannot be kept from public observation, and which if not repented of, and restitution made, deserve divorce.

After having tried in vain to restore harmony, and it is evident that the mis-mated pair cannot endure each other's society, come the terms of separation. It is better then that the settlement of affairs should be submitted to arbitration, rather than that private disagreements should be brought into Court, and made public, to the scandal of both parties. If this again fails through obstinacy on either side, the final and unavoidable necessity of resorting to a legal tribunal must be had. But to whatever tribunal the adjudication is submitted, it should be composed in part of women, as suggested by Mr. Weiss. The justice of this suggestion will be apparent to every well-meaning person. Where woman's interests are concerned, either as aggressor or aggrieved, the sympathy, the appreciation of equality of right, and even-handed justice, can be secured only by her being represented, and in part adjudged by her own sex.

In framing a divorce law, its terms should not only afford relief to cases which now need its provisions, but it should be prospective in its operation, so as to prevent some of the marriages which would be entered into by unscrupulous adventurers. For example a proper cause of divorce being proved, the property which has been held by the one party, which constituted the attraction in the eyes of the other, should revert to the original owner, after suitable provision has been made for children. But if the possessor of wealth also has the positive power, using the attraction to bring about a marriage of convenience, and afterwards chooses practically to annul it, from a capricious fancy, the partner thus chosen should be fairly compensated by a division of the property.

Laws have embraced various causes as sufficient ground of divorce, such as wilful neglect and abandonment for a certain length of time, habitual intoxication and brutal treatment, infidelity to the conjugal relation, and some have held incompatibility of temper to be sufficient, while in one State, the law has been so accommodating to the dissatisfied as to allow divorce for any cause satisfactory to the judge. This last opens the door for corruption, and unfortunately we have too much evidence that judges, selected from among educated men, for supposed impartiality, are not invulnerable when approached by interested, scheming politicians with a consideration.

The division of property accumulated by the joint industry of the contending parties should be in accordance with the principles of justice, based upon the evidence which may be adduced.

In regard to the subsequent care of children, a decision would be in some cases difficult. It would depend upon the evidence, which of the parties should be intrusted with so responsible a duty.

COMMUNISM.

Community of property has been advocated by some as a doctrine of spiritualism, and hence needs a passing notice. As an abstract theory, it is a very agreeable source of consolation to the unfortunate who have failed, notwithstanding the most faithful industry and honesty, to accumulate a fair proportion of this world's goods. As a fundamental principle in the great Fourier movement, which enlisted the sympathy of many benevolent men, a quarter of a century ago, it was full of humanity, and intended to be a fair and just practical measure. It seemed as if the millenium was approaching, when the hard workers in both physical and mental fields of labor, would be allowed an equal share of the fruits of their industry, instead of much the larger share being appropriated by mere capitalists and drones. The principle of association, recommended itself to all by the promised fruits, in the form of privileges and enjoyments, which could not by any possibility under the isolated and selfish system, be obtained by the masses. But notwithstanding the co-operation of intellect and philanthropy with practical thought and active industry, the experiment failed at last.

It has been effectually carried out among the Shakers, and by some other societies, whose bond of union embraced some particular religious creed. These have become entirely independent of the world in respect to property, and enjoy all physical comforts, with freedom from that worst of all sources of anxiety, pecuniary embarrassment.

So long as the competitive system obtains, which in business affairs is too much like every man's hand being lifted against his neighbor, it is practically impossible to secure equality of compensation for equal services.

In the present state of the world's activity in business competition, if a division were made to day, the equilibrium would scarcely last till to-morrow, so unequal is production and consumption. Hence it is regarded by practical minds as utopian. It is unquestionably impracticable to-day, but when selfishness shall be superceded by the mutual helpfulness of a universal brotherhood, the obstacle will be removed.

The argument against an attempt to equalize the distribution of property is that it would be injurious to the interests of the human family by taking away ambition, responsibility, and aspiration, making life a monotony; and if all persons in the earth sphere had wealth, and the resulting ease, comfort, and pleasure, there would be no progress; while as it now is, the world makes progress, notwithstanding all opposing obstacles.

A bed of ease, and relief from the struggle to obtain the means for material support is pleasant to contemplate, but in such a life there is no impetus to exertion for active usefulness. Many of those now wealthy have acquired it through long continued struggle with adversity; while many who were born in affluence know not the value of money, and have become spendthrifts and profligates.

Successful, enterprising merchants are not necessarily dishonest or unjust. Their energetic activity is needed in the world. It is true that rapid accumulation by appropriating the proceeds of others' labor is too common, and there are too many questionable ways for sudden enrichment. We know persons who do not own a dollar's worth of property, who have no skill to accumulate, and who scarcely know where to get the next meal, yet have been benefactors of mankind. Of such are inventors, who scarcely ever receive any reward for their contributions to the worlds' convenience and comfort, but pave the way for great profit for others. Such also are the martyrs in most benevolent undertakings.

It is a blessed hope that looks forward to a juster life in the spirit-world where dollars have no further use, and at last worth will make the man.

We find the following paragraph in point: "After all is said, I still believe that whatever is, is essential, and in the end an even balance will be struck between all men—no one to have any advantage of the other, but the experience of one is relatively the experience of all. The millionaire must be a pauper some day, and vice versa. At all events I do not see the necessity of troubling ourselves about this apparent inequality, as we cannot make the rich divide with the poor, and we all know that an equal division of property is impossible, and even if possible, there would be no equality unless there was a division every hour. To-day some men are richer in log-cabins than others in palaces, and would not exchange places. Millions might make some men happy, but would make others miserable. Diogenes in his tub was gratified and satisfied, and the only thing the wealthy and willing prince could do for him, was to "stand out of my sunlight," to use his own words, for the philosopher would not accept of any other favor when offered him. He was superior to all material accumulations and conveniences, sublimely satisfied to simply exist, and after all he was the millioniare, and possessed that which money cannot buy, supreme contentment, and a philosophy to comprehend the true value of all earthly possessions.

There is something radically wrong in the operation of methods of accumulation, as compared with ordinary industry. Enormous salaries operate unjustly, inasmuch as no person, however well trained in any one line of service or usefulness, can give to the world more than the service of one person.

Stock-gambling sometimes yields large sums with

nothing more employed than an unenviable talent, but instead of its being an advantage to the world, some one or more individuals are direct losers by the transaction.

The accumulation of millions in the hands of one person, diminishes the number of property owners, impoverishes the industrious toilers, and concentrates power in to the hands of the few, who can use it for the building up of aristocracy, and the restriction of the common liberty, when so disposed.

But we cannot treat this subject at sufficient length to show all its bearings. Individual right to property, in whatever way it may have been obtained, so that it is held in accordance with the forms of law, is guaranteed by all governments. How to equalize it is a difficult problem to solve, and requires the clearest heads, and the noblest, unselfish hearts. Certainly it is not the right way to arouse the jealousy of a badly educated, although ill-paid multitude, by revolutionary harangues, to the subversion of good order. The co-operation of active industry perseveringly carried on, will gradually and quietly overcome the evil.

To prevent the accumulation of enormous fortunes in the hands of the few, who thereby absorb the proceeds of the labor of the many, a sliding scale of taxation with an increasing ratio in proportion to the amount of the income is a just measure, the poor of course being exempt. An income tax, it is true, is complained of by those who receive large incomes, because the desire of accumulation becomes morbidly active, when the best energies of the soul are directed to plans for that purpose ; even when a liberal exemption is made, sufficient for reasonable needs. The poor, as human beings are entitled to more of the comforts of life, and more educational advantages than they get. And if the precepts of justice are instilled into the minds of the more fortunate, by plans of education which train the moral faculties as well as the intellect, mutual rights will be secured, selfishness will be overcome, and all can work together harmoniously for the common good.

PART IV.

RELIGIOUS ASPECTS AND RELATIONS OF SPIRITUALISM.

COMMENTS ON RELIGIOUS ORGANIZATIONS.

The religious aspects of Spiritualism, in view of the great commotion caused in the religious world by its teachings, the upturning, indeed, of dogmatic theology by the light of its revelations, merits some consideration at our hands, before the task which we have undertaken can be completed. A short critical sketch of the more prominent denominations, more particularly as regards their relations to Spiritualism, and their treatment of the subject and its believers, will therefore be in place.

This must, of course, be but·a partial sketch, for it would be a literary feat to even enumerate the vast variety of sects now existing in the world, and an almost endless task to point out their distinctive peculiarities, great and small.

It is a remarkable fact that teachers of religion, occupying pulpits, from which they can say what they please, without the inconvenience of their utterances being questioned or controverted on the spot, and but little danger of criticism from their hearers subsequently, should object to a truth stated in their own teachings, because additional proof of it is given in some other way. Now it has not been an uncommon thing for preachers to declare that departed friends, come from their heavenly home, and hover about us, affording us consolation in trouble, and impress the hearts and minds of the kindred whom they have left behind, with evidence in their continued love and sympathy. Have they been sincere in this, meaning just what they said; or have they been hypocritical? Have they merely indulged in flights of fancy, when speaking of a sacred subject, and thus trifled with the sorrows of the bereaved sufferers of their audience? If their words were not mere sounds, and they believed there was a reality in the presence of a loving friend in spiritual form, so near to individuals, directly within their personal sphere, as to enable them to feel an affectionate response to their longings, why do they fly off in a tangent when they are told that what they have said is true, for here is the proof by circumstances which have tested it.

But they say, "this proof that you bring us in the shape of a kindly greeting from a beloved one, is a deception. It is not your dear relative, but the devil in disguise who has been assuming the character of another for the purpose of beguiling you." To such the answer may be given "Then it must have been the devil you spoke of in the pulpit, when you uttered tender words of comfort, and you must have been executing the devil's commission when you represented that those dear spirits were hovering about the bereaved on earth, to relieve the burden of their sorrowing hearts.

Between the Jewish religion, which had its origin many centuries ago, and the Christian religion founded by Jesus and Paul, there is a wide difference, as regards the Deity. The former believe in one God, who is essentially their God, and they his favored people, in contra-distinction to neighboring nations. Many Israelites in modern times have become liberalized, so that they can fraternize with the Free Religionists. They consistently retain the seventh day as the sabbath. Jesus did not claim to be God, but his followers in the latter days claimed for him God-like rank and power.

There is a wide distinction between the Roman Catholic branch of the Christian church and the numerous sub-divisions of the Protestant branch. All believe Jesus to be God—part of a triune God, as they term it —co-equal with the Father, if such an idea can be conceived of by the mind. They shroud it in mystery, but require human beings with reasoning powers, to believe it without understanding it. This belief, together with belief in the further dogmas of a personal devil, the great adversary of God and man, a local Heaven with streets paved with gold, shut in by gates, a throne whereon the three Gods, three in one, and one in three sit, surrounded by saints with harps in their hands, singing psalms perpetually ; a local Hell where the vast majority of God's children are to burn and suffer in torments forever, are doctrines common to most of them.

"What !" exclaims one, "our Father, the Jehovah of

the Universe, the Infinite God sacrifice his Son to ap-
pease his own wrath and vengeance—it is a reproach to
the character of Deity, and a libel on common sense.
Shame should crimson the cheek of all those who profess to believe in a God of love and mercy, and then
attribute such an action to him!"

Total depravity is a concomitant doctrine. It is necessary that a nature depraved beyond description should
be proved, in order to justify the necessity of peopling
a place of indescribable and endless torment. It requires
a blind and unreasoning faith to accept such a doctrine,
but if there is a human being on the face of the earth
who believes absolutely that a beneficent father could
originate such a system of rewards and punishments,
and the fear of endless torture in a burning hell will be
the means of his refraining from evil and doing a soli-
tary good deed, let him hug his idol, until he can learn
to do right for the sake of right. This slavish fear is
unquestionably losing its hold upon the minds of thinking men and women. This mental slavery reminds us
of a circumstance which occurred in New Jersey some
years ago. Travelling with one of the pioneers in Spiritualism, we came in sight of a dark stone church with
a square belfry. Said he "that is a prison." We thought
it a church. "No" he added, "a prison for the soul."
It looked doleful, and its dismal aspect has haunted us
almost ever since. The progress of free thought has
effected an improvement both in the external architec-
ture of such buildings, and the inner arrangements.
The boxes like sheep pens have been replaced by open
pews or slips, with a more friendly look, although it is

taken advantage of to note the prevailing fashions, and gossip about the appearance of strangers.

The Catholics, in addition to these, attach a divine character to the mother of Jesus, in the doctrine of immaculate conception ; and claim supreme anthority over the church militant, which, as their name imports is universal—a curious universality with a local prefix. They anathematize every one who is not in the bosom of their church, and teach that eternal perdition is the doom of all who choose to remain outside of its pale.

The conflict of church authority with persons exercising the healing power independently of it, is sometimes exhibited in an arbitrary manner. In July 1868 the sexton of a church in Saratoga, while digging a grave for the interment of a person who died of sunstroke was himself sun-struck, and removed to his house in a cold and unconscious state. The priest, as is customary, and two physicians were sent for. A magnetizer passing in the meantime was called in. By his manipulations the man began to revive. Reaction was so strong that it required two men to hold him. The priest and physicians arriving, the magnetizer left. Croton oil was applied to irritate the surface. In a few weeks he was restored, but we think it might have been done in as many hours. Three years afterwards the magnetizer called again, and although friends were invited in to see the person who had done so much towards her husband's restoration, the wife ignored the "power," as her religion strictly forbade its use. In reply to the statement that her husband's life had been preserved, she said God cured him first, and the physicians afterwards.

The various Christian sects have their foundation laid virtually in spiritualistic facts. In the Catholic church what is the supposed protection of a patron saint, and the interposition of saints with the supreme ruler of the Universe but an acknowledgement of communication between them and the suppliants here?

All the Protestant sects acknowledge all that Spiritualists contend for, as regards ancient times. They differ so far as denying their continuance down to the present day, but in their pulpit declarations above referred to, they are essentially the same. They deny and affirm as the essential truth, or the support of a formal dogma may require them to do.

The Swedenborgians are theoretically the most spiritual of all denominations, but like other sects who claim to have the pure gospel, they think they alone have true spiritual revelations, and that all others teach a false spiritualism. The founder of their sect was a seer, and received communications from the spirit-world. He taught the personality of God, in human form, and claimed to have seen and talked with the Lord. He had some eccentricities, and his followers are exceedingly illiberal toward believers in the modern spiritual phenomena, exhibiting in this way inconsistency and intolerance. They set a plate on the table for the departed friend, in recognition of the spiritual presence, yet they will not allow that friend to communicate with them through a medium, lest they should entertain a deceiver. Some go so far as to compare spiritual communications to the diffusion of poison.

Furthermore, while they term the exercise of gifts by

others the work of the devil, they are willing to call upon such for their healing power in time of affliction.
Some in all denominations are equally inconsistent.

We have found this people well-to-do, and genial,
but inactive as far as entering a protest against, or
adopting measures to reform the errors of the day. As
regards the success of such movements, the denomination might be blotted out and no loss felt. It is comfortable to slide along easily in this world, but no advance
would be made, if we had none but fair-weather christians.

What is called the Protestant Episcopal church, the
State religion in England, is a modified Catholicism.
Its ritual is beautifully framed, but a dead formalism.
To hear the humble and penitent responses intoned by
grandiloquent persons in the highest style of fashion is
a solemn farce. Yet there are sincere and good people
who follow the routine because their fathers did.

The Quakers or "Friends," both Orthodox and Hick-
site, are a spiritual people, who go on the even tenor
of their way, speaking and acting as the spirit moves
them. . They are humane and generally tolerant. Many
have fully accepted the truths of the modern revelations.

The Shakers are more decidedly mediumistic, and have
had communications even before they became general.
Ann Lee, their great leader and founder, is regarded with
as much veneration as Jesus is by Christians. They
are pure-minded, self-denying and honest. We think
they lose much in discarding the beautiful in art, and if
their idea of celibacy was carried out, the world would

before another century, become depopulated. It is their conscientious conviction, however, that self-denial in this respect is essential to holiness of life.

The Second Adventists are now of two sorts, one taking the seventh, and the other the first day as the especially holy day. Originating with the preaching of Miller, they believe in the destruction of the world at an early day, and their literal ascension to heaven. Different days have been set for this event, but the world has continued to turn upon its axis. They are generally bitter opponents of Spiritualism, attributing its phenomena to the devil, though one of the sub-divisions has its medium, through whom spiritual manifestations are received. She has been regarded as a prophetess among them, and has written a great quantity of manuscript. They claim that the cure of diseases has followed prayer. A case of cancer was undertaken which proved obstinate, but by renewed devotion it disappeared. Her husband is the Elder. The ceremonies simply placed her in a state of receptivity, so that healing power could be exerted through her.

The faith of the Adventists is mixed with a little worldly wisdom. Some of them in Miller's time sold their property and took good care to get the money for it before their balloons were inflated for the trip to heaven. Recently an enthusiastic member published a small pamphlet explaining Daniel's vision, which is sold at ten cents a copy. He took the precaution to get a copy right, thus having an eye to business. We do not know whether or not he anticipates inter-mundane benefits from it.

About twenty years ago a farmer near Boston got ready to go up higher in Miller's company, and had visions, seeing from one to seven angels at a time. One day he stood in the road looking upwards, his feet remaining in one position, but his face turning with the sun, a woman who expected a remarkable revelation through him, standing by and wiping his eyes all day. He saw a spot, about ten feet square, with four corners, as John saw in Revelations with angels standing at the four "corners" of the earth.

They are patient waiters, or they might be tempted to think that the Lord, as of old, had put a lying spirit into the mouths of the prophets.

The Methodists were originally mediumistic, and more enthusiastic in their devotions than now. Fashion has crept in among them, so that but few retain the primitive character of the sect. Although they preach love to God, inflammatory appeals, based on the fear of an endless hell, are still made at their camp meetings.

These spasmodic gatherings, where the psychological power of bold, enthusiastic and fanatical declaimers is exercised over persons susceptible to magnetic attraction, chiefly females, are sometimes serious in their consequences, by the havoc they make in unbalancing the mind, temporarily or permanently. The subjects are readily brought under the control of boisterous spirits, who cause them to commit extravagances of which, in their sober moments, they are heartily ashamed. Not long since, a young woman in Rhode Island, after a high pressure conversion, entered the pulpit, and seizing the minister by the nape of the neck. called him very

hard names.   Since then she has been quite insane.
We have already quoted the fact that religious excitement is the second in degree among the most prolific
exciting causes of insanity.

Jealousy has been manifested among the various denominations on such occasions.   The projectors and
managers, as a matter of course, expect to reap the benefit for their own particular denomination.   But converted sinners must have the liberty to go where they will,
and so there must be a division of spoils, no one denomination appropriating the benefit.

We witnessed a conversion.   A young lady brought
up as a Universalist, who had always lived a good life,
attended a revival meeting, and "found Jesus."   She
was excited; life was full of delight; for four days she
talked about it incessantly.   Friends became surfeited
with the new manifestation.   She was sent to Boston to
enjoy it with friends of like persuasion; but she was
no more contented than among sinners.   She was told
that the devil was trying to overpower her; she must
give up to Jesus.   Her wailings becoming intolerable,
a magnetizer was called in, and with the magnetic influence of one visit, she was tranquilized, the psychological power broken, and she was restored to her former
condition.   She married and is now happily situated.

The Unitarians, Free Religionists and Universalists,
in common with Spiritualists, believe in the final salvation of the whole human family, without reference to
creeds.   They do not in all cases fraternize with each
other.   We regard the system of the first as Spiritualism with the spirit left out.   The conservative portion

seem to be getting fossilized. Some Unitarians and Universalists call their denominations "twin sisters." Many Free Religionists are also Spiritualists : those who are not, treat others with liberality and courtesy. The Universalists seem to be retrograding. If they would more freely co-operate with Spiritualists in reformatory and progressive measures, their usefulness would be much increased.

The Congregationalists, on the other hand, are getting liberalized. Some of their ministers preach Spiritualism, using the inspirational power given them, to the general acceptance of their people. Those among them who set aside creeds and dogmas, and speak "as the spirit giveth utterance" are infusing among the masses the germs of an improved life and character. Some who are recipients of spirit power get perplexed with the antagonism of their previous sectarian predilections. There is no remedy for them but to accept the light of natural truth in all its fulness.

The Rev. Dr. Hall of this denomination has taken the alarm, and published in a recent number of the N. Y. Ledger, a one-sided article, cautioning persons against the dangerous tendency of investigation of the subject. Like many others, he admits the phenomena, which he classes with Mesmerism and Magnetism, quoting the first report of the French Commission in 1784, but in a spirit of unfairness omits to mention the second, containing the results of five years' experiment and inquiry, published in 1826. He cautions his readers against associating such phenomena with the world of spirits ; but why this caution, if spirits do not or cannot communi-

cate? He sees harm in explaining the scripture cases of
the cure of disease by natural law, rather than by miraculous power.

Of the peculiarities of the Mormons, none is of particular consequence but polygamy. This is a selfish, de-
basing institution, entirely in opposition to equality of
right, and spiritual order; and destructive of happiness
to most of the female victims. Yet they quote the
practice of the Bible heroes, such as Solomon and David. Their argument is good—if the latter were right,
the former must be also: but no one need quote the de-
basing, lecherous practices of the wise king, nor the
man after God's own heart as precedents for decency in
domestic life.

Indian worship is spiritual. They worship the "great
spirit;" many of the manifestations witnessed among
the civilized occur among them. They have intuitive
perceptions of truth, and believe in a future life, as indicated in their burial ceremonies and in other ways. If
they had been humanely and honestly treated by the cultured white race, less brutality would have come to
light, and greater spiritual progress would have been
made for the benefit of both.

In every country village, there are from two to four
different societies, each employing a minister to preach
the same doctrines, as far as relates to what are called
essentials. They differ upon non-essentials, such as
baptism, close communion, free grace, and many really
minor distinctions. But when we hear a Baptist preach
upon the institution, one would think there is no possibility of salvation without it. Each sect has its building

called a church or meeting house, costing a sum of money to erect and keep in order. Now if the extra peculiarities were trimmed down to what each one considers the absolute essentials, would it not be a great economy to let one person preach for all, giving a better compensation than is now paid to each in detail, and appropriate the surplus, now utterly wasted, for the relief of the poor and other works of charity, and mental improvement.

Spiritualism, in the sense of sectarianism, is not a religion, yet it is one practically. Its adherents claim it to be the religion of the divine humanity. It has no general organization, with a specific bond of union, because, by common consent, every individual is allowed independence of opinion. Being classed by sectarians as a sect, we may allude to it in connection with the foregoing items. Nearly all the points of interest have been already stated in previous pages.

It has no creed, nor is its teaching dogmatical; neither is it on the other hand negative. It has definite characteristics. It rejects the fearful theories of old theology; but teaches man's responsibility for every act and word. If a law is transgressed, the penalty of its infringement is inevitable. There is no such thing as compromise. It rejects the idea of vicarious atonement, as a theory which makes man cowardly and unjust, and represents God as vindictive and cruel, destroying faith in his wisdom and fatherhood.

Its platform is world-wide; its philosophy comprehends faith in the infinite plans of the Divine ruler, the redemption of all human beings from sin and sorrow and the progressive development of all towards perfection.

It furnishes a key wherewith to unlock the doors which have closed the chambers of mystery. What has been enveloped in uncertainty is now positive, and what was hidden is now brought to light. Human life here with its imperfect adjustment of rewards and punishments has been to many, an enigma. Now we can see that it is an imperfect development, which another sphere of existence will complete.

Immortality has never been satisfactorily settled in the minds of students of the Natural Sciences. Gradual development was seen in all the kingdoms of Nature, but the spiritual was unseen. Theologians taught that hope, or at all events desire, afforded proof. It may be admitted that this innate longing was presumptive proof. The scriptures teach that only a certain class attain to immortality, and not that it is the inheritance of all. But now we have the proof which from being audible, has become visible and tangible, so that instead of saying "I hope" we may with all assurance say "I know."

Its progress is steadily onward. Whatever hindrance it has met with, has been more from treacherous enemies within than from foes without.

Opposition, because of the innovation which has been made upon the prerogatives of privileged orders or individuals, is precisely the same as all new and valuable discoveries have met. Their evangelists have had to suffer ignominy and ostracism; as history shows in a marked degree with reference to Astronomy. Incredulity beat back progress in the applications of Steam and Electricity ; and thus the conservative opposition has dealt with all who have been instrumental in opening the way to a knowledge of the life beyond the tomb ; even to the extent of pronouncing them insane, as the enemies of Jesus did eighteen centuries ago.

There is a point of difference, concerning the use of arbitrary power, which should not be passed over. It has not unfrequently been declared from the pulpit, that when affliction of a particular kind has befallen a family, as in the loss of one who was especially beloved for amiable, virtuous and other excellent qualities, it is a punishment inflicted by God upon the survivors. A passage is quoted containing a self-contradiction, to the effect that the Lord chastens those whom he loves. A beautiful little child who has been doatingly beloved by its mother, is suddenly removed. God punishes the mother, it is said, for idolizing the child. If the mortal life is destroyed outright, the child itself, entering its heavenly abode, has no physical suffering ; but some go farther and say that sickness and suffering is brought upon the child, although not to a fatal issue, in order to punish the mother. To a spiritualist, this is nothing less than diabolical.

With reference to prayer it is not held that the supplications of any individual are answered by the interposition of what is called a special providence. There is no change in the operation of any natural law ; for all such laws are immutable. God was the same yesterday as he is to-day, and will so remain forever. Everything is in its order, and nothing can be changed by a special plea. The act of prayer is, however, one of aspiration; and the frame of mind in which the petitioner must be, is a condition of receptivity, and is good for the soul. If it were possible to get answers to all prayers, it could only be when the being implored was like a vacillating pendulum, now having one purpose, and again another, directly opposite. Nor could some of them be allowed without inhumanity—indeed positive wickedness. Prayer to merit an answer should be consistent with divine law.

This part of the subject may be summed up in the following eloquent passage, which the reader may have heard from the lips of one of our best speakers :

"Spiritualism is a religion—the religion of the divine humanity; it comes to prove how beautiful and holy should be our affections, and not how groveling and licentious; it comes to show the stern, strict rule of morality—a law of right more absolute and potential than any that has yet been eliminated; it comes to show that the glory of our intellectual achievements is nothing, so long as we stand baffled by the very power by which we investigate our own mind.

"This is the religion which Spiritualism has come to teach us, and as long as we can thus interpret it, I do believe it has come to us, in this day, as our savior. It has come to save us from the darkness of atheism and the grossness of materialism; to teach us to make every hour an hour of worship, and every act of our lives an act of prayer; to prove to us the presence of ministering angels, and the existence, nearness and care of a better world, to prove to us the divinity that is within us, and to give us a conclusive assurance that though clouds may rise, and stormy oceans roll, there is an ever-living and deathless tablet within us, upon which the law of life and eternity is inscribed; there is an altar upon which the fires of inspiration shall never be quenched—and that is in our own spirits, instructed by the spirits that have gone on before—the full revelation of which will preach to us the religion of the divine humanity."

SPIRITUALISM IN THE BIBLE.

There is no book extant, which contains more satisfactory proof of Spiritualistic phenomena than the Bible. The events therein recorded were given from time to time, in a gradual manner, extending over a period of more than four thousand years. One revelation is said to have been given to Adam, and one to Noah: Abraham, Isaac and Jacob; Samuel, David and others also received them. Those of each age, received that which belonged to them and their time, and nothing more; and so it has continued down to the present time.

The most remarkable medium of whom we have any historical account is Jesus, whose whole life was characterized by spiritual manifestations. Before he was begotten, his mother was foretold of his birth. An angel or spirit, informed Joseph concerning him. Soon after his birth, angels announced his advent to some shepherds. While he was an infant, a spirit gave warning to Joseph, to flee with him into Egypt, in order to escape Herod's wrath. After the death of Herod, an angel came to Joseph and stated that he could return in safety.   After his baptism there came a voice from heaven, (a spirit) saying, "this is my beloved son in whom I am well pleased;" angels came and ministered unto him.   Moses and Elias came and held intercourse with him. Who are they but human spirits? An angel came to him in the garden to strengthen him, shortly before his arrest, as Luke informs us. Matthew says he taught the doctrine of special providence, by the interposition of angels; declared that guardian spirits were assigned to little children, also that he could pray to the Father, and that he would presently give him more than twelve legions of angels.

At his physical death his spirit rose out of his dead material body, and he manifested himself by form and voice.   He made frequent manifestations of himself to his disciples, and Paul declares "that he was seen of above five hundred brethren at once." - He showed himself to Mary Magdalene, and the other Mary.   He showed himself alive to the apostles after his passion by many infallible proofs, being seen of them forty days, and speaking of the things pertaining to the kingdom of God.   The Pharisees said of Jesus "This fellow doth not cast out demons, but by Beelzebub, the prince of the demons."   Jesus was not only surrounded and assisted by angels in the peformance of his wonderful works; but he asserted that he was a medium for God the Father, and that the Father communicated through him directly.   "The words that I speak unto you, I speak not of myself, but the Father that doeth the works."

Jesus also had physical manifestations. At one time it is stated that he walked upon the waters and did not sink. The Bible also gives an account of an axe floating upon the water.

In Exodus we read "I send an angel before thee, to keep thee in the way, and bring thee into the place which I have prepared." In Numbers, "The Lord sent fiery serpents among the people, and much people of Israel died;" then the Lord said to Moses "Make thee a fiery serpent, and set it upon a pole ; and it shall come to pass that every one that is bitten, when he looketh upon it shall live ;" which was fulfilled. In the same book we are told that an angel would have slain Balaam, if his ass had not saved him by speaking. If a humble animal like this was selected as the mouth-piece of the Lord, can a human being in modern times be degraded, when controlled by a higher power to speak? Balaam prophesied the happiness of Israel, and concerning the star of Jacob. Again, "Moses spake unto the Lord, saying, 'Let the Lord, the God of all flesh set a man over the congregation.'" * * "Take thee Joshua the son of Nun, a man in whom is the spirit, and lay thine hand upon him." An angel rebuked the people at Bochim (Judges ch. ii.) In I. Samuel, it is stated that Saul put away those who had familiar spirits, and wizards out of the land, and then plead with the woman to call up the spirits, promising when detected by the clear vision of the medium, not to harm her, if she would yield to the influence of the spirits. After calling up the spirit of Samuel, he consulted him on his future prospects. Saul was satisfied of the truth of

Spiritualism in his day, as he recognized Samuel at once by the description of the seeing medium.

In other portions of the Old Testament there are numerous indications of spirit influence. Solomon has two visions; Jehu prophesies against Baasha; Ahab is seduced by false prophets and is slain; Isaiah has a vision, and the birth of the future child Jesus, was supposed to be foretold; an angel slays the Assyrians; Sennacherib's destruction is prophesied; Jeremiah also prophesied evils, the utter ruin of the Jews, and a hard seige; the restoration of the scattered flock; the seventy years' captivity; he prophesied against Edom etc. Hananiah prophesied falsely; one of the prophets was imprisoned for so doing.

Exekiel (ch. ii.) says "Then the spirit entered into me, and set me upon my feet, and spake with me." What is this but mediumship? A famine was foretold; visions were seen, women exercised their gifts as prophetesses; Ezekiel spoke in prophecy against Jerusalem. In the same book sighing is mentioned as an emotion of the prophet, and in a symbolical way. The sigh is one of the most common physical circumstances in the experiences of mediums now, when taking on another's condition. Nebuchadnezzar forgot his dream: it was revealed to Daniel, with the interpretation. Daniel's vision was interpreted by Gabriel. So now mediums have visions which other mediums interpret. Daniel was comforted by an angel, as are modern mediums.

Amos, a herdsman, was told to go and prophesy unto the people of Israel; Micah spoke of false prophets; an angel sent to measure Jerusalem foretold its flourishing condition ; at one time it was purged of unclean spirits.

The Apocrypha is filled with prophecy, and other spiritual manifestations. We read "For the good angel will keep him company, and his journey will be prosperous, and he shall return safe," and similar passages. After a communication had been given, it continues "Then she made an end of weeping," thus exhibiting confidence in the spirit, whose communication had moved the hearer to tears. He tells them that he was an angel, and was seen no more.

In the New Testament, we have much more proof that spirits held converse with earth's inhabitants. The angel of the Lord descended from heaven, and came and rolled back the stone from the door, and sat upon it. His countenance was like lightening, and his raiment white as snow, and for fear of him the keepers did shake, and became as dead men ; and the angel answered and said unto the women, Fear not ye : for I know that ye seek Jesus that was crucified. He is not here : for he is risen, as he said ; Come see the place where the Lord lay ; and go quickly and tell his disciples that he is risen from the dead. And they departed quickly from the sepulchre with fear and great joy ; and did run to bring his disciples word."

And as they went to tell the disciples, behold Jesus met them, saying, All hail ! and they came and held him by the feet and worshipped him. Some doubted that spirits could return after the change called death.

Jesus had great inner perception and clear sight. By his psychometric power he could read the lives of persons as clearly as if from a book, and divine their mo-

tives.   When eating the passover he said "Verily I say
unto you, one of you that eateth with me shall betray
me." They began to be sorrowful. (See Matt. ch.
xxvi.)   He told the woman at the well, facts concerning
her social relations.   On his reminding her that she had
several husbands, she went away and reported that he
was God.   Spiritual clairvoyants and psychometrists
state to their visitors not only the number of their wives,
but point out their associates, and reveal what they had
supposed to be the secrets of their lives.

Jesus "walked not after the flesh but after the spirit,"
and religious teachers exhort us to take him as our ex-
emplar, yet in these days, if any one speaks of walking
after, or according to the spirit, they call it by an unholy name, and caution their parishioners against it.

Paul saw that his brethren did not fully appreciate
spiritual gifts.   He spoke to them as "unto carnal," and
not spiritual persons.   He considered them as babes,
which had to be fed with milk and not with meat.   He
speaks also of being absent in the body, but present in
spirit.   It seems therefore that he was a believer in the
appearance of the "double."

It is stated that "the spirits of the prophets, are subject to the prophets." In another place it is asked "Are
ye so foolish, having begun in the spirit, are ye now
made perfect in the flesh?"   Falling back into the do-
minion of the passions was a fault among the christians,
as it has been the fault of ministers and mediums in modern times.

The following passages contain good precepts : "If
we live in the spirit, let us also walk in the spirit;"

"Despise not prophesying;" "quench not the spirit;" "Prove all things, hold fast that which is good." Paul prophesies that in the latter times some shall depart from the faith, giving heed to seducing spirits and doctrine of devils; speaking lies in hypocrisy, having their conscience seared with a hot iron, forbidding to marry, and commanding to abstain from meats. He says "neglect not the gift that is in thee, which was given by prophecy, with the laying on of the hands of the presbytery."

Paul's belief underwent a change while on earth, which clearly shows that his knowledge was not perfect, and when partially initiated into the spiritual philosophy, he could realize his imperfection, and so go on towards a perfect state of knowledge and wisdom.

Peter admonishes his hearers of the gifts and promises, and foretells the destruction of false teachers. He says, "try the spirits by the Catholic faith." Jude foretells the punishment of certain false teachers. John was commanded to write to the angels of the church. He has a vision, wherein the four angels are loosed.

St. John, called the divine, is said to have seen in vision, angels of different grades of knowledge. In one place he says "And I John saw these things, and heard them, and when I had heard and seen them, I fell down to worship before the feet of the angel, which showed me these things. Then saith he unto me, See thou do it not, for I am thy fellow-servant, and of thy brethren the prophets, and of them which keep the sayings of this book: worship god. And he saith unto me, Seal not the saying of the prophecy of this book, for the time is at hand." Afterwards he says "Neither add too nor

diminish from the prophecy." Here is an apparent
contradiction. The passages may be compared with
I. Kings ch. xxii. v. 21,22. The angel did not make
the vision clear, hence much contention, misunderstand-
ing, and opposing argument has been caused among
many who regard the Bible as an infallible book, to be
accepted as authority for all generations and ages.

In a part of this vision, four angels are described as
standing on the four "corners" of the earth, making its
form square. The angel who showed John the scenes
of the vision handed him a book, saying "Take it and
eat it up; and it shall make thy belly bitter, but it
shall be in thy mouth sweet as honey." Modern mediums have sometimes been ridiculed for their enigmatical
visions, but it would be difficult to find anything more
fantastic than this, and other strange figurative passages with which the vision abounds.

We have not fully quoted the passages in reference
to gifts, as these have been already embraced in the
pages of "Vital Magnetic Cure."

CONCLUSION.

We have endeavored to place in consecutive order, the facts which have been developed in reference to Spiritualism, and the various arguments which have been adduced, first against its claims to the merit of a truthful natural revelation, and secondly, those in its support, leaving the reader to compare them, and deduce his conclusions in all fairness. The unwise conduct and conversation of neither set of controversialists have been concealed, but openly stated, so that the subject itself might stand upon its own merits, unaffected by the individualism of its advocates or opponents.

It was found necessary to abridge certain portions in order to keep within the limits assigned for the book.

The scriptural portion is submitted, for the same reason, almost without comment, though there are passages which need amplification.

The reader having before him both sides, can study

the facts, the phenomena and the philosophy of the subject, and by exercising his reason in the premises, arrive at a just conclusion, independently of all authority. Whatever will stand the test of fair criticism may be allowed to stand, and be placed among the annals of scientific and religious truth. Whatever fails to pass this ordeal should be discarded as dross.

"Let truth and falsehood grapple; whoever knew truth to be put to the worse in a free and open encounter."

VITAL MAGNETIC CURE.

AN EXPOSITION OF VITAL MAGNETISM;

AND ITS APPLICATION TO THE TREATMENT OF MENTAL AND PHYSICAL DISEASE.

BY A MAGNETIC PHYSICIAN.

A more useful book for the student or family cannot well be found. It is selling well, and gives satisfaction. It is a work that will not lose its interest in an age.—BANNER OF LIGHT.

There can be no doubt of the general and eager interest everywhere manifest in the infant science of vital magnetism. No skepticism opposes the facts slowly brought forward concerning it. Gratifying as the book is in both manner and matter, its glimpses and hints do scarcely more than whet the spirit of inquiry to know more.—WOMAN'S JOURNAL.

I am much pleased with it; consider it a very useful book, and one that the public need.—MRS. CAROLINE COBB.

This book deals with a subject that will grow strongly in favor when rightly presented,—since the tendency is to the disuse of medicines, so far as can be, in the treatment of disease.—SO. BOSTON INQUIRER.

This is an interesting book, and contains useful hints in regard to health and sickness, so far as they refer to human beings and human agencies.—BOSTON INVESTIGATOR.

It contains much valuable information for the general reader. —AM. SPIRITUALIST.

Its high moral tone must be an additional recommendation of the work. That the human magnetic force, when properly understood and applied, is a powerful curative agent; especially in all nervous complaints, is now too well established to be denied—and the writer of Vital Magnetic Cure, by an array of facts in his experience and that of others, has greatly helped to strengthen if not to settle the fact of its utility, both for the preservation of health and the removal of disease.—DAVID PLUMB.

A very valuable work, entitled as above, which deserves to be widely read, if not for the stand taken by the author in favor of a somewhat questionable remedial agent certainly, however, for the many suggestions he throws out respecting the preservation of health. The time will come when it will be better known, and we therefore commend just such books as the one now spoken of, because they will at least familiarize people with that thing which will some day be better understood.—MILFORD JOURNAL.

I have read during the last ten years nearly everything published on the application of Magnetism to the cure of disease, and I deem this work an important addition to the literature of the subject, and of great practical value to every one who would learn how to successfully use this most efficient sanative agency. W. F. EVANS M. D. Author of Mental Cure.

First edition exhausted in a few weeks.

For sale by BY Wm. WHITE & Co. PRICE $1 50. Postage 20c.

THE MENTAL CURE.

ILLUSTRATING THE INFLUENCE OF THE MIND ON THE BODY, BOTH IN HEALTH AND DISEASE,

AND THE PSYCHOLOGICAL METHOD OF TREATMENT.

By REV. W. F. EVANS.

This book has created a lively interest, not only among spiritualists, but in the minds of members of the medical profession, and among persons of various religious denominations. It is an able treatise, and should be in the library of every thinking person, sick or well. It has received the enconiums of able critics. A reviewer in the Banner of Light says :

"For originality of thought and treatment, for a certain intrepid directness which is the chief merit of a treatise of this character, and for a plain practicalness that commends its broad and profound truths, together with its more acute and intricate speculations, to the general readers, we think this volume will take its place at once among the remarkable productions of the day, and vindicate its reputation by the marked revolution it will set on foot in reference to common life and thinking."

"Along with this discussion, he sets forth the mode of regulating the intellectual and affectional nature of the invalid, under any system of medical treatment."

This is one of the best books we have on our shelves.—R. P. JOURNAL.

Table of contents annexed. About 1500 copies of first edition sold. A second edition to be issued soon. 364 pp. For sale by Wm. White & Co. Publishers, 158 Washington St. Boston. N. Y. Agents, The American News Company, 119 Nassau St. Price $1.50. Postage 20c.

CONTENTS.

CHAPTER I.

THE RELATION OF THE HUMAN MIND TO GOD.

CHAPTER II.

THE MIND IMMATERIAL, BUT SUBSTANTIAL.

CHAPTER III.

ON THE FORM OF THE MIND.

CHAPTER IV.

THE DIVISION OF THE MIND INTO TWO DEPART-MENTS.

CHAPTER V.

THE RELATION OF THE INTELLECT TO THE LOVE.

CHAPTER XII.

THE HEART AND LUNGS, AND THEIR RELATION TO THE LOVE AND INTELLECT.

CHAPTER XIII.

CORRESPONDENCE OF THE STOMACH AND THE MIND.

CHAPTER XIV.

THE REFLEX INFLUENCE OF THE STOMACH UPON THE MIND.

CHAPTER XV.

EXCRETIONS OF THE BODY AND THE MIND, AND THEIR RELATION.

CHAPTER XVI.

THE SKIN. ITS CONNECTION WITH THE INTER-NAL ORGANS, AND CORRESPONDENCE WITH THE MIND.

CHAPTER XVII.

THE SENSES. THEIR CORRESPONDENCE, AND INDEPENDENT OR SPIRITUAL ACTION.

CHAPTER XVIII.

THE MYSTERY OF LIFE EXPLAINED.

CHAPTER XXI.

THE MIND NOT LIMITED BY SPACE IN THE TRANSMISSION OF PSYCHOLOGICAL AND SANATIVE INFLUENCES.

CHAPTER XXII.

APPETITES, INTUITIONS AND IMPRESSIONS, AND THEIR USE.

CHAPTER XXIII.

THE SANATIVE POWER OF WORDS.

CHAPTER XXIV.

THE RELATION OF MENTAL FORCE TO PHYSIC-
AL STRENGTH AND HOW TO CURE GENERAL
DEBILITY.

CHAPTER XXV.

SLEEP AS A MENTAL STATE, ITS HYGIENIC VALUE, AND HOW TO INDUCE IT.

CHAPTER XXVI.

THE WILL-CURE, ACTIVE AND PASSIVE.

CHAPTER XXVII.

THE INFLUENCE OF THE SPIRITUAL WORLD UPON MENTAL HEALTH AND DISEASE.

www.ingramcontent.com/pod-product-compliance
Lightning Source LLC
Chambersburg PA
CBHW020808060726
47498CB00017B/1103